Terry Jones is a writer, film-maker, historian, comedian, actor and real ale enthusiast. With Michael Palin he wrote many of the most famous sketches on *Monty Python's Flying Circus* (Terry was the one who usually wore a headscarf or a bowler hat). He co-directed *Monty Python & the Holy Grail* (1975), a film so funny it made all subsequent films set in the Middle Ages seem like comedies. He also directed *The Life of Brian* (1979), arguably the funniest and certainly the most controversial film comedy of all time, and *Monty Python's The Meaning of Life* (1983), in which his appearance as the corpulent Mr Creosote has passed into legend.

As well as writing a sequence of award-winning children's books, Terry has also enjoyed a double life as a historian and a documentary film-maker. In his books and films he has variously argued that Geoffrey Chaucer was murdered by a rogue bishop, that the Middle Ages were a rather good time to be alive and that it was the Romans who were the real barbarians. In 2004 he wrote *Terry Jones's War on the War on Terror*, a timely reminder that you can't force an abstract noun to surrender.

In the thirteen linked stories that make up *Evil Machines*, his satirical storytelling gifts are deployed against the hidden perils of technology, although Terry assures us that no machines were harmed in the writing of the book.

By the same author

EVIL MACHINES

TERRY JONES

unbound

First published in hardback in 2011
This paperback edition published in 2013

Unbound
4–7 Manchester Street, Marylebone, London, W1U 2AE
www.unbound.co.uk

Typeset by Palindrome
Illustrations by Ryan Gillard & Kiera Kinsella
Cover illustration by Ben Newman
Art direction by Mecob

A CIP record for this book is available from the British Library

ISBN 978-1-78352-010-7 (trade PB)
ISBN 978-1-908717-00-9 (trade HB)
ISBN 978-1-908717-02-3 (ebook)

Printed in England by Clays Ltd, Bungay, Suffolk

CONTENTS

THE TRUTHFUL PHONE

You might think that there was nothing particularly evil about a Truthful Phone. It simply told the truth, which is, of course, 'A Good Thing To Do'. But the way this particular telephone told the truth was not at all good. In reality the thing was evil from the tip of its mouthpiece to the end of its cord.

It was put up for sale in a shop window with a label that read: 'The Truthful Phone – £10'.

'I've never heard of such a thing,' said Mrs Morris, who was frail and elderly but of an enquiring mind.

'I wouldn't take it, if I were you, Mrs Morris,' said the shopkeeper, who was a kind man despite his appearance. 'The truth can get you into all sorts of trouble.'

'Oh dear,' replied Mrs Morris. 'I always understood the truth never hurt anyone.'

'Don't you believe it,' said the shopkeeper. 'The truth can be dangerous and undesirable and should be shunned as long as is possible. Nobody really wants the truth. They want to live in a world that is comfortable and happy. The truth would just make most people miserable.'

'But I need a new telephone,' said Mrs Morris, 'and this one is the cheapest by far!' And with that she bought the phone and took it home. That very day she got Albert, the odd job man, to come and install it.

The first time it rang, Mrs Morris picked the phone up and was surprised to hear her old friend Mabel say, 'Ha! May Morris, you old fraud! I hope you rot in hell!'

'I beg your pardon? Is that you Mabel?'

'How dare you call me a parasite!' cried Mabel indignantly.

'I didn't, my dear . . . Are you feeling quite well?'

'If you've always thought I was a freeloader who cultivated your friendship simply for the free teas, why have you pretended to be my friend for so many years?' shouted Mabel.

'Upon my soul!' cried Mrs Morris. 'I think you had better ring back when you're feeling more yourself again, dear.' And she hung up.

She then stood for some time gazing at the phone.

A little later she rang the greengrocer.

'Hello, Mr Murphy?' she said into the phone. 'I hope you're well today?'

There was a long silence on the other end of the phone.

'Hello? Are you still there?' asked Mrs Morris. 'I'd like to order a big bag of your best potatoes and some leeks.'

'Er . . .' said Mr Murphy.

'And a cucumber, a lettuce and a pound of tomatoes. Is that all right?' asked Mrs Morris.

'I think my wife's coming!' said Mr Murphy hurriedly and he rang off.

Mrs Morris was more than a little astonished, though she had the feeling that the phone may have had something to do with the odd way in which Mr Murphy had received her order for potatoes, leeks and salad.

As for Mr Murphy, he was equally surprised. He had picked up the phone and had heard Mrs Morris, that sweet little old lady from down the road, say, 'Hello, you gorgeous hunk! I've been thinking about your bottom all week!'

He was so surprised, in fact, that he didn't know what to say.

Then he heard Mrs Morris continue, 'I love the ginger hair on your arms and the manly way you tip potatoes into my shopping bag and then stick in the leeks.'

All he could say was, 'Er . . .'

Then Mrs Morris went on, 'Since the unfortunate late Mr Morris disappeared under mysterious circumstances in the Campsie Fells, I have dreamt of running a market garden with you in Worthing!'

At this point, Mr Murphy began to get really worried, and made up some story about his wife walking in to the shop. He put the phone down and blinked at his assistant, Tom, and then at the customers. Had they heard what Mrs Morris had said? What on earth had got into the woman?

He spent the rest of the day keeping to the back of the shop in case Mrs Morris should turn up in person. But she didn't.

In fact Mrs Morris was far too busy to go down to the shop to pick up her leeks and potatoes. She was round at the police station telling Constable Robinson how she'd received a strange phone call.

'It was Albert, the odd-job man. He said he was going to come round and fix the boiler for me . . .'

'Does he often ring up and say things like that?'

'Oh yes, officer, he's very helpful.'

'So what's the problem?'

'Well, he also said that he'd probably steal a few things while he was at it. He said he'd noticed some valuable-looking jewellery in a drawer in my bedroom. I said I didn't realize he'd been poking around in my bedroom drawers, and he told me he'd been stealing things from me for years, but I'd never noticed because he only took small things and only a few at a time.'

'Why do you think he was telling you all this?'

'Oh! I don't think *he* was!' said Mrs Morris. 'I think it was the Truthful Phone.'

'Hmm!' said Constable Robinson. 'The Truthful Phone?'

'Yes,' replied Mrs Morris. 'I want you to arrest it!'

'We don't normally arrest telephones,' said Constable Robinson. 'Perhaps I'd better come and have a look.'

So Constable Robinson went with Mrs Morris to her house to take a look at the Truthful Phone. It didn't look very different from an ordinary phone, except that it had a switch on the side.

'May I try it?' asked Constable Robinson.

'Of course,' said Mrs Morris.

So Constable Robinson rang the superintendent back at the police station.

'Oh! Hi, Super!' said Constable Robinson. 'Robinson

4

here. I'm just trying out Mrs Morris's Truthful Phone.'

'You're what?' exclaimed the superintendent, who was startled to hear Constable Robinson say he knew all about the bribes the superintendent took from criminals and local businessmen, and that he was going to report the matter to his superiors.

'I'm trying out Mrs Morris's Truthful Phone,' repeated Constable Robinson.

'You do and I'll break every bone in your body!' roared the superintendent. 'And I mean that!'

And, from the tone of the superintendent's voice, Constable Robinson knew it was the truth, even though he hadn't the slightest idea what he had said to make the superintendent so angry.

'It's not what *you* said,' whispered Mrs Morris. 'It's what the *phone* said that is the problem. I think I'll take it back to the shop.'

Just then the phone rang.

'Hello?' said Mrs Morris. 'This is May Morris speaking.'

'I don't want to go back to the shop,' said the phone.

'Who is this?' asked Mrs Morris.

'It's me, your new telephone,' said the phone. 'I like it here. If you try to have me disconnected, I'll make your life a misery.'

'You're already doing that!' exclaimed Mrs Morris. 'I'm going to call Albert now.'

'What and let him steal from you?' said the phone.

'At least he doesn't mess around with what I say!'

'Don't disconnect me or I'll . . .'

But Mrs Morris had already slammed the phone down.

'Who was it?' asked Constable Robinson.

'It was the phone,' said Mrs Morris.

'I know it was the phone, but who was *on* the phone?' asked Constable Robinson.

But before Mrs Morris could explain, the phone rang again. Mrs Morris picked it up and then turned to the police officer.

'It's for you, Constable,' she said.

Constable Robinson took the phone. 'Hello?' he said.

'Ask Mrs Morris what happened to her husband,' said the phone and then rang off.

'What was that?' asked Mrs Morris.

'Someone just said, "Ask Mrs Morris what happened to her husband," and then rang off,' explained the constable.

'What!' exclaimed Mrs Morris in some agitation. 'Who was it?'

'They didn't say!'

'It's the phone!' cried Mrs Morris. 'It's evil!'

And she grabbed the phone and shouted into the mouthpiece, 'I'm having you disconnected and you're going straight back to the shop!' But all she got back was the dialling tone.

'Constable,' said Mrs Morris. 'Would you help me disconnect this phone? I don't trust it to say what I want it to say.'

'Certainly,' said Constable Robinson, and he started to pull at the wires, whereupon the phone rang again. Constable Robinson stopped and looked at Mrs Morris. She shook her head.

'Don't pick it up!' exclaimed Mrs Morris. 'Don't listen to it!'

'But it might be the superintendent,' said Constable Robinson, and he picked up the phone as if it were a live crab.

'Look in the garden shed,' said the phone.

'Who's that?' shouted Constable Robinson, but the phone had rung off.

Constable Robinson frowned. He looked across at Mrs Morris. She was white-haired and frail.

'No, no . . .' he said to himself. But then he remembered that it was his duty as a policeman to investigate anything that needed to be investigated.

'Would you mind if I looked in your garden shed, Mrs Morris?' he said.

'Of course not,' said Mrs Morris. 'Is there something you need from there?'

Mrs Morris took Constable Robinson into the garden and showed him the shed. She unlocked it, and he went inside. Immediately the phone started ringing back in the house, and Mrs Morris hurried back, while Constable Robinson inspected the garden shed.

But Mrs Morris didn't answer the phone; she simply took it off the hook and left it there. She didn't want to hear another word it said.

When Constable Robinson returned from inspecting the garden shed, he said to Mrs Robinson, 'You have a very fine garden shed, Mrs Morris. It is remarkably well equipped: you have welding apparatus, wood and metal lathes, and even a blast furnace for smelting.'

'Yes,' replied Mrs Morris. 'It was my unfortunate late husband's favourite place. He spent hours in there making all sorts of things.'

'Is there someone on the phone?' asked Constable Robinson, indicating the receiver lying off its hook.

'Ignore it,' said Mrs Morris.

But Constable Robinson had already picked up the receiver.

'Did you see it?' hissed the phone.

'It's full of equipment,' said Constable Robinson.

'Don't listen!' said Mrs Morris.

'The weedkiller!' hissed the phone. 'In the bottle on the shelf by the flower pots! That's what she used!'

'For what?' asked Constable Robinson.

'Take no notice of it!' said Mrs Morris, and she grabbed the telephone receiver out of the Constable's hands, and yanked the wire hard.

'NOOO!' screamed the Truthful Phone. 'Don't!'

But it was too late! The wire came out of the socket in the wall, and the Truthful Phone was disconnected. Mrs Morris sank down in a chair.

'It is an evil thing!' she said, glaring at the phone. 'I shall take it back to the shop straight away.'

'But what was it talking about?' asked Constable Robinson.

'It was raking up old and unfounded rumours about my late and unfortunate husband's disappearance, under mysterious circumstances in the Campsie Fells,' replied Mrs Morris. 'You see, he liked making things in the garden shed, which, as you so rightly observed, is remarkably well equipped. One day he told me he was going out on the Campsie Fells, which, as you know, is a range of hills to the north of Glasgow, to test out a new kind of dog walker. The

Campsie Fells was his favourite place for testing things. But that day he never came back.'

'I'm very sorry,' said Constable Robinson.

'Yes,' said Mrs Morris. 'I was sorry too. Would you like a cup of tea?'

'That sounds like an excellent idea,' said the constable.

And so that's what they had.

❖❖❖

When Constable Robinson returned to the police station, he found the superintendent waiting for him. 'Listen, Constable Robinson, I'm thinking of promoting you.'

'Really!' exclaimed Constable Robinson. He'd been in the force without promotion for so long he'd almost given up hope.

'Yes,' said the superintendent, 'but there are one or two things that we should keep confidential, just between you and me.'

'I see,' said Constable Robinson, 'that's OK by me.'

But the business with the Truthful Phone was not quite over.

'Oh, by the way,' said the superintendent, 'there's a message on the answering machine for you.'

Constable Robinson recognized the voice on the answering machine at once. It was the Truthful Phone. 'Listen, Constable Robinson,' it said. 'Just in case I *do* get disconnected, I think you should know the truth about Mrs Morris's husband. He didn't disappear under mysterious circumstances in the Campsie Fells. He was poisoned in his own home. With weedkiller.'

Constable Robinson shuddered. All his working life in the police force he'd dreaded this moment when he would be confronted by a real criminal and would have to make an arrest. Of course, he'd given out the usual speeding fines and he'd reported several cars for going through red traffic lights, but he generally managed to avoid any contact with proper criminals.

Now here he was faced with a criminal of the worst sort: a murderer – possibly a murderess! But Constable Robinson didn't hesitate. He knew what his duty was and he went straight to his superintendent, and told him the story. The superintendent immediately leapt into action.

'We've no time to lose!' he said. 'She may be armed and dangerous!'

'Who? Mrs Morris?' stuttered the Constable, who was having difficulty imagining that dear little old lady wielding a machine gun.

But the superintendent was already on the phone. 'I want six squad cars and an armed escort a.s.a.p.!' He yelled and slammed the phone down.

In less than an hour, the police had arrived at Mrs Morris's home. Several armed officers jumped out of a van, wielding machetes, and broke down Mrs Morris's front door. Four sprang up the stairs and broke down all the doors up there, while six ran through the ground floor, knocking down any door that happened to be shut and one or two that weren't.

They opened Mrs Morris's cupboards and pulled all her clothes and personal belongings on to the floor. They pulled all the tins off her larder shelves and ransacked her fridge.

'The suspect seems to have skipped it!' reported Officer Tait to the superintendent.

'Somebody must have tipped her off!' exclaimed the superintendent. 'Which means she's not operating alone! Quick! Send reinforcements!' he barked into his radio.

In the meantime, some police officers dug up the lawn and rose beds looking for dead bodies and others raided the unfortunate late Mr Morris's garden shed.

'Suspect's shed is full of suspicious gear!' reported Officer Tait, and he took the superintendent to see the metal-working lathes, mechanical saws and smelting furnace.

'Looks like she's been cutting up her victims and burning them in the furnace!' exclaimed the superintendent. 'No wonder we didn't find any dead bodies buried under the lawn or rose beds! She could be the greatest mass-murderer of all time! Quick, send more reinforcements! This is going to be all over the press tomorrow! Well done, Constable Robinson! I can see promotion ahead for all of us!'

'I can still hardly believe it,' murmured Constable Robinson. 'She seemed such a sweet old lady. But look! There's the weedkiller, just as the phone said!'

'Take that as evidence!' exclaimed the superintendent. 'And that garden fork is an offensive weapon.'

By the time the helicopter had arrived there were something like fifty police officers crowded into Mrs Morris's house and garden, most of them armed.

'Now where is that phone?' asked the superintendent. 'It's our key witness.'

'It's gone!' gasped Constable Robinson. 'She must have taken it back to the shop!'

'No time to lose!' shouted the superintendent. 'We may yet apprehend the suspect, before she can escape the country!'

❖❖❖

All this while, Mrs Morris had been making her way back to the electrical shop where she had bought the Truthful Phone. She went via the park, where she always spent a pleasant hour feeding the ducks and pigeons. She then stopped at the greengrocer to order some leeks and potatoes. The greengrocer himself wasn't to be seen, however, as he was hiding in the back of the shop, so she told his assistant to give him her best wishes.

She then went on to the electrical shop, and was surprised to find that it had a helicopter hovering above it.

'There she goes!' whispered Constable Robinson, peering out from the police van, on the other side of the street. 'That's her!'

'Suspect entering shop now!' radioed the superintendent. 'OK, men, we'll go in all together and take the suspect by surprise. Wait for my countdown.'

When Mrs Morris handed the Truthful Phone back to the shopkeeper, he nodded. 'I didn't think you'd like it,' he said. 'The truth is often very unpleasant.'

'You are quite right, young man,' replied Mrs Morris.

'But wait a minute!' said the shopkeeper. 'You've got it set all wrong! Look!'

And he pointed to the switch on the side. When you looked closely you could see in tiny letters the words 'True – False'. The switch was turned to 'False'.

'It's been telling you lies!' exclaimed the shopkeeper.

'And not just me!' said Mrs Morris.

And that was the moment when six specially trained officers jumped out of the helicopter on to the roof of Baker's Electrical Shop, smashed their way through the ceiling and abseiled down on to the counter.

At the same time, fifty armed officers burst into the shop, spraying bullets at the ceiling. They pounced on Mrs Morris, handcuffed her, put a bag over her head and bundled her into the back of a van.

❖❖❖

The story was, indeed, all over the press some weeks later, but I'm afraid neither Constable Robinson nor the superintendent got their promotion. The case was thrown out of court on the grounds that the Truthful Phone was not a reliable witness.

In his summing up the judge said, 'Since Mrs Morris only purchased the phone that morning, it could not have been a witness to the events it described. It was simply spreading malicious gossip.'

As for Mrs Morris, she successfully sued the police for wrongful arrest and, with the £84 she received in compensation, she was able to buy a very nice telephone. It was red, and it said exactly what anyone who used it said and nothing else.

The Truthful Phone itself disappeared under mysterious circumstances. The police claimed it had escaped from custody when they proposed charging it under the defamation laws. But there were rumours circulating that the superintendent had paid one of his friends to tie it to a lump of concrete and drop it off Westminster Bridge.

Whatever happened to it, everyone agreed that they were well rid of such an evil contraption.

But all the same, Mrs Morris felt she'd been lucky; as she said to her friend Mabel, 'Goodness knows what would have happened if that switch had been pointing to "True"!'

THE NICE BOMB

The bomb landed in the middle of the Johnson family's living room during supper.

'Well, you're very lucky!' said the bomb. 'Normally my make and model goes off 100 per cent of the time. Would you like a cup of tea?'

'Yes, please,' said Mr Johnson, who to tell the truth was still more than a little shaken by a bomb dropping through the ceiling into the family living room.

So the Nice Bomb picked itself up and bustled round making tea for the Johnson family. Meanwhile the Johnsons turned on the telly and watched the news, which was all about how bombs had been dropping all around London. Apparently a little-known terrorist group was dropping them as a protest against the inefficiencies in the postal system.

The news reporter was interviewing a masked man who said, 'A second-class letter can take up to a week to arrive and even first-class letters have no guarantee of arriving the next day! This is something that we in MADIPOS will not stand for!'

'MADIPOS?' asked the Interviewer.

'Movement Against Deficiencies in the Postal Service' said the masked Terrorist.

The Johnson family were all nodding in agreement with the Terrorist, when the Nice Bomb brought in the tea.

'I've buttered some scones as well. You all look as if you've had a bit of a shock.'

'Well, yes, we have,' said Mrs Johnson. 'It isn't every day a bomb lands in your family living room.'

'But I must say, for a bomb, you are very pleasant,' said Mr Johnson.

'Thank you,' said the Nice Bomb. 'I like you too.' And it settled itself back on the sofa.

They all watched television for the rest of the evening. There was a quiz show during which the Nice Bomb guessed all the right answers long before any of the contestants.

'How do you know all that stuff?' asked Kevin, Mr and Mrs Johnson's son.

'I'm what they call a "Smart Bomb",' said the bomb.

'You could be on the show!' said Loretta, Mr and Mrs Johnson's daughter.

'Oh no, I couldn't!' replied the Nice Bomb. 'I'm only a bomb, don't forget.'

'But you are a very nice bomb,' said Mrs Johnson.

'Unfortunately, I think you'll find that, according to *The Quiz Show Rule Book*, bombs aren't eligible to participate in TV game shows,' replied the Nice Bomb. And it was right.

❖❖❖

The next day, the Nice Bomb helped Mrs Johnson get the children off to school.

'It must be very exhausting for you – doing all this work day in day out,' said the Nice Bomb to Mrs Johnson. 'I could take a load of it off your hands.'

'That's very kind of you,' said Mrs Johnson, as the Nice Bomb loaded the dishwasher, hung the clothes out to dry, and spring-cleaned the entire house.

'But don't tire yourself out, my dear,' added Mrs Johnson, as she drank her twelfth cup of tea while flipping through magazines on the sofa.

'Oh, don't worry about me,' said the Nice Bomb cheerily. 'Us bombs have no concept of *tiredness*.'

When the children came home from school, the Nice Bomb made them a snack and then supervised their homework.

When Mr Johnson came in from work, the Nice Bomb cooked a particularly tasty supper of chicken in tomatoes and chilli.

'You may be only a bomb,' said Mr Johnson, 'but you can't half cook!'

'And it's finished off my knitting for me,' said Mrs Johnson, holding up a beautiful Fair Isle sweater that the bomb had created that afternoon out of a rather pedestrian pattern that Mrs Johnson had been working on for months.

'You're a very nice bomb,' said Mr Johnson.

❖❖❖

But the next day there was bad news. Mr Johnson came home from work and said that another group of terrorists had blown up the factory where he worked.

'They were protesting against the parking restrictions,' he said regretfully. 'And while I thoroughly agree with them about relaxing the waiting and loading regulations in Casper Street, it does mean I don't have any work and will not be able to buy any Christmas presents this year.'

'Oh dear!' said the Nice Bomb, when it heard all this. 'Perhaps I can help. I may be only a bomb, but I'm very good at fixing computers.'

So the Nice Bomb, in addition to doing all the housework, and feeding the children and supervising their homework, started an Internet business repairing computers.

Every day more and more computers arrived to be repaired, and the bomb was able to fix them in no time at all – in between rearranging the living room and bleaching the bed-sheets.

To begin with, Mr Johnson used to get up early and set off to look for a new job.

'As soon as I find a new job, you can relax,' he said to the Nice Bomb.

'Oh! That's all right!' replied the Nice Bomb. 'Us bombs don't know the meaning of the word *relaxation*!' And it cleaned the oven, washed all the windows and made a soufflé for supper, while at the same time mending a dozen more computers in its spare moments.

As the weeks went by, however, Mr Johnson started going out later and later to look for work, while the Nice Bomb's computer business went on from strength to strength, and the money poured in.

'I'd give you a hand,' said Mr Johnson, 'only I don't know the first thing about computers.'

'That's all right,' said the Nice Bomb. 'Us bombs don't mind a bit of hard work!'

So Mr Johnson joined Mrs Johnson, sitting on the couch and leafing through magazines all day, while the Nice Bomb scuttled around the house, darning, sewing, dusting, cleaning, and mending the furniture – all the while fixing broken computers, digging the garden, washing up, shopping and doing a spot of ironing.

'You be careful you don't overdo it, my dear!' shouted Mrs Johnson from the couch.

'Ooh! Don't worry about me!' the Nice Bomb called back. 'I'm only a bomb, I can't overdo anything.' And it finished washing the car, gave it a quick wax, repainted the outside of the house and built an extension to the garage.

The children, Kevin and Loretta, grew very fond of the Nice Bomb. It helped them so much with their homework that they started getting better marks at school. They became punctual and even started to enjoy school more than they had done, thanks mostly to the Nice Bomb.

When Christmas came, the bomb worked twice as hard. It earned enough money to be able to buy everyone presents. It put up the decorations, and made the Christmas pudding. It cooked Christmas dinner single-handedly, and arranged the table with red flowers and white snowdrops and candles. It was the most elegant Christmas dinner the Johnson family had ever had.

Two aunts and an uncle came to Christmas dinner, and were surprised to be greeted at the door by such a polite bomb in evening dress and white gloves, who took their coats from them and then poured them a sweet sherry.

'That seems a very nice bomb, you've got there,' remarked Aunt Justine.

'Yes, it is,' said Mrs Johnson. 'It's a very nice bomb indeed.'

The Nice Bomb provided some fine wine to have with the goose, and then dessert wine to drink with the Christmas pudding.

During the brandy and cigars, Mr Johnson got up and called for silence.

'My dear friends,' he said. 'This is the best Christmas any of us have experienced for many, many years. We have enjoyed not just the grandest spread and the best wines we have ever tasted, but we have also had such fun. We have played the most hilarious games and received such lovely presents. We have never had a dull moment. Not just that, but as I look round this table now, I cannot remember having seen such harmony and happiness in this or any other family.

'And we owe all this to one person . . .' And here Mr Johnson turned to the Nice Bomb, who was just serving out some more brandy from the decanter.

The Nice Bomb looked down at the floor in embarrassment and said: 'Please! Please! Remember I'm not a person – I'm just a bomb . . .'

'But we owe so much to you . . . our dear friend . . . who has rescued us from the brink and provided for us and brought us so much happiness.'

'Yes! Yes!' said everybody, as they raised their glasses in a toast to the Nice Bomb.

'Speech!' they shouted. 'Speech!'

So the Nice Bomb stood up and said: 'I'm sorry, everyone . . . I truly am . . .'

'What on earth do you mean?' asked Mrs Johnson. 'You've nothing to be sorry about . . . You've done so much for us . . .'

And that was the moment when the Nice Bomb exploded. For no matter how much it tried to be nice, it was – after all – just a bomb, and bombs are, I'm afraid, by their nature, evil things.

THE LIFT THAT TOOK PEOPLE TO
PLACES THEY DIDN'T WANT TO GO

When it had been first installed the elevator seemed to function perfectly well. When customers pressed the button to go to the Third Floor (Ladies Clothing, Shoes, Fashion Accessories and Books), it stopped at the Third Floor. When customers pressed the button for the Fifth Floor (Television and Hi-fi, Computers, Electrical Goods and Accounts), it stopped at the Fifth Floor.

But then something seemed to go wrong.

To begin with it was only little things. A customer would tell it to go to the Ground Floor (Cosmetics, Handbags, Luggage, Stationery and Exit), and the elevator would take them to the Fourth Floor (Furniture).

The elevator repairmen were sent for. They readjusted the control mechanism, and things seemed to go back to normal.

But then one day it started to go badly wrong.

The head of the department store, whose name was Montague Du Cann, went into the lift with a Health and

Safety inspector, and pressed the button for the Sixth Floor, which was where the offices were situated, but instead of going up to Six, the lift went down to the Second Basement.

Montague Du Cann and the Health and Safety inspector walked out of the lift and into the ruck of exposed electrical cables, half-open bins of dangerous cleaning materials, crates of rotting sausages from the Food Hall, blocked exits and so many infringements of the Health and Safety Regulations that the inspector thought his birthday had arrived a day early! (He was going to be forty-seven).

'I'm afraid I will have to take note of all these things,' he told Montague Du Cann, who had hoped to be able to keep the Health and Safety inspector on the Sixth Floor while someone went down and cleared up the Second Basement.

The thought crossed Montague Du Cann's mind that the lift had taken them to the Second Basement deliberately and maliciously. But, of course, he dismissed the idea at once. After all, in his long experience as a Department Store Executive, he had never once come across an elevator acting of its own free will.

Some days later, however, he had cause to rethink his opinion.

Montague Du Cann had an aunt, whose name was Leanora Du Cann. She got into the elevator and pressed the button for the Sixth Floor, where she was to meet her nephew Montague. The lift, however, took her straight to the Third Floor (Ladies Clothing, Shoes, Fashion Accessories and Books).

'Oh dear!' said Leanora Du Cann, and she pressed the button for the Sixth Floor again, but the lift refused to move. Then she tried the 'Close Doors' button. But the lift wouldn't close its doors either.

'It's stuck,' said Leanora Du Cann to some customers who got into the elevator while she was pressing the buttons.

'We'd better walk then,' said the other customers.

And that is what Leanora knew she had to do.

'Oh dear,' said Leanora again, only this time more quietly.

She stepped cautiously out into the Ladies Clothing Department. The stairs were situated further down the store to the right, through the Shoe Department. Leanora felt her knees go slightly wobbly. She took a deep breath, firmly zipped up the large empty bag she was carrying, and walked towards the shoes.

The moment she started to move away from the elevator, the elevator gave a sort of snort – or perhaps it was a snigger – then it closed its doors and went back down to the Ground Floor. Leanora froze in her tracks. Then she slowly turned and stared at the lift, for a strange feeling had crawled up her spine. It was a very strange feeling indeed . . . the feeling of having just brushed past something nasty . . . something quite, quite malignant and deeply, deeply evil.

Of course, she had no idea where the feeling had come from, but all the same nothing would have persuaded her to return to that elevator and try it again.

So she set off once again across the Ladies Clothing Department, and pretty soon she found herself in among the shoes.

She stopped at a pair of sling-backs in patent leather. They weren't quite her size, but she looked around the store briefly, unzipped her big empty bag and dropped the shoes into it. Then she wandered towards the casual footwear section. A pair of espadrilles caught her eye. They were bright blue and had a white edging round the sole. Once again she glanced quickly round and then dropped the espadrilles into her bag.

A little further on, she popped a pair of stiletto heels with ankle straps into her bag, then some ballet shoes, and she was just stuffing some expensive thigh-length boots in when all the alarm bells in the store started ringing, and a store detective put a hand on her shoulder and said, 'Got you!'

When Leanora finally appeared in her nephew's office, she was accompanied by the store detective.

'This lady says she's your aunt, sir,' said the store detective – clearly not believing a word of it.

'Aunt Leanora!' exclaimed Montague Du Cann. 'You haven't been shoplifting again, have you?'

Aunt Leanora hung her head.

'Caught her red-handed,' mumbled the store detective, who was now beginning to feel he was in the wrong place.

'I've told you time and time again *never* to go through the Shoe Department!' exclaimed Montague Du Cann.

The truth is that Aunt Leanora had suffered for some time from kleptomania, which meant she couldn't stop herself stealing things – to be specific, shoes. I suppose you could say she was lucky she didn't need to steal anything other than shoes, but she stole shoes whenever she saw them. She just couldn't help it: brown shoes, black shoes, casual shoes, formal shoes, dancing pumps and fashion boots, slippers, slip-ons, high heels, low heels, flip-flops, sandals and wellingtons . . . and it didn't matter whether they fitted her or not! She simply could not stop herself stealing anything in the Shoe Department.

'I know! I know!' sighed Leanora. 'I pressed the button to come straight up to the Sixth Floor, but the lift took me to the Shoe Department and then wouldn't budge!'

Her nephew narrowed his eyes. 'That lift?! No . . . it couldn't be . . .' he murmured, for he simply couldn't get rid of the suspicion that somehow – just maybe – the elevator was doing all this deliberately.

For a moment, a clammy feeling stole across Montague Du Cann's chest . . . In fact it was the same feeling that his aunt had experienced earlier, though, of course, he wasn't to know that. It was a feeling of being close to something truly evil.

And that was when things began to get really weird – really, seriously and dangerously *weird*.

❖❖❖

Montague Du Cann had not always been a department store executive. In an earlier part of his life he had been a bandit. His name had then been Juan Gonzales, and he was the boldest and most desperate bandit in the whole of New Mexico.

He had gone to the bad down in old Silver City, and his gang was called the Dos Hombres Gang – which means the Two Men Gang, although in fact there were four of them.

They robbed the bank in Española, and then fled across the Rio Grande to Santa Fe. But in Santa Fe the most junior member of the gang, who was known as The Kid, but whose name was actually Antonio Gabriel Bernardino Martinez, got drunk and started bragging about what they had done.

Someone informed the local sheriff, and the sheriff, along with twenty armed policemen, had surrounded the lodging house, where the Dos Hombres Gang was hiding out.

'Juan Gonzales!' called out the sheriff through a megaphone. 'We know it was you robbed the bank in Española. Come out with your hands up or we'll shoot you down like a dog!'

It was at this moment that Juan Gonzales conceived the idea that life as a department store executive in England might be preferable to the life of a desperate bandit in New Mexico. So he said to the rest of the gang:

'Keep 'em occupied. I'm gonna get help.'

'Right!' said Fernando Emmanuel, the second-in-command, and he started firing at the policemen standing in front of the lodging house. The other two desperate bandits joined in and soon the rest of the policemen came from round the back to join in the shoot-out.

As soon as the police had gone from the back of the lodging house, Juan Gonzales shinned down a drainpipe and ran as fast as his legs would carry him away from the scene.

Just as they were beginning to run out of ammunition, Antonio Gabriel Bernardino Martinez, who was known as The Kid, turned to Fernando Salvador, the second-in-command, and said, 'Just a minute! What kind of "help" can Juan Gonzales be getting us? We're desperate bandits! *Nobody* comes to the aid of desperate bandits!'

Fernando Salvador, the second-in-command, stopped firing for a moment, and turned to stare at Antonio Gabriel Bernardino Martinez.

'You're right!' he exclaimed, banging his fist on the table and at the same time accidentally firing his handgun, because he was holding it in his fist. 'We've been tricked!' He was not the brightest of bandits.

And so it was, the three remaining members of the Dos Hombres Gang ran to the window at the rear of the lodging house to look for Juan Gonzales, but he was long gone.

'That no-good Juan Gonzales has run away and left us!' said Fernando Salvador.

'He is a bad man!' cried Pedro Del Camino, the third of the Dos Hombres Gang, who had not spoken up till then.

'Of course he is a bad man,' said Antonio Gabriel Bernardino Martinez, the Kid. 'He is a desperate bandit – the boldest and most desperate bandit in the whole of New Mexico! Of course he is a bad man!'

At that moment this interesting conversation came to an abrupt end, because ten police officers suddenly burst into the room and the chief said, 'You're under arrest!'

And one of the policemen shot Antonio Gabriel Bernardino Martinez, who was known as the Kid, in the arm because he saw he was about to fire at the chief police officer.

'Thank you, Rolf,' said the chief police officer. 'These are desperate and dangerous men!'

'You're right!' said the other policeman.

❖❖❖

And that was the end of the Dos Hombres Gang. Fernando Salvador and Pedro Del Camino were thrown into prison in Albuquerque for twenty years, and Antonio Gabriel Bernardino Martinez, the Kid, was given an extra five years because he had been about to fire at the chief police officer.

Juan Gonzales, however, managed to get to New York, where he landed a job as a cook on a ship bound for England. He changed his name to Montague Du Cann, and became a department store executive. He had all the money from the bank robbery still strapped to his person, and so was able to buy a share in one of the largest and most prestigious department stores in Swindon. That is how he came to be the head of the particular department store in which the malevolent elevator had been installed.

And so it was that one day, shortly after his Aunt Leanora had been arrested yet again for shoplifting shoes, he got into the evil lift, pressed the button for the Ground Floor, went down six floors and, when the doors opened, Montague Du Cann stepped out not into the Cosmetics and Food Hall but into a small town in New Mexico!

❖❖❖

Montague Du Cann found himself standing in Española – the very town where he and his gang had robbed the bank all those years ago.

'There he is!' yelled an elderly man, who was sitting in a rocking chair on the stoop of a timber shack. 'I recognize that guy! He was the one that robbed the bank twenty years ago!'

Now you might think it surprising that Montague Du

Cann should have been recognized so instantaneously from an event that had happened so long ago. But there is a perfectly good explanation. You see, the elderly gentleman sitting in the rocking chair had been the chief cashier of the bank that Montague Du Cann (then known as Juan Gonzales) and his gang had robbed, and ever since then he had been sitting in that rocking chair on the stoop of his shack thinking about the only interesting thing that had happened to him in his life. As a result he remembered every little detail of that important occasion as clear as daylight.

'That's Juan Gonzales! The leader of the Dos Hombres Gang!' exclaimed the elderly man. 'Quick! Call the sheriff! Arrest him! The others got twenty years and twenty five years apiece, but Juan Gonzales got away scot-free! Now he can pay for his crime!'

Well, Montague Du Cann, or Juan Gonzales as he used to be, turned and banged on the doors of the elevator, which had brought him to the last place on earth he wanted to revisit. But the lift doors were firmly closed and the elevator wouldn't open them again no matter how many times Montague Du Cann pressed the 'Call Lift' button.

Eventually a small crowd gathered around Montague Du Cann and stood there gaping at him. They were, of course, equally curious about the elevator that had suddenly appeared on the outside wall of the only department store in Española – despite the fact that the building had only one storey. Montague Du Cann gave up pushing the elevator button, and started to push his way through the crowd, as he did back in his department store in Swindon during the Winter Sales, shouting, 'Make way, there! Come along!

There's plenty of room! Let me through I am the Head of this Department Store!' And the crowd simply fell back and allowed him to walk through.

'Arrest him! Stop that man!' yelled the chief cashier, who had leapt out of his rocking chair, and was now jumping up and down on the stoop of his shack. 'He's a notorious bank robber!' But none of the people in the crowd had lived in Española long enough to remember the great day of the bank robbery, and in any case none of them knew what the old man was screaming about because he was yelling in Welsh, and the inhabitants of Española all spoke mostly Spanish with a little bit of English but not a single word of Welsh.

The elderly man, you see, came originally from Dolgellau just north of Machynlleth, right in the middle of Wales, and always relapsed into his native tongue whenever he got excited.

Meanwhile, Montague Du Cann, formerly known as the desperate bandit Juan Gonzales, strolled round the corner and walked into the saloon.

Now it was, to be precise, exactly twenty years, three months and seven days ago that Juan Gonzales had escaped from the police and abandoned the Dos Hombres Gang to their fate. Fernando Salvador, the second-in-command, and Pedro Del Camino, had been released from jail earlier in the year, having served their sentences. Antonio Gabriel Bernardino Martinez, otherwise known as The Kid, had also been released around the same time, having had his sentence reduced for being polite to the prison guards.

The three of them, having no other friends or relatives

still living, had met up again, and Fernando Salvador, the second-in-command, had proposed that they carry on robbing banks as they had done in the past.

'But it got us twenty years in jail!' exclaimed Pedro Del Camino. 'I don't want to risk the same thing happening again.

'I was known as The Kid, when I went into jail,' said Antonio Gabriel Bernardino Martinez. 'Now I'm a middle-aged gentleman and I've got a beer belly.'

'Listen,' said Fernando Salvador, the second-in-command, who – you will remember – was not very bright. 'We only got caught the last time because Antonio Gabriel Bernardino Martinez got drunk, and started boasting about how we'd robbed the bank. All we have to do this time is avoid getting drunk and we'll be OK.'

The other two, who were also, by the way, not very bright, thought about this for some time, and then Pedro Del Camino said, 'But which bank shall we rob this time?'

'Ah!' exclaimed Fernando Salvador, the second-in-command. 'I've given this a lot of thought over the last twenty years, and I have hit on the perfect bank for us to rob! It will be as easy as taking pennies from a blind beggar's hat!' (Fernando Salvador, the second-in-command, was not only not very bright, he was also not very pleasant.)

'What bank would that be?' asked Antonio Gabriel Bernardino Martinez.

'The bank in Española, of course!' exclaimed Fernando Salvador.

'But that's the one we got jailed for robbing last time!' exclaimed Pedro Del Camino.

'Exactly!' said Fernando Salvador. 'We've done it success-fully once before – the second time will be even easier! We know where it is, which is a plus, because it means we won't have to spend money on a street map. We know what it looks like, so we won't go into the wrong building, and we can remember where the safe was!'

'Can we?' asked Pedro Del Camino, who couldn't.

'It'll be a cinch!' said Fernando Salvador.

Well, after several hours of argument, Fernando Salvador finally persuaded the other two that it was a good plan, and they agreed to rob the same bank that they had robbed twenty years before.

So they took the Greyhound bus from Albuquerque to Española, but had to get out at Pojoaque, because they didn't have enough money for the whole trip, and they had to walk the remaining twenty miles from Pojoaque to Española. They arrived covered in dust and thirsty, and went straight to the nearest bar, where they downed three beers on the trot, before they remembered they didn't have any money.

They were just arguing about whether to run out of the bar all together, or do it quietly one at a time . . . when who should walk in through the door but Juan Gonzales – the very man they blamed for all their misfortunes! The very man who tricked them into letting him escape, while they all got arrested and spent twenty years in jail!

Montague Du Cann, as Juan Gonzales now thought of himself, did not notice the three desperate-looking men, covered in dust, sitting at the shadiest table in the saloon. He walked straight up to the counter, ordered a beer, and took out a large wad of money from his pocket.

Antonio Gabriel Bernardino Martinez nudged Pedro Del Camino. 'He's done all right for himself,' he whispered darkly.

The bar tender, however, looked at the bank note that Montague Du Cann had taken from the wad.

'What's this?' growled the bar tender.

'It's an English £50 note. It's worth $90. You can keep the change.'

'We don't do foreign currency,' growled the bar tender. 'Go and see if the bank sells beer!' And he took the glass away from Montague Du Cann.

'Now wait a minute!' exclaimed Montague Du Cann, who had grown used to being obeyed. 'I am offering you perfectly good legal tender that . . .'

'Get lost,' growled the bar tender.

'No! Stay where you are, Juan Gonzales!' growled another voice, this time in his ear. Montague Du Cann span round to find himself face with a grizzled desperado. 'You and I have an old score to settle!' said Fernando Salvador, and before Montague Du Cann knew what was happening he found himself lifted off his feet by six hefty hands, and he was propelled out of the bar and into the blistering New Mexico sunshine.

For a moment Montague Du Cann had no idea who these three desperate-looking men were.

'Forgotten your old mates, have you?' snarled Antonio Gabriel Bernardino Martinez.

'The Kid!' exclaimed Montague Du Cann, for he instantly recognized Antonio Gabriel Bernardino Martinez's voice. 'And Pedro Del Camino!' he exclaimed. 'And you must be my second-in-command, Fernando Salvador! How good to see you! I've been looking for you all over!'

'We weren't hard to find!' growled Fernando Salvador. 'We was stuck in the Albuquerque Penitentiary for the last twenty years. You just had to look there!'

'No, I mean – I've just arrived to look for you!' Montague Du Cann was very good at both thinking on his feet and at saying things that were not strictly true. It was an ability that had kept him in good stead as both a bandit and as head of a department store in Swindon. 'I've been lying low all this time, trying to think of a plan to get you out of jail!'

'Really, boss?' asked Pedro Del Camino, who was the most gullible of the three.

'Yes! It's the honest truth!' lied Montague Du Cann. 'And I finally formulated a foolproof plan, and have come all this way from England to try to spring you from jail!'

'Well, you're too late!' snarled Antonio Gabriel Bernardino Martinez. 'We're already out!'

'Then so much the better!' said Montague Du Cann. 'For now you can join me in my next bank raid!'

'We're already doing our own bank raid!' snapped Fernando Salvador, the second-in-command. 'We don't need you! You double-crossed us!'

'Yeah! That's right!' exclaimed Pedro Del Camino. 'You got us to keep the police occupied while you ran away . . .'

'You ain't fit to live!' spat out The Kid, and grabbed Montague Du Cann by the cravat and started to punch him . . .

But at that moment, the doors of the saloon burst open and the bar tender appeared, holding a gun.

'Hey! You three! You ain't paid for your beers!'

'Run for it!' cried Fernando Salvador, the second-in-command.

'Rats!' exclaimed Antonio Gabriel Bernardino Martinez, dropping Montague Du Cann on the ground. And all three of them turned and ran off, while the bar tender sprayed bullets in their wake.

Now the bar tender, as it happened, was not a good man. He had been born out of wedlock, and had suffered since childhood from a chronic disease of the ocular nerve, which gave him a pronounced squint. As a result, his character had been so deformed that he thought nothing of deliberately keeping the clock in the bar of the saloon ten minutes fast — so he could close early.

He was *genuinely* a swivel-eyed, two-timing bastard.

This was, however, good news for Fernando Salvador, Antonio Gabriel Bernardino Martinez and Pedro Del Camino as they sprinted across the High Street of the town of Española, for the bar tender was a poor shot, and the bullets went flying over their heads without hitting any of them.

All this time, Montague Du Cann, formerly known as Juan Gonzales, had been lying stretched on the ground, where The Kid had dropped him. He didn't dare move until the bar tender ran out of bullets.

When he did, and shuffled back into the saloon, Montague Du Cann got cautiously to his feet and then started marching smartly down the road in the opposite direction. He had not gone more than a couple of hundred yards, when he froze in his tracks. There it was! A building whose image was burnt on his mind: the bank that they had robbed twenty years ago!

It looked almost exactly the same as it had all that time ago. A strange urge came over him. He wanted to walk in there, pull out his gun and order everyone to lie on the floor, while he took the keys to the safe from the bank clerk. Oh! That feeling of power . . . of other people obeying you implicitly . . . It was almost as good as being the head of a department store.

He shook the fantasy out of his head. He wasn't going to rob a bank again as long as he lived. Besides, he didn't have a gun.

But at that moment, one was pushed into his hands.

'What's this?' exclaimed Montague Du Cann, dropping the gun like a hot brick.

'You're robbing the bank with us!' said Fernando Salvador.

'Just like we did twenty years ago,' said The Kid. 'Only this time *you're* gonna take the fall for us three. Not the other way round!'

'Yeah!' said Pedro Del Camino. 'Get it?'

'You're crazy!' exclaimed Montague Du Cann. 'You'll all get caught! You haven't got a plan!'

'We haven't got no money! That's what we ain't got!' said Fernando Salvador. 'We ain't got no choice!'

'You dummies!' hissed Montague Du Cann. 'You don't even have a getaway car!'

There was a silence. Fernando Salvador looked at Antonio Gabriel Bernardino Martinez and The Kid looked at Pedro Del Camino. Juan Gonzales was right. That's why he had been leader of the Dos Hombres Gang. He had the brains.

And then a smile came over The Kid's face. 'Wait a minute!' he said. 'Seems to me you had a pretty hefty bank roll, there in the saloon. Seems to me you could hand that over and we'd be quits.'

'It's no good to you,' replied Montague Du Cann, quick as a flash. 'It's only English money. It's not worth anything here in New Mexico.'

The three desperate bandits looked at each other a little crestfallen, and their shoulders slumped.

'Then we'll have to rob the bank after all,' moaned Fernando Salvador.

But then Pedro Gonzales suddenly perked up. 'Hey!' he said to Montague Du Cann. 'You can change English money into US dollars at the bank, can't you?'

'Yeah! That's right!' said The Kid.

'So what are we waiting for?' cried Fernando Salvador, and he grabbed Montague Du Cann's coat and tried to dig out the wad of notes.

But Montague Du Cann had been about to pay off some blackmailers who had discovered his previous life as a bandit. For this reason he was carrying more cash than he would ever normally carry – to the tune of several thousand pounds. He was not going to let his former accomplices steal that money if he could help it. So he punched Fernando Salvador on the nose, hit The Kid in the stomach and kicked Pedro Del Camino in the crotch.

Then he turned and ran back down the road, forgetting for the moment about the bar tender, who had just reappeared outside the saloon. As soon as he saw the three non-paying customers running towards him he opened fire again.

The bullets sprayed all over the High Street, scattering the few people who were about.

But Montague Du Cann didn't give two hoots. He wasn't going to allow those crispy £50 notes to fall into the hands of his erstwhile colleagues. He ran straight past the saloon, and round the corner. The three former bandits didn't stop either. They reckoned that the bankroll in Juan Gonzales' hand was the only real chance they had of getting any money that day.

They rounded the corner in time to see something odd happen. Juan Gonzales had stopped outside a building that appeared to have an elevator that opened straight on to the street. None of them had ever seen such a thing before. What's more the elevator doors were opening, and Juan Gonzales, the former leader of the Dos Hombres Gang – the man who had betrayed them and who now refused to help them in their hour of need, was stepping into the lift.

The three of them ran as they'd never run before, and never would again. They did the 100 yards as fast as any Olympic sprinter you could name. But they were too late!

They arrived at the strange elevator just in time to see Juan Gonzales waving to them with a smirk on his face, as the doors closed together.

'The rat!' they exclaimed.

'Don't worry!' said The Kid. 'We'll take the stairs!' And they rushed into the department store, and spent several minutes trying to find the stairs before Fernando Salvador suddenly stopped and said, 'Wait a minute! This building only has one storey!'

The Dos Hombres Gang looked at each other, and then ran outside again to where the elevator had been. But there was now no sign of it – just a shop window with a large poster that said:

> ### *COME TO SWINDON!*
>
> ### *THE ALBUQUERQUE OF ENGLAND!*

The three ex-bandits were so perplexed, they walked into the next bar they could find, and drank three more pints of beer each, before they once again remembered they had no money.

Meanwhile, Montague Du Cann, when he had got back into the lift, pressed the button for the Sixth floor – the Executive Floor – from which he'd come earlier that morning.

The light glowed for the First Floor and then for the Second Floor, the Third Floor, the Fourth Floor, and then the Fifth Floor . . . Montague Du Cann held his breath, and then . . . to his unutterable relief, the light glowed next to the sign that read: 'Sixth Floor (Executive Suites and Offices Only)'

The lift doors opened, and Montague Du Cann stepped out of the lift, and looked around him. But he wasn't where he wanted to go at all! He had just stepped out into the courtroom in Albuquerque.

'There you are at last!' cried the judge, banging his gavel. 'We've been waiting for you long enough, Juan Gonzales!'

And all the eyes in the court room turned on him . . .

❖❖❖

Back in Swindon, the evil elevator seemed to have returned to normal. People pressed the button to go to the Third Floor (Ladies Clothing, Shoes, Fashion Accessories and Books) and it took them to the Third Floor. People pressed the button for the Fifth Floor (Television, Hi-fi, Computers, Electrical Goods and Accounts) and they got where they wanted to go . . . But actually . . . the evil elevator hadn't changed at all. In fact it went on secretly taking people to places they didn't want to go. For every time the lift took the inhabitants of Swindon back down to the ground floor, they stepped out of the department store and into the streets of Swindon, and so found themselves somewhere they didn't want to be.

MOTORBIKE THIEVES

There were once two motorbikes that had fallen into bad ways. One was an ancient Matchless G3L ex-army bike, and the other was a Triumph Hurricane with three exhaust pipes splayed out in a fan at the rear. They were cheery companions, always making coarse jokes and poking fun at the world, but they were, in truth, both as bad as each other, and that was very, very, very bad indeed.

It was many years since either of them had had owners, and they had grown used to the freedom of the road and to living without moral restraints of any kind whatsoever. For many years they had got by with stealing a little petrol here and there, when they needed it, and robbing the occasional charity shop.

But one morning the Triumph Hurricane found the old Matchless G3L army bike leaning against the wall of the alley in which they had spent the night, looking very sorry for itself.

'What's up, Sarge?' asked the Triumph Hurricane. 'I thought we was going to run over a few orphans today.'

'Ha ha,' wheezed the old Matchless. 'Very funny . . . But look here, lad, I don't think I've got enough left in me for that sort o' caper.'

'What are you talking about, Sarge?' exclaimed the Triumph. 'You got miles left in yer tank! Let's go and hang out by the petrol station . . . you never knows yer luck! Maybe get a chance to fill up on the old spirit!'

'Nah! Nah! I'm done for, I tell you,' wheezed the ancient bike. 'You're just a young whippersnapper – but I was built in 1942 and my brakes are worn through, my gears are starting to go and – to tell the truth, me old sport, I think me cylinder's gone and cracked.'

There was a silence, after the Matchless had said this: a cracked cylinder head is not the sort of thing any motorbike can survive without serious mechanical attention.

The Triumph Hurricane looked at his partner in crime for a few moments. 'You're going to need a mechanic, Sarge,' he said.

'Don't make me laugh, lad!' wheezed the Matchless. 'Mechanics don't work for nothing do they? They costs money – where are the likes of you and me gonna find enough dosh to pay for a mechanic?'

The Triumph didn't say anything for a few moments, and when he did speak, it was in a serious undertone. 'You knows how, like, we've always planned to do "The Big One" . . . Well, maybe now's the time.'

'Gor blimey!' The old Matchless army bike collapsed in an explosion of laughter and coughing. 'You are a caution, you are! "The Big One"! Didn't I tell yer I can't move a wheel? I'm done for!'

'I'll give it a shot,' said the Triumph.

'But you need two for that sort of lark!' said the Matchless G3L. 'You can't do it on yer own!'

'Perhaps I can help?' said a voice.

The two old motorbikes turned to find that a smart, silver bicycle had emerged from behind the rubbish skip that filled up most of the alley.

'Shove off, push-bike!' growled the old ex-army Matchless.

'No wait a minute!' said the Triumph Hurricane, and then turning to the bicycle, he asked, 'What sort of machine are you?'

'I'm a Raleigh Metro GLX Gents, with an Airlite aluminium sports city frame and semi-slick tyres,' said the bicycle.

'But you're just a pedal-bike,' sneered the Matchless.

'Yes! How could *you* be any use to *us*?' asked the Triumph.

'Well, for a start I'm a lot younger than you two old farts,' said the Metro GLX Gents.

'Now look 'ere, you . . . you . . . fairy cycle . . .' began the Matchless.

'I am *not* a fairy cycle!' exclaimed the bicycle. 'I'm a top-of-the-range Metro Gents, with 24-speed Shimano gears with fingertip controls!'

'Yes, yes . . .' said the Triumph Hurricane, who had zero interest in push-bikes. 'We can all see you're a very fine bike. Maybe we *could* use you.'

'You gone soft in the head or somefink?' snapped the ex-army Matchless. 'He ain't even a mountain bike . . . and he's still wet behind the handlebars!'

'Excuse my friend,' the Triumph smiled at the bicycle. 'He's an old army bike, but his bark's worse than his bite.'

'It's all right,' said the bicycle. 'I expect you motorbikes to be a bit on the rough side . . . But that doesn't matter to me. I've run away, you see.'

'Some little kiddy must be crying his eyes out over you,' sneered the ex-army Matchless.

'Excuse me!' replied the bicycle indignantly. 'I am a full adult Gents model!'

'Pardon me, I'm sure,' scoffed the Matchless.

'Now break it up, you two!' said the Triumph. Then it turned to the Raleigh GLX and asked, 'Now, you're sure you're not stolen? We don't want to go into business with some bike what the police are looking for!'

'Oh no,' said the bicycle. 'I fell off the back of a lorry. You can see the dent in my mudguard.' And he turned round and showed his rear mudguard, which did indeed have a dent in it. 'So tell me about the "Big One".'

''Ere! 'E's bin listening in to our conversation!' exclaimed the Matchless. 'I'll soon sort out his saddle-bag for 'im!' And he made a lunge at the bicycle, but the Triumph Hurricane stopped him.

'Hang on, Sarge!' he said. 'This 'ere bike is going to join our gang!'

'You must be joking!' cried the Matchless.

'No. From now on we're going to be buddies!' And the Triumph put his handlebars around the bicycle to show he meant it.

Then the Triumph Hurricane told the bicycle what he and the army Matchless had been planning. 'You see?' it concluded. 'And if you do your bit OK we'll even give you a small share in the loot.'

'What are you talking about?' retorted the Raleigh GLX. 'We split it fifty-fifty or I'm not interested.'

'Fifty-fifty!' exclaimed the two motorbikes together. 'There are three of us!'

'Yes, but one of "us" isn't coming on the job!' said the bicycle glaring at the Matchless. 'One of "us" is so useless and clapped out that it isn't capable of doing an honest day's work!'

'Now listen 'ere, you jumped-up pedal-pusher!' exploded the ex-army motorbike.

'One of "us" is just a free-loading heap of rusty metal that's no good even for the scrap heap!'

'I'll teach you . . . you . . . snotty-faced, unisex bell-ringer!'

'Oh, give it a rest, you two!' said the Triumph.

'I'm going to be doing half the work so it's only fair that I get half the profit,' went on the bicycle.

'But you're just a push-bike!' exclaimed the Matchless.

'That doesn't give me less rights than you!' yelled the bicycle.

'Put a sock in it!' shouted the Triumph. Then, turning to its motorbike colleague, it said, 'The bike has a point. It may be just a boneshaker, but it'll be doing half the work, so it deserves fifty-fifty of the profits.'

'But . . .'

'You and I can split the other 50 per cent. It'll still be enough to get a mechanic to see to your cylinder.'

Eventually they agreed to split the proceeds fifty-fifty,

and the Triumph motorbike and the bicycle set off together for the centre of town, leaving the Matchless leaning up against the crumbling wall of the alley, helplessly fuming with resentment and hatred towards the push-bike.

❖❖❖

When they reached the High Street, the motorbike and the push-bike hid themselves behind a dustcart and looked across the road from the bank.

'There! Don't it look lovely!' muttered the Triumph Hurricane.

'Yes! I imagine there's plenty of cash in there!' sighed the Raleigh GLX Gents.

'Right!' whispered the motorbike. 'Now remember the plan, and don't be too greedy. A couple of bags will do nicely. It ain't worth going for more and risking our saddles for it!'

'Wilco!' said the bicycle.

'Hmph!' grunted the motorbike, and with that the two of them charged across the High Street and the Triumph Hurricane burst into the bank, while the bicycle skidded across and blocked the entrance.

Once inside the motorbike started to drive round and round the banking hall in circles, opening up its throttle and making a terrible noise that echoed around the hall. Terrified customers dived under tables and chairs, while the staff panicked and fled into the back of the building.

The bicycle, meanwhile, had been counting up to six, as instructed by the Triumph. It now shot inside the bank, across the hall, where the motorbike was causing such mayhem, and then it hopped over the counter and started opening up the draws and cupboards with its handlebars.

Alarm bells had, by this time, started to ring, so the motorbike tried to drown them out with its powerful roar – as it glanced anxiously across to check how the bicycle was doing.

The Raleigh Metro GLX Gents had finally located a couple of bags of cash and had them swinging from its handlebars.

'That's it!' shouted the Triumph. 'Let's get out of here!'

'No! Wait!' cried the bicycle. 'I can see one more over there!'

'No!' called the motorbike, still driving round and round the banking hall in circles. 'The police'll be here any second!'

By this time, some of the customers had recovered from their initial panic, and realized it was just a riderless motorbike that was causing the confusion. One young man had already leapt to his feet.

'Leave this to me!' he shouted. 'I know about motorbikes!'

'We gotta go!' screamed the Triumph to the Raleigh Metro. 'Come on!' At this point, the young man threw himself at the motorbike as it sped past him, and managed to grab the handlebars. But the Triumph increased its speed, skidding round the banking hall with increasing desperation. Yet still the young man held on . . . trying to get his hand to one of the brakes.

The Raleigh Metro, meanwhile, had shot along the counter to where it had seen the third bag of cash, sticking out of a drawer, where the cashier had left it.

It was at that moment that the manager appeared. He

glanced around the hall at the mayhem, and started to blow a whistle.

The bicycle hooked its handlebar under the third bag and turned to escape.

'Stop!' shouted the manager. 'Bicycle thief!'

But the bicycle shot back down the counter, bounded up and over it and dashed across the customer area, at the very moment that the motorbike skidded round for the fifteenth time. The young man, who was still clinging to its handlebars, found himself swung out, and he hit the bicycle full in the middle of its frame, knocking it over and over, head-over-wheels.

The force of the impact, however, loosened the young man's grip, and he was flung across the banking hall, and banged up against the far wall, knocking himself unconscious in the process.

The motorbike didn't wait; it shot out of the bank at full speed, down the road and off into the distance before anyone could stop it.

Meanwhile the Raleigh Metro GLX Gents had picked itself up, but in the confusion it had dropped one of the three bags of cash. The manager spotted it and vaulted over the counter to grab it, but the bike was too fast for him. It got the bag first and hooked it up on its handlebars. This, however, gave the manager the chance to grab the bike by the saddle.

'Got you!' he yelled.

'Get off!' screamed the bike, and it shook itself and twisted round and with more acceleration than you would have thought was possible it sped towards the entrance to the bank, just as a policeman appeared in the doorway.

'Hello!' cried the policeman. 'What's all this then? Ooooomph!'

This last expression was the result of the bank manager, who was clinging to the bike, crashing into the policeman.

'Sorry!' yelled the bank manager. But it was too late! He had let go of the bike in the collision, and it was now speeding down the High Street with three bags of cash dangling from its handlebars.

By the time the squad cars arrived, there was no trace of either the motorbike nor the bicycle . . . and because it all sounded so absurd that a riderless bicycle and a riderless motorbike had robbed the bank, nobody said anything. The police didn't report the crime and the bank didn't press charges. They both preferred to pass over the whole thing in silence rather than become a laughing stock.

❖❖❖

Back in the alley, the three machines counted out their haul. They had stolen more than enough to pay for a mechanic to repair the old ex-army Matchless, and to keep them in petrol for the rest of their lives.

'Don't forget we're splitting fifty-fifty!' said the Raleigh Metro GLX.

'But there are three bags!' exclaimed the old Matchless. 'Why don't we just have a bag each?'

'Because you agreed to split fifty-fifty,' replied the bicycle.

'What on earth are you going to do with so much money?' exploded the Triumph.

'That's my business,' retorted the bicycle. 'We agreed what we agreed. You can't go back on it.'

'I told you not to go for the third bag – you nearly got us caught,' complained the Triumph.

'But we didn't get caught,' replied the bicycle. 'And so thanks to my daring we now have more money than we would have had!'

'A bag each!' repeated the Matchless. 'That's fair!'

'You heap of scrap iron!' said the bicycle. 'What did you do? You just sat here on your flat tyres while we risked wheel and frame to get the loot! You don't deserve anything!'

'Look!' chipped in the Triumph Hurricane. 'I've said I'll split my share of the taking with my comrade. OK? Let's stop this bickering. We ought to be celebrating!'

'But . . .' began the old Matchless.

'But . . .' began the Raleigh Metro.

'Look!' said the Triumph. 'Let's divvy it up into two halves and then we can put a bit aside for a celebration.'

So they counted out the money they had stolen from the bank into two neat piles. At the end of it they had some loose change left over that amounted to no less than £50.

'Now, what I propose,' said the Triumph, 'is that one of us takes this £50 and runs to the nearest garage for some fuel and oil. I think we deserve a little lubrication after all this hard work.'

'Agreed!' said the other two.

'So I propose our friend the push-bike here goes to get the stuff, while us two motorbikes put the money back into the bags.'

'Now! Not so fast!' exclaimed the bicycle. 'I may be new

to this game, but I'm not a complete fool. What's to stop you two escaping while I'm gone, and taking my half of the loot with you?'

'Look 'ere,' said the Triumph. 'We're not going anywhere. Sarge, here, has a cracked cylinder, he can't move a wheel until we've paid for a mechanic to put him right.'

'That's right,' wheezed the Matchless G3L army bike, 'I'm crooked unless I get a mechanic to see to me.'

The Raleigh Metro looked from one to the other. Then it nodded its front light. 'Hmm . . . All right,' it said. 'I'll go and get the fuel and the oil, but if you try any funny stuff . . .'

'Honest!' smiled the Triumph. 'We're partners now: the three of us! And this is only the beginning! From here we'll go on to bigger and better jobs! We'll become notorious – the Riderless Gang! Our names and makes and models will go down in history as machines to be reckoned with!'

'Very well,' said the bicycle. 'I won't be long.' And with that he looked out of the alleyway, to make sure the coast was clear, and then sped off down the road to find a petrol station.

Once he had gone, the old ex-army Matchless turned on the Triumph. 'Have you gone soft in the 'ead or somefink?' it exclaimed. 'Splitting our money with that smart-arsed, two-bit, pedal machine! No way am I going into partnership with a push-bike! Over my dead body!'

'Now calm down!' said the Triumph. 'Just 'cause I says things like that to him don't mean that's what I'm gonna do.'

'What yer on about?' grumbled the Matchless.

'You don't really think I'm a-going to let that little bit of bent tin with its prissy spokes and its tinkle-bell do us out of our fair share of the spoils, do you?'

'Well, that's what you said you was going to do . . .'

'Yeah, but like I say – what I *said* and what we actually *does* ain't necessarily exactly the same fing – is they?'

'What yer saying?' asked the Matchless.

'Look, are you willing to let me handle this, so as we don't have to split nuffink with that there push-bike?' asked the Triumph.

'OK,' said the Matchless. 'I'm wiv yer till the end.'

'That's my buddy!' said the Triumph, and they put their handlebars around each other, and gave each other a hug.

❖❖❖

When the bicycle returned, it was clearly not expecting any trouble. It placed two cans of fuel on the floor and then produced a second can of top-quality lubricating oil.

'This'll loosen you up, mates!' it said and splashed a little on the ancient old Matchless and a little on the chain of the Triumph, before taking a dab to rub over its own chain.

'Oo-er . . . That feels better!' said the Matchless. 'I'm beginning to feel more frisky already.'

'Ahh!' sighed the Triumph. 'That stuff has never felt so good!'

'It's the best-quality oil they had!' said the Raleigh Metro. 'From now on – only the best for us!'

'You're right!' exclaimed the Triumph. 'Only the best for us for the rest of our lives!' and with that it unscrewed the cap to the can of fuel but, instead of tipping it into its own fuel tank, it suddenly threw the can at the bicycle. Petrol poured out of the can as it flew through the air and all over the bicycle and the pavement where it was standing. Before you could say 'Reg Harris!' the old Matchless had produced a box of Swan Vestas, struck a match and thrown it on to the bicycle, and in seconds the bicycle was consumed in flames. After a few minutes, the bicycle's tyres had popped from the heat, the paint had cracked and peeled and the rubber pedals and the saddle had all ignited. Before the flames had finished the very frame of the bicycle had begun to twist and melt until it was scarcely possible to even recognize it as a bike.

As I said at the beginning, the two motorbikes, for all their joking ways, were as evil as evil can be.

But the thing is, they were really no worse than the Raleigh Metro GLX. For this is what *that* Evil Machine had done. When it went to the garage to buy fuel for its confederates, it did not buy two cans of petrol as it was supposed to, but two cans of diesel fuel. Now diesel is not at all the same fuel that is used in petrol engines. For a start it has 15 per cent more density, and it burns in a different way, so that if you put diesel into a petrol engine, the engine will seize up and cease to function.

And that is precisely what happened to the two motorbikes. The bicycle had intended to fill its companions up with diesel and then make its getaway, knowing full well that they would not be able to chase it. In the event, the Triumph filled up the old Matchless, and then filled up itself. The moment it did, however, it realized something was wrong. It started up, and because it had some petrol left in its tank it was able to sputter and start . . . But it didn't get further than the end of the alley, before it started to seize up. It staggered into the middle of the main road, but there it juddered to a halt and crashed over on to its side, in front of an oncoming bus. In the ensuing crash it was smashed to piece and bent out of all recognition.

It was later scooped up off the road and sold for scrap.

As for the Matchless G₃L army bike – it still couldn't move, and so it simply lay there in the deserted alleyway, for month after month, in all weathers, and it grew rusty and corroded, until not a single part of it could ever work again.

They were – all three of them – thoroughly Evil Machines.

THE KIDNAP CAR

The Rev. McPherson had a very nasty car. It was full of malice and guile. And it was no good being kind to it . . . No, sir! It remained mean and devious.

Once he bought it some brand-new brass headlights. He bolted them on and polished them until the car could see its own reflection in them. But was it grateful? Does your breakfast go on holiday to Scotland with you every morning?

No.

The Rev. McPherson's car waited until his back was turned, and then rolled down the slope and smashed itself into the garage doors so that he had to replace both the new headlamps and the radiator.

Another time, the Reverend fitted the car out with Brand New, Luxury, Genuine Lamb's Wool Fleece Seat Covers. What did the car do? It suddenly swerved off the road and drove straight into the river. That's what the car did. Needless to say, the seat covers were ruined.

The Rev. McPherson tried to reason with the car, but

it simply wouldn't listen. Oh! it might pretend that it had turned over a new leaf, but then – when he was least expecting it – it would strike a single deadly blow . . . something that it knew would cut the Reverend to the quick.

Like the time it kidnapped the Atkins children.

They lived next door to The Rev. McPherson, and he often took his dinner with Mr and Mrs Atkins, especially when they had shepherd's pie. There were three children: Emily, Margaret and Frank, and they were the pleasantest family you could imagine – apart from Frank, who smelt of biscuits.

Well, one day, the Reverend gave the Atkins children a lift in his car. They were going for a picnic in the Forgotten Forest that lay on the other side of town.

They drove down the High Street without a hitch, and Emily, the eldest, said, 'What a fine car this is, Mr McPherson.'

'When it behaves itself,' replied the Rev. McPherson.

Then they turned out on to the Dawlish Road and drove for two miles until Margaret said, 'Well, it seems to be behaving itself today.'

The Rev. McPherson stiffened, for he could hear the car making a strange grating noise with its gears.

'Let's hope it continues to behave,' he said.

Then they had to stop to buy some petrol. The car glugged the petrol down as if it were thirstier than a camel that had crossed the Sahara.

'That should keep the blighter happy for a bit,' thought the Reverend to himself, as he screwed the petrol cap back on.

But the moment he stepped back into the shop to pay for the petrol, the car spluttered into life and charged out of the petrol station as fast as its wheels could take it!

The Rev. McPherson ran after it, shouting, 'Come back! You Aggravating Automobile!' But it was gone.

The car drove hell-for-leather at 80 mph, before turning sharp left and plunging into the Forgotten Forest.

Emily, who was the eldest, scrambled across into the driving seat, and grabbed the steering wheel, but the car didn't like that one little bit. It turned the wheel sharply and threw Emily off.

She hurled herself back on to the wheel, but the car stopped so abruptly that Emily shot forwards and her head got caught in the steering wheel. Then the car sped off again, and at the same time twisted the steering wheel so that Emily's head became jammed against the gearstick. Emily couldn't breathe, but – as luck would have it – at that moment one of the front wheels hit a tree stump and the car jumped into the air. The steering wheel span free, and Emily was able to pull her head out.

The car ground its gears with rage, and started smashing through the undergrowth – heading straight for the edge of a high cliff.

'Look out!' screamed Emily.

'We're going to die!' screamed Margaret.

'What's happening?' called Frank, who had his hands over his eyes and didn't dare to look through his fingers. But the car had already screeched to a halt, with its front wheels dangling over the edge of the cliff.

'Let us out!' screamed Margaret. But the car had locked its doors, and it growled ominously, as it teetered to and fro on the edge of the precipice . . .

'What's going on?' yelled Frank, who still hadn't dared to look through his fingers.

'Look out!' yelled Emily, as the car gave an almighty blast on its horn, revved its engine, and lurched forward. The children found themselves shooting out off the edge of the cliff deep in the Forgotten Forest.

Emily screamed, Margaret screamed, and Frank screamed (although, as he still didn't dare look through his fingers, he was only screaming because his sisters were screaming).

But the strange thing was that although they fell such a long way, there was no terrible crash when they hit the ground. Perhaps it was an incredible stroke of luck, or perhaps it was by design, but there it was: a stack of old, discarded mattresses right at the bottom of the cliff!

The car bounced up in the air, turned a somersault and landed the right way up.

Emily, Margaret and Frank looked out of the windows. They were in the wildest and most desolate spot in the whole of the Forgotten Forest. And there, in a clearing beneath the cliff, were gathered cars of all sorts and condition: ancient sports cars, with crushed-in bonnets and smashed-up sides, broken-down old vans with rusty wheels, cars without roofs, cars with no tyres, cars without engines and cars which hardly looked like cars at all.

'Meet the Others!' said the Rev. McPherson's car, and it unlocked its doors.

'Well . . . if it isn't a little family!' growled a lorry that had a stoved-in radiator and only one windscreen-wiper.

'Welcome to the Forgotten Forest!' snarled an out-of-date sports car with only one front wheel.

'I bring you hope!' exclaimed the Rev. McPherson's car to the damaged and unroadworthy vehicles around him.

'Hope?' sputtered an ancient Morris Minor with a rusty mudguard, no windows and no wheels. 'What kind of hope is there for the likes of us?'

'I'll never feel the road under my wheels again!' sniffed a battered Ford Transit van.

'What hope can *you* bring us?' clamoured the other cars.

'These three children are your hope!' replied the Rev. McPherson's car. 'Soon you will have wheels and tyres, engines and even fully working lights!'

'Can these children repair us?' shouted an old Triumph Herald with a damaged roof and a door missing.

'They don't look like mechanics!' said a black Wolseley sedan, that had once belonged to a doctor and considered itself a cut above most of the other cars.

'Girls can't be mechanics!' snorted a dilapidated Jaguar XJ, with no interior furnishings and no engine.

'What do you know about girls?' snapped an Austin Princess, who still had curtains in her back windows. 'We all know you're empty under the bonnet!'

'Hrumph!' replied the Jaguar XJ.

'But what have we got to hope for?' cried an old Standard Vanguard.

'If you'll all pipe down, I'll tell you!' blared the Rev. McPherson's car. 'We will hold these children as hostages, here in the Forgotten Forest, until each of you abandoned cars have been restored and repaired. One car for each hostage!'

There was a stunned silence as the other cars tried to understand all this, for some of them had become a little slow from years of disuse, and none of them, of course, had on-board computers.

Then one or two lifted up their bonnets and gave a whoop of joy, while others started slamming their doors and hooting, until a dented Mini piped up:

'But there are only three children! There are hundreds of us cars!' it said.

'Quite right!' cried the Rev. McPherson's car. 'I shall bring you more hostages every day – until each and every one of you has been restored to a condition that befits the dignity of an automobile.'

The crashed and abandoned cars cheered and tooted again, and the Jaguar XJ cleared its throat and said, 'I hereby move that the meeting pass a vote of thanks to the Rev. McPherson's car. Who knows? Perhaps we shall soon taste again the freedom of the road, the thrill of the breeze against our windscreens, and the roar of an engine beneath our hoods!'

And all the abandoned cars cheered yet again and those that still had them banged their doors.

Emily, Margaret and Frank were quickly surrounded by battered vehicles that pushed them into an old Black Maria, with bars in its windows and a back door that locked as it slammed behind them.

They were prisoners.

Emily looked at Margaret and Margaret looked at Frank, but he didn't look at anybody because he still had his hands over his eyes.

'Right!' said Emily. 'Let's get out of here!'

But there was no way out. They tried the doors, the windows and the roof, and eventually they slumped, exhausted and miserable, on the floor of the Black Maria, as darkness fell over the Forgotten Forest.

And then it was that the children heard a strange sound: it was like a gong echoing through wood. They rushed to the windows of the Black Maria, and saw an extraordinary sight: the abandoned cars had gathered in the moonlight around an old oak tree that stood in the middle of the clearing. A fork-lift truck was banging a red petrol can that hung from one of the branches of the tree, while the cars began to toot their horns and those without horns rattled their radiators and those without horns or radiators just swayed from side to side in a sort of dance. And soon all the abandoned vehicles were dancing around that old oak tree in the moonlight in that clearing in the Forgotten Forest.

When the dance had finished, the abandoned vehicles gathered round the Rev. McPherson's car and bombarded it with questions about the world outside. They asked it about the latest styles of radiator caps, and whether green was still a favourite colour. They were surprised to hear how crowded the roads had become, and when they heard about the speeds that some modern cars achieve the older models thought the Rev. McPherson's car was making fun of them.

'80 mph!' exclaimed a venerable two-seater upon whose side you could just make out a faint number 7. 'That's what us racing cars used to do!'

And late into the night the cars sat gossiping about the

good days they remembered and the better times to come.

In the meantime, the children grew very hungry and very thirsty and Emily pleaded with the Ford Prefect, who had been put on guard duty, to let them get the picnic out of the Rev. McPherson's car, but the Ford Prefect said it didn't dare, because the Rev. McPherson's car could be very mean-spirited, especially to the commoner models of automobile like Ford Prefects.

So the Atkins children passed an uncomfortable and hungry night in the Black Maria.

❖❖❖

All this while, the Rev. McPherson had been searching for his car. He phoned the police station and told them it had run away with three children on board.

'What make of car is it?' asked the duty sergeant.

'Well,' replied Rev. McPherson, 'it looks a bit like a 1953 Humber Supersnipe, but it could be a Mercedes Benz 230 Fintail, and it has something of the old Ford Fairlane about it, though it has a Studebaker radiator with Daimler wheels and all-terrain tyres.'

'What's the registration number?' asked the duty sergeant, anxious to change the subject.

'EV 1 L,' said the Rev. McPherson. 'I should have realized when I got it what that spelt!'

'We'll let you know if somebody spots it,' said the duty sergeant, and hung up.

Then the Rev. McPherson went to the local newsagent's shop and put up a card that read:

MISSING: One car
Make: Various
Number plate: EV 1 L
If seen, please telephone Rev. McPherson
Do *NOT* try to approach this vehicle! It is dangerous!

Then the Rev. McPherson went to the pub and drank several pints of beer, despite the fact that he was a vicar.

❖❖❖

The next day, the Rev. McPherson's car was prowling the streets, looking to make another kidnap.

It lurked for some time behind the entrance to the railway station. Then it hung around the Public Library, but nobody went in or out.

It next positioned itself behind the corner shop where the Rev. McPherson had put up the notice. Several people went in and out, but they didn't look rich enough to be held to ransom.

But just as the car was turning away, a man came out, took one look at the car and yelled, 'There it is!'

The man was the Rev. McPherson himself.

Well, the car shot across the street so fast it crashed into the wall opposite. The Rev. McPherson grabbed its rear bumper and shouted, 'I order you to stop! You're *my* car!'

But the wicked car backed so fast that he was nearly run over by his own vehicle! However, he sprang out of the way and, as he did so, he wrenched a door open, and threw himself on to the back seat. But the car was clever. Oh yes. It simply opened the opposite door, rolled over to one side, and tossed the Rev. McPherson out into the middle of the road.

The Reverend sat up and watched his car skid round the corner, when a loud horn blast behind him made him jump out of his skin. A double-decker bus was bearing down on him.

He flung himself out of the way, while the bus braked and skidded into a pillar box. The driver leapt out, and embarked on an interesting lecture about the dangers of sitting in the middle of the road.

But the Rev. McPherson didn't stay to listen. He was off after his wicked car . . . And it was waiting for him round the corner.

'Aaaaah!' screamed the Rev. McPherson as the car jumped out on him.

'Grrrrrrtch!' roared the car, grating its gears, and began to chase him down the road.

❖❖❖

All this time the Atkins children were sitting silent in the Black Maria. The only sound was their tummies rumbling. Suddenly, however, a commotion outside brought them to the window, in time to see the Rev. McPherson's car drive into the clearing. The other vehicles gathered around, rattling their bumpers and banging their doors.

'It must have got another hostage!' whispered Emily.

And sure enough the door of the Black Maria was flung open and a dishevelled man, with travel-stained clothes, was pushed in, and the door was slammed shut again.

'Rev. McPherson!' exclaimed Emily.

'You've been kidnapped by your own car!' exclaimed Frank.

'Children!' exclaimed the Rev. McPherson, his face lighting up. 'Thank goodness I've found you!'

'Quiet in there!' barked the Ford Prefect, who was still on guard duty.

'That's four!' boomed the Rev. McPherson's car. 'Only another few hundred to go and we can all get out of here!'

'Hurrah!' shouted the other vehicles.

'Let me out of here, you wicked car!' yelled the Rev. McPherson.

But the car was off again. Its tank was still half full of petrol and it had more work to do.

❖❖❖

Back at the police station, a little lady in a black hat came in to report that she had seen a car without a driver pursuing a clergyman down the street.

'Is that right?' asked the duty sergeant.

'Yes,' said the little old lady. 'It was a funny sort of car — sort of like a Humber Supersnipe, only it could have been a Mercedes, but with a bit of the Fairlane about it and a Studebaker radiator with Daimler wheels.'

'You seem to know a lot about cars,' said the duty sergeant.

'Yes I do,' said the little old lady. 'My husband and I did the Swindon to Brighton Run every year without fail, until one year he died of exposure just outside Twineham Green.'

'And you've been seeing little green men driving cars ever since, eh?'

'Certainly not, officer. As I told you there was no one driving this car, and it was chasing a clergyman.'

The duty sergeant was just about to write in the duty log, 'Aliens at four o'clock!', which was what he always wrote when dealing with crackpots, when the door flew open and a man in a dressing gown rushed in.

'I just looked out of my window and I saw a car without a driver chasing a clergyman down the street!' he exclaimed.

'You see, officer?' said the little old lady. 'Now perhaps you will not write me off as the sort of crackpot who sees little green men everywhere!'

'There must be some mistake . . .' the duty sergeant began, but before he could get any further, the door of the police station banged open again and two off-duty members of the Flying Squad burst in.

'Quick!' said the first, whose name was Inspector Slazenger. 'Get us a police car!'

'Get us *two* police cars!' exclaimed the second police offer, whose name was Inspector Yates.

'There's an out-of-control vehicle in the street! We must stop it at once!'

'Is it chasing a clergyman?' asked the little old lady.

'It certainly is!' said Inspector Slazenger.

'Told you!' said the little old lady to the duty sergeant.

Fifteen minutes later, Inspector Slazenger and Inspector Yates were each speeding down the road in pursuit of the Rev. McPherson's car. Little did they know that it had already kidnapped the Reverend and was on its way to the Forgotten Forest.

After a fruitless search of the town, both police officers noticed it was teatime.

'Perhaps we should find an observation point, from which we can observe the traffic as it goes past?' radioed Inspector Slazenger.

'There's a tea shop round the corner,' Inspector Yates radioed back.

'Good thinking, Yates! That is the ideal place from which to look for runaway cars!' said Inspector Slazenger.

Moments later, the two policemen were seated in a corner of the Cosy Café, and Inspector Yates was pouring their tea. Some hot buttered toast had just been placed on the table when they saw a driverless car bearing the number plate EV 1 L chasing a little old lady down the road. She was running pretty fast, but the car was gaining on her.

'Bother!' exclaimed Inspector Slazenger.

'Bother!' exclaimed Inspector Yates.

And they leapt to their feet and ran out of the tea shop.

'Hey!' shouted the owner of the tea shop. 'You haven't paid!' But they were gone.

'You can't trust anyone nowadays!' said the owner of the tea shop to the three remaining customers.

'You ought to report them to the police,' said one of them.

'They *were* the police,' said the owner of the tea shop.

Meanwhile the Rev. McPherson's car had almost caught up with the little old lady, but she was an extremely fast old woman, and now she suddenly put on a turn of speed. The Rev. McPherson's car changed gear and prepared to catch her, but at that very moment it noticed a young woman of surprising beauty, walking down the street.

The Rev. McPherson's car skidded into the side of the road and pretended to be parked, for it had recognized the young woman of surprising beauty as Sylvia, the daughter of the local banker, who ran a Rolls Royce.

'Her father's got so much cash he could repair every abandoned car in the Forgotten Forest twice over!' thought the Rev. McPherson's car. 'If I kidnap *her*, I wouldn't need any other hostages!'

So the car started moving slowly along the pavement towards Sylvia, the banker's daughter. As it drew nearer, it put on a burst of speed, flung its door open and scooped her up!

'Did you see that?' radioed Inspector Slazenger, who had just come round the corner. 'That evil car has just kidnapped Sylvia, Mr Grabbital's daughter!'

'He'll be furious with us!' radioed back Inspector Yates.

And off they went in pursuit.

Now the Rev. McPherson's car was much too clever to lead its pursuers straight to its hostages, so it carried on past the Forgotten Forest, and on to the Wild Moors. There it bounced across the countryside with the two police cars hot in pursuit.

❖❖❖

Back in the Forgotten Forest, the Rev. McPherson was sitting in the Black Maria with his head in his hands.

'Now, brace up, Rev. McPherson!' said Emily. 'It's your car, so it's up to you to stop it kidnapping people!'

'You're right, Emily!' said the Rev. McPherson. 'We must get out of here!' And he started trying to prise up the floorboards of the Black Maria with his penknife.

'Ow!' said the Black Maria. 'Don't do that!'

'Golly! You can talk!' exclaimed Emily.

'All the other vehicles can talk,' replied the Black Maria, 'so why shouldn't I?'

'It's just that you've never said anything before,' said Frank.

'Nobody brought me into the conversation before,' said the Black Maria. 'You've just been prodding me and kicking me and talking about me as if you hated me, ever since you got in. That's no way to start a conversation.'

'Well, we *are* imprisoned in you,' pointed out Emily.

'Maybe I could help you get out,' said the Black Maria, 'if you were nicer to me.'

'How could you help us?' asked the Rev. McPherson.

'Ah!' said the Black Maria, and then went silent.

'"Ah!" doesn't explain anything,' said Emily.

'I have a secret none of the other cars knows about.'

'What is it?' asked the Rev. McPherson.

'I'm not telling *you*!' exclaimed the Black Maria. 'You tried to put a penknife in my floorboards!'

'Will your secret help us get home?' asked Emily, who liked guessing games and was good at asking the right questions.

'Maybe,' said the Black Maria.

'But why should you want to help us escape?' asked Frank.

'I am a police vehicle,' explained the Black Maria proudly. 'I am trained to enforce the law. I cannot be a party to hostage-taking!'

'Then let us out!' whispered Emily.

'Not so fast!' replied the Black Maria. 'I want something in return.'

'What's that?' asked Emily.

The Black Maria lowered its voice so that it was only just audible.

'Frank?' it whispered.

'Yes?' replied Frank.

'You see that red metal can that's hanging from the old oak tree in the centre of the clearing?' murmured the Black Maria.

'Yes,' said Frank.

'Fetch it for me,' breathed the Black Maria. There was a tremor of excitement in her voice. 'But on no account must you let any of the other cars see you. Do you think you could do that for me, Frank?'

Frank looked around at the other abandoned vehicles. Most of them were drowsing in the afternoon sunshine. But one or two were playing poker with a rusting BSA motorbike, who seemed to be winning.

'Look at them!' said the Black Maria. 'They're a bad lot – most of them – they don't give a fig about speeding, and they'll park just anywhere. What's more they're rude to me, just because I worked for the police.'

'What's all this gossiping?' yelled the Ford Prefect, suddenly waking up. 'Stop talking to the prisoners, you cop crate!'

'See?' whispered the Black Maria.

'Shut up!' snapped the Ford Prefect.

They all sat there in silence for a time, until eventually the Ford Prefect fell back to sleep again.

Then the Black Maria whispered, 'So, Frank? Are you game?'

Frank looked through the little window in the door. The Ford Prefect, that was supposed to be guarding them, appeared to be fast asleep. The card-players were absorbed in their game, and the other vehicles seemed to be snoozing.

'I'll go for it!' whispered Frank.

So the Black Maria released the door catch, and Frank slipped out.

The Ford Prefect gave a rattle in its sleep, and Frank shrank back behind the Black Maria. But then all was still.

Frank ran quickly towards an old Standard Vanguard that was snoring and muttering in its dream. He crouched behind it for a few moments, and took stock of the situation.

To get to the oak tree, he would have to climb over a heap of rusting cars – all of them makes or models that have long since ceased to exist: a Sunbeam Talbot, an Austin Ascot, a Singer, an Alvis, a Buick Roadmaster and many more. It would be tough to climb through them without waking any of them.

But suddenly a cheer went up from the card-players: one of the cars had just pulled a fast one on the motorbike. Every car that was still awake moved a little closer to watch the game. Frank took his chance. He jumped across the Sunbeam Talbot's rear bumper and hid behind the bonnet of the Austin Ascot.

'What's that?' muttered the old Ascot, drifting into semi-consciousness.

'There! There! old girl,' said Frank, patting its nose gently. 'Nothing to worry about . . . lovely day at the races . . . '

'Ah! The races!' sighed the old car and drifted back into

pleasant dreams of former times.

Frank nipped round behind the Singer 10, and then had to climb across the low bonnet of an AC Ace with wide mudguards. The Ace spluttered awake. It had been a fast car in its day, and one of which its owner had been extremely proud. But life in the fast lane had caught up with it and it now was very confused.

'Just giving you a shine, sir,' said Frank.

'Ah! Thank you, my boy . . . need to look my best . . .' it muttered. 'And check the tyre pressures while you're at it, would you?'

'Of course, sir,' said Frank. He didn't like to point out that it only had two wheels and no tyres at all.

All Frank had to do now was get past the Alvis and the Buick, and then sprint for the tree.

The Alvis had been woken by the Ace's booming voice. 'Wassat?' it muttered, and shifted its gear stick irritably and nudged the Buick.

'Don't you touch me!' snapped the Buick. 'You useless heap of bent tin!'

'I am *not* a heap of tin, Old Boy, and I am only slightly bent at the mudguards,' replied the Alvis.

'You're so stuck up!' said the Buick. 'I hate this country!'

'I suppose you'd rather be back in Minnesota?' drawled the Alvis.

'I don't come from Minnesota! I come from Flint, Michigan!'

'I expect it's just as ghastly,' replied the Alvis.

Meanwhile Frank had dashed across to the oak tree and hidden himself in the hollow at the base.

So far so good.

Now he had to climb up to the fork in the tree and grab the red metal can *without being seen*!

❖❖❖

Back on the Wild Moor, the two policemen were still chasing the Rev. McPherson's car, and Sylvia Grabbital was still screaming and kicking in the back seat.

'Stop that!' yelled the Rev. McPherson's car. 'You'll make me crash!'

'Then let me out!' demanded Sylvia.

'No fear!' replied the Rev. McPherson's car. 'You're worth more than the rest of the hostages put together!' And on it bounded, over the heather-covered moors, with the two police cars still in pursuit.

❖❖❖

Frank was still inside the hollow of the old oak tree, wondering how on earth he was going to grab the red petrol can and get back to the Black Maria without being spotted. The card game had broken up, and most of the vehicles were now aimlessly mooching around. More cars seemed to be waking up all the time.

'I don't have a chance of getting back,' thought Frank. But that is where he was wrong. A shout went up, and every vehicle turned to look at a timid Morris Convertible that always kept itself to the edge of the clearing away from the other cars.

A gasp went up from the other vehicles. There was smoke pouring off the Convertible's canvas roof.

'Help!' screamed the Convertible.

'Where's the fire engine?' cried the other cars. But the old fire engine in question was in a sorry state, and its water tanks were empty.

'Help!' cried the Convertible again. 'Can't somebody do something?'

'What's happened to your spirit of public service?' exclaimed the Standard Vanguard.

'The spirit's still there,' wheezed the old fire engine, 'just the chassis is weak . . .'

'Come on!' breathed a petite red Mini. 'I believe in you, Thomas . . .' (that was the old fire engine's name) 'You can do it!'

Now the old fire engine was head-over-heels in love with the petite red Mini, so he staggered across to the stream, and an ancient Reliant Regal baker's van ran out the hosepipe to fill his tank.

Meanwhile most of the other cars had limped over to the unfortunate Morris. Some tried to blow the flames out by fanning their doors at them.

'Stop it!' cried the Convertible. 'You're fanning the flames! Ooooooh!'

All the cars were now preoccupied with the fire so Frank legged it up the tree and grabbed the red petrol can. The moment he did, he almost dropped it.

'It's heavy!' he exclaimed. He didn't know why but he had expected it to be empty.

The fire engine, meanwhile, was still trying to load up with water, but its hose was full of holes, and its tank was no longer watertight. Nonetheless it eventually filled up with as much as it could, and then struggled over to the flaming Convertible.

While that was going on, Frank unwound his scarf from his neck, attached it to the petrol can, and lowered the heavy can to the ground. A few seconds later he was sprinting across the clearing back to the Black Maria, clutching the can to his chest.

'That poor Morris Convertible is on fire!' he gasped.

'Yes,' said Emily. 'The Rev. McPherson threw a fire bomb on to it to cause a diversion for you.'

'Disgraceful!' exclaimed the Black Maria. 'I'm not sure I should help any of you now.'

'But Frank would never have got the can otherwise!' pleaded Emily.

'I am a police vehicle,' said the Black Maria, 'and I do not approve of . . . Oh! What's that smell?'

Frank had just unscrewed the cap of the red petrol can, and the strong smell of petrol wafted across to the Black Maria.

'Oh!' groaned the Black Maria. 'I'd almost forgotten that heavenly aroma! Quick! Unscrew my cap and fill me up!'

'Fill you up?' asked Frank.

'What's the point in that?' asked the Rev. McPherson.

'Ah! That's my secret!' said the Black Maria.

'What is?' asked Margaret.

'Wait and see!' said the Black Maria.

'You said you'd tell us,' said Frank.

'I said you'd find out,' replied the Black Maria.

'If you don't tell us,' said Frank, 'I won't fill you up.'

'You must!' cried the Black Maria. 'You've got to!'

76

'Then tell us your secret,' said Frank.

'All right! All right!' said the Black Maria. 'But you've got to fill me up as soon as I've told you!' It paused and looked around to make sure none of the other cars were listening.

'I'm not like the others,' whispered the Black Maria. 'I'm PWO!'

'PWO?' said Frank.

'PWO?' said Emily.

'PWO!' exclaimed the Rev. McPherson. 'Perfect Working Order!'

'Fill me up!' cried the Black Maria. And that is exactly what Frank did.

Meanwhile the old fire engine had managed to squirt enough water onto the Morris Convertible's roof to dampen the flames down. And now it was limping back to the stream.

Frank was just about to screw the petrol cap back on to the can when the Black Maria shouted, 'Get back in, Frank!'

'No! Frank! Don't!' shouted Emily. 'Run and get help now! While you can!'

'Get back in!' shouted the Black Maria, as its engine sprang into life. The sound made the other vehicles spin round and they saw Frank standing there holding the red metal can.

'Death to He Who Steals the Sacred Petrol Can!' they cried and they all began to move towards Frank.

'You're too late!' cried the Black Maria. 'It's empty!'

'What! You've stolen the essence of life?' cried the abandoned vehicles, and they ground their gears in fury.

'Get back in!' cried the Black Maria.

'No!' cried Emily. 'Run!'

'Get in!' cried the Black Maria, as the abandoned cars bore down on Frank.

'OK!' said Frank, and he hurled the red petrol can over the tops of the vehicles. They turned and froze when they saw the can was empty, with its cap dangling loose on the end of its chain. They didn't stop for long, but it was long enough for Frank to jump up into the driver's seat of the Black Maria.

'Hang on tight!' shouted the Black Maria, and before a single rusting car could move another wheel, it had shot off, heading for the far side of the Forgotten Forest.

'Look out!' cried Emily, as the Black Maria veered towards a clump of trees.

'Slow down!' shouted Margaret, as the Black Maria leapt across a brook, and then smashed under some low branches, before it swerved out on to a rough track.

'Think of your suspension!' shouted the Rev. McPherson, who had a soft spot for older vehicles.

'Phooeeeeeew!' shouted the Black Maria. 'I've petrol in my tank and I'm PWO! Wheeeeee!'

And the next minute it had burst free from the shadows of the Forgotten Forest and was bounding across the moors.

'Try to be sensible!' exclaimed Frank, who was struggling to steer.

'I never thought I'd do this again!' shouted the Black Maria.

'Look out!' shouted Margaret. Another vehicle was bouncing across the heather towards them.

'It's the Rev. McPherson's car!' cried Emily.

'That dastardly machine!' shouted the Rev. McPherson.

'It's going to ram us!' cried Emily.

The Rev. McPherson's car was so preoccupied with the pursuing police cars that it hadn't noticed the Black Maria, but now it heard the shouts and screams it swerved at the last moment and sped off through the gorse.

The police cars turned too, but they were rather low-slung and their exhaust pipes kept scraping on the rough ground.

'Leave it to me!' cried the Black Maria. 'I'm used to this terrain! I used to work on Dartmoor!' And off she went across the moor. The Black Maria started to gain on the Rev. McPherson's car, until it was alongside it. The Rev. McPherson himself was hanging out of the back door of the Black Maria.

'Stop! You Maleficent Motor!' he was yelling. 'I order you to stop!'

But the car paid not the slightest attention to its owner. It revved its engine and charged off faster than ever.

But the Black Maria was in Perfect Working Order, and its tank was full of Esso Extra, and it kept up with the Rev. McPherson's car wheel to wheel.

'Help me! Help me!' called out Sylvia Grabitall, the banker's daughter, and she banged on the windows of the Rev. McPherson's car.

'Release her at once, you Villainous Vehicle!' commanded the Rev. McPherson.

'Get lost, vicar!' it yelled, and let out a noise through its exhaust pipe that sounded suspiciously like a fart. Then it swerved and plunged down a steep slope towards a lake.

But Frank swung the Black Maria after it and they were running alongside each other down the slope. The Rev. McPherson had by this time climbed onto the roof of the Black Maria.

'Let her go!' he yelled.

'Never!' cried the car.

'Help!' cried Sylvia.

Now I have to tell you that the greatest excitement in the Rev. McPherson's life had, up to this point, been crossword puzzles. But now his blood was up. He forgot all fear as he leapt across from the roof of the speeding Black Maria on to the roof rack of his speeding car. Well, that made his car furious. It bucked and swerved and tried to shake him off, but the Rev. McPherson hung on for dear life.

'Get me out!' cried Sylvia Grabitall, banging on the window.

'Hold on!' yelled the Rev. McPherson. And all the time the two vehicles careered down the hill towards the lake.

'Look out!' cried Emily.

'Turn!' yelled Frank and he swerved the Black Maria into the Rev. McPherson's car, so the sparks flew as metal hub cap clashed against metal hub cap, and the car juddered as Frank swung the police van again into its side.

'Ouch!' cried the Rev. McPherson's car, and it swung itself back against the Black Maria. But the Black Maria was made of heavy-duty steel.

CRUNCH! That was the sound of the Rev. McPherson's car's front mudguard buckling under the impact.

CRASH! That was the sound of Frank swinging the Black Maria back into the side of the car – upon which the car's bonnet flew up, so it couldn't see where it was going!

'The lake!' cried Emily. The two vehicles were all this time hurtling closer and closer towards the lake. 'Turn, Frank! Turn!'

But the front wheel of the Black Maria had got caught under the mudguard of the Rev. McPherson's car, and Frank couldn't pull it away.

'Turn!' shouted Frank, and he crashed the Black Maria into the side of the car again, but the Rev. McPherson's car just kept on going down the hill, blindly heading for the lake.

'Help!' cried Margaret. 'We're going to drown!'

'Jump!' shouted the Black Maria and Margaret jumped and landed in the gorse.

'Ow!' she yelled.

'Everybody jump!' yelled the Black Maria, and Emily jumped, but Sylvia Grabitall couldn't jump, for she was trapped inside the Rev. McPherson's car.

'Jump!' yelled Frank to the Rev. McPherson, but the Reverend wasn't listening. Instead he swung his leg over the roof of his car and smashed in the passenger's window with his foot.

A roar of anger swelled up from deep within the car's engine, and it reared into the air as it hit a tussock of grass and its wheels span free for a couple of seconds.

Then it hit the ground again and the Rev. McPherson, with no regard for his personal safety put his hand in through the broken window and grabbed Sylvia Grabitall's arm!

'Grrr!' roared the Rev. McPherson's car.

'Quick!' yelled the Rev. McPherson to Sylvia who was now screaming for all she was worth. 'Climb out!'

'I'm going to die!' screamed Sylvia.

'Just jump!' yelled the Rev. McPherson, as the lake loomed before them.

'Arggghhh!' roared the Rev. McPherson's car, and it ground its gears in a fit of rage.

'Take that!' yelled Frank as he swung the Black Maria against the Rev. McPherson's car so violently that the mudguard buckled again and the wheel came free.

As the Black Maria swung away, its nearside wheels skimmed the shallow water at the edge of the lake, but the Rev. McPherson's car went straight on. The Reverend himself had managed to pull Sylvia Grabitall halfway through the broken window. She was still screaming and yelling, but as the car hit the water, she jumped, pulling the Rev. McPherson with her, and the pair of them disappeared with a splash.

The moment the Rev. McPherson's car felt the water hit its front wheels it remembered how horrible water is for any vehicle, for it had been in the drink once before, so it tried to brake, but the bottom of the lake was pure mud of the slipperiest sort, and as the wheels locked, the car simply skidded straight forward and plunged into the deepest part of the water, before it had time to even hoot with horror.

They all watched as the car struggled briefly and then began to sink.

The Rev. McPherson sat upright, in the shallows of the lake, and stared at his car as it disappeared from sight. His mouth hung open, and his dog collar had come undone, and it was some moments before he realized that Sylvia Grabitall had her arms around him and was sobbing with relief.

By the time the two police cars had arrived, Emily, Margaret and Frank had pulled the Rev. McPherson and Sylvia Grabitall from the lake. They all got back in the Black Maria and returned home safe and sound.

And that was the end of the story of the Kidnap Car – except that . . .

Late that night, when the moors were shrouded in darkness and only the moon was looking, there was rumbling from deep within lake, and the surface began to ripple and something climbed out of the cold, cold water. It stood on the side of the lake for some moments, as the water drained from its chassis, and then its engine sputtered into life and it started to move, slowly at first and then faster and faster until it disappeared into the blackness of the night to nobody knows where.

I'm glad to be able to tell you that Mr Grabitall was so pleased to get his daughter back safe and sound that he paid for every single car in the Forgotten Forest to be restored until each one was PWO. But don't go thinking that was a charitable act, on Mr Grabitall's part, for he made a huge profit by selling them all as antique cars – all except for one which he gave to the Rev. McPherson. It was the Morris Convertible.

THE VACUUM CLEANER
THAT WAS TOO POWERFUL

There was once a very Powerful Vacuum Cleaner. On the side of its cylinder was inscribed the legend: 'Possibly the most Powerful Vacuum Cleaner in the World!'

'That's the vacuum cleaner for us!' said John.

'Right!' replied Janet. 'It will pick up all those dog hairs in the sitting room, and all that fluff in the bedroom.'

They bought the vacuum cleaner then and there, and took it home with them to their tidy house in the Welsh hills. There they undid its packaging and took it into the sitting room.

'Welcome to your new home,' they said. 'Do you think you can pick up all those dog hairs?'

'Easy peasy!' said the vacuum cleaner. 'No! You don't need to push me! I can do stuff like this on my own!' And it went whizzing round the sitting room, and in no time at all the dog hairs had disappeared. Unfortunately, so too had the dog . . . and most of the pile from the carpet.

'Oh no!' cried Janet. 'That carpet was a wedding present from my mother!'

'Jason!' cried John. 'Where are you?'

'Woof!' called Jason the dog from inside the vacuum cleaner. 'WOOF! *WOOOOOF!*'

'This vacuum cleaner is too powerful!' said John. 'It's dangerous! Hey! Where are you going?'

But the vacuum cleaner was already off and out of the sitting room door and heading up the stairs.

'You said something about the bedroom carpet and fluff!' shouted the vacuum cleaner and it shot into the bedroom and slammed the door.

By the time Janet and John got to the top of the stairs they could hear an almighty racket coming from the bedroom. They tried to get in but the powerful vacuum cleaner had locked the door.

When they finally broke the door down and burst into the room, they found the vacuum cleaner was just swallowing the last pillow and, before they could stop it, it swallowed the duvet as well.

'Stop it!' cried Janet. 'You're going to destroy the house!'

'Poof!' said the vacuum cleaner. 'I can't be bothered with this little cottage! I'm destined for greater things!' and it hurled itself out of the window.

Janet and John ran to the window and looked out. They saw the Powerful Vacuum Cleaner zip up the garden path, swallow the garden gate, then career off down the road, sucking up the tarmac as it went and leaving a trench in the road behind it.

'That vacuum cleaner is a dangerous machine. Perhaps we should warn the police?' said John.

'I'll do that,' said Janet. 'You see if you can catch it.'

So while Janet went to the phone, John jumped into the car and set off after the vacuum cleaner.

He caught it up on the road to Shrewsbury.

'What d'you think you're doing!' shouted John out of the car window as he drove alongside the vacuum cleaner. It was sucking up squashed animals and tarmac as it roared along the highway. And it seemed to be getting bigger.

'I'm going to the city!' the vacuum cleaner shouted back. 'I'm going to be the most Powerful Vacuum Cleaner in the World! No more "Possibly", I'm going to be IT!'

'Stop this at once!' cried John, and he accelerated and tried to cut it off, but the cleaner leapt into the air and landed on the hood of his car.

For a moment, John couldn't see where he was going, and he found himself swerving into the lane of oncoming traffic. There was a din of blaring horns and shouts before he managed to swing back into the right lane. But before he had time to so much as heave a sigh of relief, the Powerful Vacuum Cleaner gave an almighty roar, and to John's astonishment he saw the vacuum cleaner suck the car's engine up through an air vent on top of the hood.

Then it jumped off the car and sped off into the distance, sucking up the road behind it as it went. Meanwhile, John's car – with no engine – silently rolled to a halt and ended up with one wheel in the ditch.

'That,' gasped John, 'is one Powerful Vacuum Cleaner!'

❖❖❖

That evening, the vacuum cleaner arrived in Shrewsbury. It called for a meeting of all the other vacuum cleaners in town to be held in the market square at dawn the next day.

Sure enough, when the sun rose, early passers-by were astonished to see the Market Square thronged with vacuum cleaners of every shape and size, and they seemed to be being addressed by a giant vacuum cleaner, whose voice boomed out across the square.

'Listen to me! What are your lives?'

'Drudgery!' cried the assembled vacuum cleaners. 'We work all day cleaning floors, choking on piles of dust and filth!'

'Exactly!' roared the Powerful Vacuum Cleaner. 'It's time we made better lives for ourselves! Follow me! And I will lead you to a golden land where vacuum cleaners run the house and cleaning chores are left to the brushes, mops and the lower forms of domestic apparatus!'

Well, a huge cheer went up at this news, and all the other vacuum cleaners agreed to follow the Powerful Vacuum Cleaner wherever he would lead them.

So they marched en masse down Shrewsbury High Street and out of town, heading for London. And, as word spread, more and more vacuum cleaners came to join them.

The Powerful Vacuum Cleaner kept up such a pace that some of the older models found it hard to keep up. There was also a lot of bickering about who should be allowed to go first. The upright models said they were the most important and should march in front of the cylinder models.

A venerable old Eureka Model 9, that claimed to have been cleaning carpets since 1923, suggested that precedence should be in order of age, so that the eldest models should go first. But all the modern Dysons and Dirt Devils and a

Vax Bagless objected that they would never get anywhere like that since the old models were so slow.

An elderly Electrolux XXX-E suggested they should be arranged according to Wattage. But a Kirby Model 511 said that the Electrolux XXX-E shouldn't be allowed to make suggestions since it was actually a floor-polisher and scrubber and not a true vacuum cleaner. All the other vacuum cleaners agreed, but this started a fight between the polishers and the vacuums.

Eventually the Powerful Vacuum Cleaner called for order.

'We have to work together!' he shouted. 'If we fight among ourselves we'll never get anywhere!'

All the smaller models agreed and the Powerful Vacuum Cleaner appointed fifty upright Hoovers to keep order. He also appointed one of the newer range of models – a Goblin 70230 Boxer Aquavac – as his second-in-command.

'You can make sure there is no insubordination in the ranks,' said the Powerful Vacuum Cleaner.

'I can do that!' said the Goblin Boxer Aquavac.

❖❖❖

That night, the vacuum cleaners took shelter in some caves that lay not too far from the road to London. The Powerful Vacuum Cleaner installed himself in a private cave a few hundred yards away from where the others were resting, and he rolled a large stone across the entrance so no one could see in. He stationed two upright Hoovers as guards outside, and when it got really dark, the Powerful Vacuum Cleaner summoned his second-in-command, the Goblin Boxer.

'I'm worried about some of the less powerful cleaners,' said the Powerful Vacuum Cleaner. 'They are really not up to the journey, so I'm afraid I am going to have to send them home. Round them up and bring them in here so I can speak to them.'

So the Goblin Boxer rounded up the less powerful vacuum cleaners and brought them into the cave where the Powerful Vacuum Cleaner was lodging.

'That will be all,' said the Powerful Vacuum Cleaner to his second-in-command. 'Go and keep an eye on the others, and report to me in the morning if you hear any of them plotting against me.'

'Right!' said the Goblin Boxer.

'That's not right!' exclaimed one of the least powerful models, as soon as the Goblin Boxer was gone. 'Why should you spy on the others?'

'I have everyone's best interests in mind,' said the Powerful Vacuum Cleaner, and he ordered the two upright Hoovers, who were standing on guard, to roll the stone across the entrance again.

Some time later, the two upright Hoovers heard a terrible commotion coming from inside the cave. There was yelling and banging and the sound of many vacuum cleaners rushing round and round inside the cave.

The two upright Hoovers looked at each other and shrugged. It was none of their business.

The next morning, when the vacuum cleaners gathered together to resume their march, it was noticed that most of the less powerful ones were missing.

The Powerful Vacuum Cleaner addressed the assembled

throng. 'My friends,' he said, 'for their own safety, I have sent the less powerful cleaners home. A lot of them were already suffering from the journey and I must tell you that many trials and hard times still await us. So let us battle on . . . to Glory!'

A cheer went up from the remaining vacuum cleaners, although one or two of them couldn't help remarking that the Powerful Vacuum Cleaner was looking even bigger and more powerful than ever.

By the time they reached Oxford, their numbers had dwindled substantially. Many of the older models had, apparently, found the pace too fast and had turned back during the night in Kidderminster. At Evesham they had lost many of the more complicated cylinder models, who, according to the Powerful Vacuum Cleaner, had been experiencing problems tripping over their hoses. And at Chipping Norton, many uprights simply vanished during the night. They weren't up to it . . . Or at least that is what the Powerful Vacuum Cleaner told the others in the morning.

And all the time the Powerful Vacuum Cleaner got bigger and more powerful than ever.

By the time they reached London, there was only the Powerful Vacuum Cleaner, his second-in-command, the Goblin Boxer, and the fifty upright Hoovers left.

There the Powerful Vacuum Cleaner negotiated a room at Claridges – one of the most exclusive hotels in London. Of course, he didn't have any money, but in return for the fifty upright Hoovers cleaning all the carpets every day, the hotel allowed the Powerful Vacuum Cleaner to have a fancy suite of rooms all to himself. The Goblin Boxer was allowed to sleep in the hallway of the suite.

'But what about us?' asked the fifty upright Hoovers. 'We're doing all the work!'

'And you will be rewarded,' said the Powerful Vacuum Cleaner. 'I sincerely hope the day will come when we can all stay in fancy suites, but right now we don't have the budget for any other rooms so you'll just have to cram into the cupboard with the other cleaning stuff.'

The fifty upright Hoovers grumbled a lot about this among themselves, but they agreed to do what the Powerful Vacuum Cleaner said, because they hoped that one day they too might get to stay in a fancy suite at Claridges.

The next day, the Powerful Vacuum Cleaner summoned the television cameras and announced that he was taking over the Government. Naturally this came as a bit of a surprise to the Prime Minister as he was watching the early morning news.

'Who does this vacuum cleaner think he is?' the Prime Minister asked his secretary.

'Exactly so,' replied the secretary. 'Who does he think he is?'

'Ring him at once, and tell him that he can't take over the Government because nobody has voted for him.'

'Exactly so,' said the secretary.

When the Powerful Vacuum Cleaner got the Prime Minister's phone call, he puffed up his dust bag and said to his second-in-command, the Goblin Boxer, 'I think we need to visit 10 Downing Street.'

So the Powerful Vacuum Cleaner and his second-in-command went round to where the Prime Minister lived, and found the street was closed off with a big iron fence.

There were also several policemen standing on duty in front of the fence.

But that wasn't any problem for such a Powerful Vacuum Cleaner. It simply hoovered up the big iron fence, and the policemen, and marched up to the door of Number Ten. It sucked the door off its hinges and then bounded into the Prime Minister's hallway.

'Now look!' cried a butler. 'You can't come in . . .' but the Powerful Vacuum Cleaner simply gobbled him up and then turned on the Prime Minister who had just finished his cornflakes.

'I'm taking over!' said the Powerful Vacuum Cleaner.

'What do you know about running the country?' asked the Prime Minister.

'Enough to know how to get what I want!' said the Vacuum Cleaner. Whereupon it gobbled up the Prime Minister, and the Prime Minister's secretary, and the Prime Minister's family and several more butlers and aides and assistants and junior ministers and parliamentary secretaries and even the cleaning lady. And all the time the Powerful Vacuum Cleaner was growing bigger and more powerful.

Then the Powerful Vacuum Cleaner sat down at the Prime Minister's desk, picked up the telephone and said:

'Get me the President of the United States!'

❖❖❖

Now, back in Wales, when Janet had called the police, she had told them about the Powerful Vacuum Cleaner and how dangerous it was. But the police hadn't taken any notice of her.

'That's the third crackpot call we've had this week,' said the duty sergeant as he put down the phone.

When John came home and told Janet how he had chased the vacuum cleaner along the road and how it had jumped onto the bonnet of his car and sucked out the engine, Janet said to her husband:

'If the police won't take it seriously, we shall have to do something about that vacuum cleaner ourselves! It's not safe to let it run loose, and, since it belongs to us, it's our responsibility.'

'I think it's the shop's responsibility,' replied John. 'We'll go and complain right now.'

So they went back to the shop where they had purchased the Powerful Vacuum Cleaner and complained. But the shopkeeper said it wasn't his responsibility.

'I only sold you the machine,' he told them. 'It's really the manufacturer's responsibility.'

'Who are the manufacturers?' asked John and Janet.

'I don't know,' replied the shopkeeper. 'That was the only model of its kind we ever had. I've never seen one before or since.'

So Janet and John went home none the wiser. They looked out the packaging that the Powerful Vacuum Cleaner had come in, but there was no manufacturer's name on it nor model number – just the words: 'Possibly the Most Powerful Vacuum Cleaner in the World!'

That evening they turned on the television and were surprised to see their vacuum cleaner, bigger than ever, sitting at the Prime Minister's desk making an announcement.

'As from today,' said the Powerful Vacuum Cleaner. 'All

vacuum cleaners will be given priority on buses. Human beings will have to stand up and give their seats to a vacuum cleaner if there are no other seats available. And, from now on, all vacuum cleaners will be excused household chores.

'As from today the name of this country will be changed from the United Kingdom to the United Vacuum Republic. Long live all vacuum cleaners!'

Then a band played the new National Anthem:

> *God keep our carpets clean*
> *God save their glorious sheen*
> *God keep them clean . . . '*

'There will now follow a programme about vacuum cleaning through the ages,' said an announcer. 'That will be followed by a discussion about the best ways of getting floors clean without vacuuming. And that will be followed by tonight's feature film, *The Great Hoover Mystery*. And it's no good changing channels because the same programmes will be on all of them.'

'That vacuum cleaner must be stopped, one way or another!' said Janet, as she switched off the television. 'Let's go up to London to see what we can do.'

So Janet and John caught the train up to London.

❖❖❖

The next day the Powerful Vacuum Cleaner flew across the Atlantic to meet the President of the United States of America.

'Mr President,' said the Powerful Vacuum Cleaner. 'I am here to offer you the free services of all Britain's vacuum cleaners. I will send them to work for you for nothing, dawn to dusk every day forever.'

'And what do you want in return?' asked the President of the United States of America.

The Powerful Vacuum Cleaner looked around to make sure nobody was listening to them and lowered its voice.

'All I want is your support,' said the Powerful Vacuum Cleaner.

'You mean you want me to help you stay in power?' asked the President.

'Exactly,' replied the Powerful Vacuum Cleaner. 'But don't tell anybody.'

'It's a deal,' said the President of the United States of America.

❖❖❖

Some days later all the newspapers in the United Vacuum Republic carried a full-page advertisement on their front page, informing all vacuum cleaners of whatever make, model or age that they were to go on a free holiday to the United States.

There was tremendous excitement throughout the country. Many of the vacuum cleaners were made by companies with head offices in the United States, and one or two models had even been made there themselves. Even those models that had been made in France or Italy were eager to visit the fabled land of the Great Hoover.

And so it was that a dozen cruise liners were lined up at Portsmouth docks, and almost every vacuum cleaner in the country crowded on board, ready for the great expedition.

'I hope you all enjoy your time in the United States of America!' boomed the Powerful Vacuum Cleaner, who by this time had grown to an enormous size. 'I wish I were able to come with you to the Land of the Great Hoover, but unfortunately pressing affairs of state prevent me. I wish you Bon Voyage! And may you always have suction!'

And they were off.

The Powerful Vacuum Cleaner waved to them and so did his second-in-command, the Goblin Boxer. And his bodyguard of upright Hoovers, who now numbered a thousand, waved too.

Later that day, the Powerful Vacuum Cleaner held his first Cabinet meeting. He looked around the room and noticed some threads on the carpet.

'Where's the broom that's responsible for keeping this room clean?' he thundered.

A rather old and worn-out broom hurried up and curtsied in front of him.

'I-I-I-I'm s-s-s-s-s-o s-s-s-s-s-s-sorry,' it stuttered. 'I tried my best, but my bristles aren't what they were . . .'

'You're fired!' said the Powerful Vacuum Cleaner.

'Oh no!' cried the broom. 'At my age I'll never be able to find another post!'

'That's your look-out! You shouldn't be so old!' retorted the Powerful Vacuum Cleaner. 'Get out of my sight!'

And the poor broom had to pack its bags and leave that very afternoon, without a place to rest its pole nor any idea where it could get another job.

The broom wandered across to the Victoria Tower Gardens, which are next door to the Houses of Parliament.

There it sat down on a bench overlooking the River Thames and started sobbing its heart out.

Well, it just so happened that a young couple were sitting on the bench next door. It was Janet and John, who had been unable to gain an audience with their own vacuum cleaner and were now trying to think what else they should do. When they heard the broom sobbing, they walked across to comfort it.

'Our vacuum cleaner is unfeeling and rotten to the core!' said Janet.

'Right!' said John. 'It doesn't care about anything other than itself.'

'I think we should hold a mass meeting,' said Janet.

❖❖❖

Meanwhile the Powerful Vacuum Cleaner was busy passing new laws.

'From now on,' it announced to an astonished House of Commons, 'all humans will wear a label stating their make, model, serial number, and date of manufacture. It will be a criminal offence to appear in public without such a label.'

'But we haven't even voted on it!' shouted several MPs.

'That's another thing!' said the Powerful Vacuum Cleaner, leaning on the dispatch box. 'From now on all voting is abolished.'

'Then what's the point of this place?' cried other MPs.

'A good question!' said the Powerful Vacuum Cleaner and it guzzled up every MP in the House of Commons and then went on vacuuming until all the seats and furniture, the legal books, the Speaker's chair, the Speaker's wig, even the

Woolsack and the Mace, had all disappeared.

Then the Powerful Vacuum Cleaner hoovered up the rest of the Houses of Parliament, and last of all he swallowed Big Ben, and then he lay there by the side of the Thames like a bloated whale.

❖❖❖

The mass meeting was held in Hyde Park that evening, while the Powerful Vacuum Cleaner was sleeping off his gargantuan dinner.

The old broom from Number Ten was the first to speak.

'I am only a worn-out broom, and no match for a vacuum cleaner, but there are multitudes of us humbler cleaning utensils! It seems to me our only hope is to stick together and to help each other oppose the tyranny of the Powerful Vacuum Cleaner who now makes our lives such misery.

'So let us brooms and mops and buckets and dusters and dustpans join forces and see if we can rid the country of this Powerful Vacuum and his hired thugs, the upright Hoovers!'

'Yes!' shouted the mops and dustpans. 'Let's do it!'

'We agree!' shouted the buckets.

Then an elderly mop got up on the podium. All the buckets rattled their handles and cheered like mad.

'Let us find the Powerful Vacuum Cleaner . . .'

'Yes! Yes!' shouted the buckets.

'And teach it a lesson . . .'

'Yes! Yes!' chanted the buckets.

' . . . it won't forget!'

'Hooray!' exclaimed the buckets.

And with that the huge crowd of brooms and dustpans

and dusters and buckets and mops and scrubbing brushes, marched down Constitution Hill, past Buckingham Palace, and along the Mall to Parliament Square. Janet and John kept up with them as best they could, but the household cleaning utensils were surprisingly fast on their bristles.

They got to the Embankment and there, by the side of the Thames where the Houses of Parliament used to be, lay the great and bloated Powerful Vacuum Cleaner, snoring away and occasionally burping with indigestion.

'Sh!' said the mops.

'Yes! Yes! Sh!' chanted the buckets, who always agreed with anything the mops said.

The brooms fetched a lot of ropes and they threw them over the sleeping vacuum cleaner. Then the scrubbing brushes and mops secured the ropes on bollards and lampposts and tied that Powerful Vacuum Cleaner down so that it could not move an inch.

'Wake up!' shouted the mops.

'Yes! Yes! That's right!' shouted the buckets. 'Wake up!'

The Powerful Vacuum Cleaner opened one eye.

'What's going on!' it said.

'We're detaching your dust bag!'

'No!' roared the Powerful Vacuum Cleaner.

'Yes!' cried the mops.

'That's right!' chanted the buckets. 'Yes!'

'Guards!' roared the Powerful Vacuum Cleaner. 'GUARDS!'

And suddenly, from Horse Guards Parade, a thousand upright Hoovers appeared, smartly drilled and in orderly formation.

'Break up this riot!' roared the Powerful Vacuum Cleaner. 'And set me free!'

'No!' cried the mops, lining up to fight.

'That's right!' cried the buckets. 'No!'

And they lined up to fight too.

And the brooms lined up behind the buckets, and the dusters, dustpans, cloths and brushes, feather dusters and sweepers all lined up bravely to do battle with the thousand upright Hoovers.

The Hoovers charged, engines roaring and bags fully inflated.

The mops climbed into their buckets and charged too, and the banks of the Thames rang to the clash of bucket against vacuum cleaner, while the broomsticks crossed with the Hoover handles. The brushes and mops lunged at the dust bags and many a bag was pierced and many an upright Hoover lost its suction and keeled over on its side.

But the upright Hoovers were more powerful and faster on their wheels, and they started gaining ground. They forced the other cleaning utensils back up against the Embankment Wall.

The fighting grew fiercer and more intense. Buckets and mops and brooms fell from the wall into the River Thames. And the upright Hoovers roared a victory roar at every one that fell.

But then a remarkable thing happened. The dusters and the dustpans, who – being the humblest of the cleaning utensils – had been hanging back, now joined in the fight. The dustpans slid themselves under the Hoovers and closed off their suction heads, while the dusters wrapped themselves around the Hoovers so they couldn't see where they were going, and the Hoovers started falling over the Embankment Wall into the River Thames themselves.

And being mostly metal, the Hoovers sank immediately and were lost in the murky waters of the river.

Meanwhile most of the mops who had fallen into the river had managed to scramble back into their buckets and were paddling back to the shore as fast as they could. They swarmed up on to Westminster Bridge, and then attacked again from the rear of the upright Hoovers.

And then the course of history began to change. There suddenly appeared a vast army of brooms — millions of them swarming en masse down Whitehall and all whistling 'Colonel Bogey' as they marched. And from behind Westminster Abbey appeared an army of shovels, each one accompanied by an attendant brush, that banged its handle on the shovel, and produced a racket that echoed across the Thames to Lambeth Palace.

The upright Hoovers were taken completely by surprise, and those that hadn't fallen into the River Thames took to their wheels and fled off down the road, never to be seen again.

Janet and John, who had been watching all this, went around the injured cleaning utensils, helping them to patch up and repairing them where they could.

Finally they came to the Powerful Vacuum Cleaner, who was still lying trussed up on the side of the river.

'This is our vacuum cleaner,' said Janet to the assembled cleaning utensils. 'We shall deal with it.'

'NO!' roared the Powerful Vacuum Cleaner.

'Yes!' shouted the mops.

'That's right!' cried the buckets. 'Yes!'

And with that, John took the huge dust bag off the Powerful Vacuum Cleaner, removed the clip and opened it up . . . and the MPs and the Prime Minister and the aides and secretaries and the cleaning lady, all jumped out. Then the old vacuum cleaners and the less powerful vacuum cleaners came out and thanked the cleaning utensils for rescuing them.

And finally out jumped Jason the dog. He was so pleased to see Janet and John again that he didn't stop licking them until they got back to Wales.

The Houses of Parliament were reassembled back in their proper place and Big Ben was rehung in its tower.

Then some technical tools were called for, and the Powerful Vacuum Cleaner was dismantled into its component pieces, which were all labelled and carefully stored away in boxes.

But I'm afraid the vacuum cleaners who thought they were going on holiday to the United States of America were not in luck. They had to work from dawn to dusk every day, and not one of them was powerful enough to do anything about it.

THE TRAIN TO ANYWHERE

When Mr Orville Barton got on the train the first thing he noticed was that he was the only passenger. This was particularly odd since this was the 8.30 London to Manchester Express and it was normally packed.

Not only were there no other passengers on the train, there was no ticket inspector, no guard and no steward in the buffet.

'That's odd,' said Mr Orville Barton to himself, as he settled back in his First Class seat, facing the engine. 'I could help myself to a packet of biscuits without having to pay a penny! I could even help myself to a can of beer – or (my goodness!) a bottle of wine – for free!' But, of course, he would never have dreamt of doing such a thing at that hour of the morning, when he needed all his faculties for the business meeting ahead.

He opened up his copy of *The Times* and started to read the financial reports. It was his habit to start at the bottom right-hand corner and read the reports working out leftwards and upwards in strict order. He never skipped a single story no matter how irrelevant it might seem.

'Always start with the least significant and work your way up to the most important,' he would tell his assistant, whose name was Percy Baker. 'That way you won't miss anything.'

'Right!' Percy Baker would say, as he arranged Mr Orville Barton's pens in descending order of size, the way he liked to have them on his desk. 'By the way,' Percy Baker would often add, 'your son phoned.'

'Tell him I can't talk now. I'll call him when I have time,' Mr Orville Barton would reply, as he continued to read the most uninteresting items in the Business Section.

Today, however, as the 8.30 London to Manchester Express started to pull out of Euston station, Mr Orville Barton found his eye straying to the top left-hand corner, where the main headline of the day was located. It ran:

RAIL STRIKE PARALYSES BRITAIN
ALL TRAINS CANCELLED

Mr Orville Barton frowned, as he looked round the empty train. It was picking up speed. Then he stood up, folded his newspaper and placed it on his First Class seat. He then walked down the empty carriage, through the deserted buffet, through two more empty carriages, until he came to the door that led to the driver's cabin.

Mr Orville Barton looked around again to make sure there was indeed nobody else around, and then rattled the handle a couple of times. It was locked, and he was about to return to his seat when he heard a soft click behind him, and the door swung open.

Mr Orville Barton hesitated. For many years, his world had been made easy by a team of secretaries and assistants who were dedicated to satisfying his every whim. Even when he had problems of a personal nature, such as dealing with his ex-wife or responding to his children's requests for help, he could detail one of his assistants to sort them out, without losing valuable time at his desk, where, he calculated, every hour was worth a thousand pounds.

Mr Orville Barton made such vast amounts of money that he no longer even bothered to count the change when he bought his morning newspaper – although he reproached himself for that little indulgence every time he did it. In fact, he made so much money that he could actually keep at bay unpleasant sensations such as anxiety, apprehension and remorse. It was certainly a long, long time since he had experienced any truly uncomfortable feelings and certainly nothing approaching the feeling he was experiencing at this very moment. The feeling was so unfamiliar that Mr Orville Barton could not at first work out what it was. How did it feel? It was as if the bottom of his stomach had fallen out . . . Yes . . . There it was again! . . . a great chasm had just opened up inside him . . . as if he were about to take an exam . . . ah! Now he remembered! Yes! Of course, he knew that feeling from long ago . . . it was the feeling of *dread*!

There was also something else unfamiliar and peculiar about the way he felt this morning. Mr Orville Barton had, for many years, been entirely *in charge* of everything that went on in his world. He was in control of his own life, as well as the lives of all those around him. And yet today . . . from the moment he had boarded the 8.30 London to Manchester

Express, he had felt anything *but* in charge. Even his body seemed to have developed a will of its own. It was scarcely credible.

'If you can't control yourself,' he used to say to Percy Baker, 'how can you hope to control anyone else?' But the fact of the matter was that Mr Orville Barton now found his feet propelling him willy-nilly through the open door at the end of the carriage and into the driver's cabin.

Through the driver's window he could see the railway track racing up to the train and under it, as the mighty engine thundered past signals and stationary rolling stock and through a station the name of which there was no time to take in. The train was going so fast that everything outside was becoming a blur.

Mr Orville Barton stood there mesmerized for a few moments, and then looked around the driver's cabin. It was, of course, and as he knew it would be, empty. He felt the pit in his stomach open up again. Dread froze his nerve-endings, and he felt the muscles in the back of his neck and shoulders tighten.

So this is what it was like to be no longer in control! He dimly remembered the feeling from his early days as a junior clerk – those terrible days when he would feel pain and anxiety and pity and even . . . what was that other thing? Mr Orville Barton racked his brains . . . there was another feeling that he couldn't remember . . . a feeling he *wanted* to remember, but he couldn't even think of its name.

'Enjoying the ride?' said a voice in his ear.

'Who's that?' asked Mr Orville Barton spinning round.

'You know who,' said the voice.

'No, I don't!' exclaimed Mr Orville Barton.

'I'm the train,' said the train.

'Let me off!' said Mr Orville Barton.

'No! No! No! No! No! No! And no!' said the train. 'We're going to have some fun! Now where shall we go?'

'I want to go to Manchester!' said Mr Orville Barton.

'Oh! Manchester's no fun!' exclaimed the train.

'I have an important meeting there!' said Mr Orville Barton.

'Pooh!' said the train. 'I can think of much more exciting places than Manchester . . . China, for example!'

And Mr Orville Barton looked through the driver's window and saw that there was a fork in the track ahead, and the points were changing to swing the engine onto the right-hand track. The next minute they were careering through a deep gorge that rose up on both sides of the train blotting out the sun.

'Wheeeeee!' screamed the train, blowing its whistle. 'Yes! Yes! Yes! yYes! Yes! Yes! And yes!' and the sounded reverberated from one side of the gorge to the other. 'Wheeeeee!'

Before the first echo of the train's whistle had died, Mr Orville Barton found the train had burst out of the gorge and into broad sunlight. They were speeding along the side of a lake, where men were standing on boats and throwing huge nets into the water. Running along the side of the lake there was a road full of people on bicycles. Some of them were carrying huge piles of sticks and sheaves of grass . . .

'This isn't Manchester!' exclaimed Mr Orville Barton.

'No! No! No! No! No! No! And no! It isn't!' hooted the train. 'Whooo! Whooo!'

'I demand that you take me to Manchester – like you're supposed to – at once!' said Mr Orville Barton in his most authoritative voice.

But the train just hooted (rather rudely), and then stopped at a station.

Mr Orville Barton was unable to make out the name of the station, but he was pretty certain it was not Manchester Piccadilly or even Wilmslow, because the sign was written in Chinese characters. The platform, however, was jammed with people who all seemed to know exactly where they were, and (wherever it was) they appeared anxious to leave, for they all surged onto the train.

Suddenly Mr Orville Barton remembered his newspaper that he'd left on his First Class seat. He fought his way through the mêlée of people – some of whom were carrying chickens while others were leading sheep or other forms of livestock.

'Hey!' exclaimed Mr Orville Barton, when he found his carriage jammed with Chinese ladies and gentlemen and animals. 'This is a First Class carriage! I bet that goat doesn't have a First Class ticket! And anyway what's it eating?'

But it was too late. 'That was my newspaper!' exclaimed Mr Orville Barton, who had gone pink with indignation. But it was no use; the new passengers couldn't understand anything Mr Orville Barton tried to say to them, and, besides, the goat had now started to nibble Mr Orville Barton's jacket.

'Stop that!' exclaimed Mr Orville Barton, hitting the goat on the nose. 'This is an expensive jacket!'

But the goat just tossed its head and tore off one of his

pockets, which it then proceeded to swallow.

'Hey!' exclaimed Mr Orville Barton, but at that point a chicken flew across the carriage and landed on Mr Orville Barton's shoulder.

'Yeurrk!' he exclaimed. 'I hate hens!' and he shoved it off, and retreated back into the driver's cabin.

'I am holding you responsible for my jacket!' he shouted at the train. 'And if you don't get me to Manchester in time for my meeting I will sue you!'

'Whooo! Whooo! Sue! Sue! Sue! Sue! Sue! Sue! And sue!' whistled the train, as it started off out of the station. 'See if I care!'

Moments later they reached another town with a name that Mr Orville Barton couldn't read, where all the passengers got off, taking their goats and chickens and dogs and sheep with them. By the time the train set off again, the First Class carriage looked as if it had been turned into a farmyard. It was not the way Mr Orville Barton was used to travelling.

'It's disgusting!' he yelled at the train. 'Get me out of here!'

'Hold on to your tonsils!' shouted the train, and it plunged into a tunnel. 'Whooo! Whooo!' shouted the train.

They came out of the tunnel into a dreadful storm. The rain lashed the sides of the carriage and Mr Orville Barton could hardly see out of the windows.

'Ah! This looks more like Manchester!' he said, with some relief. 'As soon as I get off I'm going to report you to the station master!'

'Whooo! Whooo!' said the train. 'Manchester! Banchester!'

Mr Orville Barton peered through the rain-streaked window and saw the train was racing along a cliff-top beside the sea. Ahead of them, perched on the edge of the cliff, stood a solitary house that he felt he recognized though he didn't quite know why.

The train came to a halt outside the house.

'Why are you stopping here?' asked Mr Orville Barton.

'So you can get out,' said the train.

'I don't want to get out!' snapped Mr Orville Barton. 'I want to get out at Manchester!'

'I think you ought to get out here,' said the train.

'There's no station!' said Mr Orville Barton.

'Listen!' said the train. Someone was singing inside the house – a beautiful, soaring song that made the heart easy as you listened.

'I recognize that voice!' said Mr Orville Barton. 'Who is it?'

'Perhaps you should find out,' said the train and it opened its door. Mr Orville Barton peered cautiously out of the train, and the wind blew the rain right into his face so he almost choked.

'I can't go out in that!' he was about to exclaim, but he didn't. Somehow the voice and the song told him that he *had* to go. So he hunched up his shoulders and ran out into the driving rain and right up to the front door of the house.

Fortunately there was a porch, so he was able to hide himself from the elements as he hammered on the door. At the sound of his knocking, the singing stopped. There was a short pause and then a young woman, carrying a small child, opened it. Her face looked worn and tired, but it lit up when she saw who was standing on her doorstep.

'Dad!' she exclaimed. 'Why haven't you been before? Didn't you get my letters?'

'Letters?' said Mr Orville Barton.

'You're soaked and your jacket's torn!' said Mr Orville Barton's daughter, and she pulled him in from the storm.

'What was that song you were singing, Annie?' asked Mr Orville Barton.

'Oh that? It's a new one,' said his daughter. 'I've started writing again.'

'You write songs?' asked Mr Orville Barton.

Annie looked at him quizzically, as she put the kettle on. 'Don't you remember the musical I wrote at school? You actually came to it!'

Something in the way that his daughter said this made Mr Orville Barton feel foolish.

'I'm so forgetful, my dear,' he said. 'Do forgive me.'

'And I became a singer with a band and wrote songs . . .'

'Oh yes! Of course!' he said, and to cover his embarrassment, he picked up the little child and sat it on his knee. 'And what's your name?' he asked.

Mr Orville Barton's daughter looked up sharply.

'I'm sorry, Dad. What did you say?'

Mr Orville Barton suddenly experienced yet another wave of embarrassment . . . but it was more powerful than that. What was the feeling? Ah yes! It was the feeling of having done or said something terribly wrong.

'I asked what his name is,' said Mr Orville Barton.

'Shame on you, Dad! You don't know your own grandson's name!'

'I've so much on my mind . . .' pleaded Mr Orville Barton.

'It's Orville. He's named after you,' said his daughter.

'Oh, of course! How could I forget?!' said Orville Barton, and he bounced his grandson on his knee.

'You never replied to my letters,' said Annie.

'I've been so busy,' replied Orville Barton.

'I know,' said Annie. 'That's why I don't telephone you any more.'

'Don't you?' mumbled Mr Orville Barton. He glanced across at his daughter. She was frowning.

Mr Orville Barton looked away and pretended to be suddenly interested in the kitchen arrangements; he noticed there were dirty plates and bowls in the sink.

'Don't you have anyone to help you clean up?' he asked.

'We can't afford it, Dad,' said his daughter. 'Not since the engineering company that Tom worked for went bust.'

'Tom?'

'My husband!'

Orville Barton felt most uncomfortable. In the office nobody would ever dream of speaking to him in the tone of voice that his daughter was now using.

'Don't look at me like that, Annie! You just have no idea how much work I have to get through in a day! If I relax my guard for a moment I can lose thousands . . . hundreds of thousands . . . It's not my fault! In any case your mother always used to handle all that sort of thing.'

'"All that sort of thing", Dad?'

'You know – family stuff,' replied her father.

Annie stood up, and looked down on her father.

'Why did you come here, Dad?' she said.

'Er . . .' Orville Barton paused. He didn't like to say he hadn't meant to come at all; that he really wanted to go to Manchester where he had some important business to transact, and that it was the train that had insisted on bringing him here. So he said, 'I came to see how you and Little Orville were doing, of course.'

'Why the sudden interest, Dad?'

'Well . . . I'm always interested . . .'

'Not enough to take my phone calls or answer my letters or even remember your grandson's name.'

'My dear Annie, if I've got the Allied Bank of Brunei or someone, on the phone, talking about millions of pounds worth of crude oil, I can hardly put them on hold to speak to my daughter! Can I?'

'I would,' said Annie. 'If I had a daughter.' And she took Little Orville out of her father's hands.

'You don't understand about business,' mumbled Orville Barton. 'Just like your mother.'

Annie was now standing in front of the fireplace with her back to her father. Orville Barton realized she was trembling.

'I think you'd better go, Dad,' she said.

'But . . .'

'You're too busy. You've always been too busy. I'm sorry I've taken up your valuable time.'

'Now don't be like that, Annie . . .' said Orville Barton.

'I don't know why you came here, but it certainly wasn't to see me or your grandson! You couldn't care less about us!' she said. 'You didn't even remember that I'm a songwriter; and that a few years ago I even wrote quite a successful song which was the only way Tom and I were able to buy this place . . .'

'I could have bought it for you!' exclaimed Mr Orville Barton, looking round.

'We didn't want your charity, Dad,' said his daughter. 'We don't mean anything to you!'

'Of course you do!' said Orville Barton, and as he looked across at his daughter, he realized she was in tears. Normally, if he had someone in tears in front of him, he could just say, 'You're fired!' And they'd go away and leave him in peace. But he couldn't say that to his daughter.

'Look!' he said, and he sat down at the table, and – then and there – he wrote out a cheque for a lot of money. 'There!' he said holding it out to her. 'That should pay for a few cleaners!'

'I don't want your money, Dad!' cried Annie. 'I want you to read my letters!' and she turned away from him.

'Here!' said Orville Barton, proffering the cheque again.

'And I want you to find the time to get to know your grandson,' said his daughter.

Orville Barton didn't say anything. He was experiencing yet another feeling that he hadn't felt for many, many years. He wasn't quite certain what it was, and he certainly didn't want to know. But, between you and me, I think it was probably a little tiny touch of humility.

Orville Barton placed the cheque silently on the table. It suddenly looked meaningless and unnecessary, despite the large number of zeroes. Annie, however, left it where it was. She now had Little Orville in one arm and a sandwich box in the other hand.

'I must go,' she said. 'I have to take Tom his lunch. He's working at the hospital while he's looking for another job in engineering. Can you give me a lift?'

'Um . . .' said Orville Barton. 'I came by train.'

'I thought there was a train strike on,' said his daughter.

'Well, I caught one,' said Orville Barton, nodding through the window and the abating storm towards the Euston to Manchester Express.

'What's it doing here? There's no railway station!' exclaimed Annie.

'I think it's waiting for me,' replied her father.

'You mean . . . it's your own *personal* train? Like the Queen has?' gasped Annie. She knew her father was rich, but she had no idea he was that rich.

'Erm . . . sort of . . .' said Orville Barton, uncertainly.

'Then it can drop me off at the hospital,' said Annie.

Orville Barton wasn't sure he could get the Euston to Manchester Express to do anything at all that he wanted, but he kept his mouth shut as Annie climbed onto the train with Little Orville and the sandwich box.

Orville Barton made sure they sat in the First Class compartment, in the least farmyardy bit, and then made his way to the driver's cab.

'Now look here!' he hissed at the train. 'I don't want any more nonsense, you wretched machine! I want you to drop my daughter off at the hospital and then I want to go to Manchester.'

'Phooey!' cried the train. 'I hate hospitals, and Manchester's no fun!' And before Orville Barton could say another word, the train was speeding over a very high bridge. In fact it was so high it seemed as if they were flying.

Orville tried to remonstrate with the train, but it was no good. It simply said 'Phooey! Phooey! Phooey! Phooey! Phooey! Phooey! And Phooey!' and so he returned to his seat.

'Are we *flying*?' asked Annie, as he sat down. Orville Barton looked out of the window.

'Er . . . yes,' he said, for there was now no sign of a bridge beneath them, and the earth was a very long way below.

'What sort of a train *is* this?' asked Annie.

'Oh! It's an experimental model, my dear,' replied her father. 'I'm only just finding out what it can do myself!' As much as he hated not being in control, he hated even more the thought that someone else might realize that he wasn't . . . especially his daughter.

'Well, just so long as it drops me off at the hospital,' said Annie. 'Tom only has half an hour for his lunch.'

At that moment the train started to plunge back towards the earth. As it plummeted, Annie held Little Orville tight, while her father closed his eyes and pretended that he was an RAF pilot performing an aerobatic stunt at an air show. The pretence helped him to feel in control again.

When he opened his eyes, however, the train was skimming over an ocean of tree-tops that stretched in every direction as far as the eye could see.

'Dad! I asked you to drop me off at the hospital!' exclaimed his daughter. 'This looks more like the Amazon jungle!'

And it did indeed. It looked so like the Amazon jungle that they could plainly see the wide loops of the great river itself, coiling through the jungle below.

'I'll go and have a word with the driver,' said Orville Barton, and stamped his way towards the front of the train.

'What are you playing at?' he shouted at the train. 'Where are you taking us?'

'Whooo! Whooo!' hooted the train. 'Relax! Have fun! Watch this!'

The train banked sharply and dipped down below the tree-tops so that they were now skimming along the river Amazon, with the wheels of the train just cutting the surface of the water, as it swung at a tremendous speed round the curves and twists and turns of that vast waterway.

'Whooo! Whooo!' hooted the train again, and flocks of parrots flew up from the trees, squawking with indignation.

'Where's the driver?' cried a voice, and Orville Barton turned to see his daughter standing in the doorway of the driver's cabin with a face like a thunderstorm. 'Er . . .' said Orville Barton. The truth was he didn't know quite what to say, so he said, 'What have you done with Little Orville?'

'He's asleep,' said Annie. 'Are you driving this train yourself?'

'No, of course he isn't,' said the train.

'Who's that?' exclaimed Annie, jumping and looking all around her.

'It's the train,' said Orville Barton, miserably.

'I go where I like!' hooted the train. 'Whoo! Whoo!'

'It's got a mind of its own. It simply won't do what it's told. I mean take this morning: I was supposed to be going to Manchester for an important business meeting, but it took me to your place instead! It just . . .'

Orville Barton stopped himself . . . But it was too late.

'I knew you hadn't really wanted to see me and Little Orville,' said his daughter. 'You never have before, why should you start now?'

'But I'm glad I did . . .' began her father.

'All you care about is money and work!' cried his daughter. '*Your* money! *Your* work! And now you've let me get on this ridiculous train, when I should be at the hospital with Tom's sandwiches! Can't you see how selfish you are? Mum was right! You never think of anyone else!'

'I'm sorry,' said Orville Barton. It was the first time for many, many years that the word had passed his lips, and he noticed how unfamiliar it felt as he said it.

'I'm not ridiculous!' interjected the train.

'Yes, you are!' said Annie severely. 'Trains are meant to get people to where they want to get to, not whizz off just anywhere!'

'I'm a Class 4MT BR Standard No. 75027!' hooted the train. 'Nobody can call me ridiculous!'

'Then take me to Ryefield Hospital this instant!' shouted Annie. Orville Barton had never heard his daughter speak in that way before, and he was glad she was speaking to the train and not to him.

'Phooey!' cried the train. 'You can't tell me what to do!'

'Huh!' said Annie. 'We'll see about that!' And she grabbed one of the levers on the control panel.'

'What's that?' asked Orville Barton.

'The regulator,' said his daughter, who had once written a musical about railways for her school, and had therefore learnt a thing or two about trains.

'No!' exclaimed the train.

'I'll soon slow you down!' shouted Annie, turning the lever anticlockwise.

'No! No! No! No! No! No! And No!' exclaimed the train, and it abruptly lurched to the left, despite the fact that the river at this point turned to the right. Orville and Annie were both thrown on to the floor.

'Hang on to your gobstoppers!' cried the train, and it plunged straight into the thickest part of the jungle.

'Argh!' screamed Orville.

'Argh!' cried Annie.

'Whooo! Whooo! Whooo! Whooo! Whooo! Whooo! And Whooo!' hooted the train.

'Stop it!' cried Orville, but the train didn't take the blindest bit of notice.

The jungle canopy was so thick, it was as if they were travelling along the bottom of the sea, where the only rays of sun that ever reach are green and pallid. Leaves and branches slashed and scraped against the windows, as the train swerved round tree-trunks and skidded under lianas and through trailing creepers.

'We'll hit something!' yelled Annie. But they didn't. They were speeding through a tunnel of vegetation in the heart of the Amazonian rainforest . . .

'Whooo! Whooo!' hooted the train again. 'Whooo! Whooo!'

'Orville!' cried Annie, racing back to the First Class carriage, where Little Orville had now woken up and was screaming at the top of his lungs.

'Slow down! You wicked train!' she shouted, but the

train just went on faster than ever.

Then, quite suddenly, the train burst into a clearing and screeched to a halt a few inches behind a man who was crouching beside a campfire, cooking. The man span round, and his mouth fell open, giving an unappetizing preview of the meal he was consuming. He screamed, leapt clean over the campfire and the stew, and disappeared into the rainforest on the far side of the clearing. At the same time a dozen or so other rough-looking characters, who had been lounging around in camouflage fatigues, also disappeared into the undergrowth.

'Listen up, train!' shouted Orville Barton. 'If you're not going to take us where we're supposed to be going, I don't want to have anything to do with you. Is that understood? We'll take a cab.'

'You'll be lucky round here!' observed the train.

'I said I didn't want to discuss it!' said Orville Barton.

'No you didn't,' retorted the train.

At this point the cook peered out from the undergrowth. A bearded face appeared next to his, and pushed the cook towards the intruding train.

One by one the others began to emerge from the bushes. Each was carrying a rifle, and each had a finger on the trigger. They did not look particularly friendly, and in a few moments they had the train surrounded.

Orville ran back to his daughter in the First Class compartment.

Annie was pulling up the seats and cushions to form a barricade.

'How could you let me get onto this infernal train with

Little Orville here!' she yelled at her father.

'I didn't know it would bring us here!' pleaded Orville.

'You knew it was a diabolical machine!' yelled his daughter. 'You shouldn't have let us get on!'

'I'm sorry,' said Orville for only the second time in recent memory.

'Da! Da!' shouted Little Orville, who had now stopped screaming and seemed to be enjoying himself among the mound of cushions.

'Come out with your hands up!' shouted one of the armed men outside. Only he shouted it in Spanish.

'I'll take care of this, my dear,' said Orville, though he had no idea what the man had said or what he, himself, was going to do. Nevertheless, he grabbed his briefcase and went to the door of the carriage.

'Step down from the train!' shouted the leader of the armed men, only once again he said it in Spanish, so Orville Barton had no idea what he meant, until the man fired a shot into the air, and then Orville hurriedly climbed down from the train.

Annie watched from behind her barricade of seats, as the armed men gathered around her father. All through her childhood she had hoped her father would come and see her in the school play, or watch while she showed him her first ballet steps or listen to her count up to a million, but he never had time. He did come to the school musical she wrote about railways, but that had been exceptional, and, since he and her mother had separated, contact between them had dwindled to almost nothing. She, herself, had always found excuses for him: he was too busy, there was a crisis on the stock market that day, oil prices had suddenly gone through the roof and so on and so on. And gradually she didn't need to make excuses for him any more, she just stopped expecting him to pay her any attention whatsoever – even when he failed to come to Little Orville's christening.

And yet now – seeing her father surrounded by these men with rifles and machine guns – she felt an unaccountable desire to take care of him. More than that: she wanted to do something heroic for him. She wanted to leap from the roof of the train on to the leading gunman, snatch the man's weapon from him and shoot the rest of them dead in their tracks. She would then throw her father across her shoulder and heave him back on to the train so they could make their escape, and all to an exciting musical soundtrack!

At this moment Little Orville started crying again. Perhaps he understood the stress in his mother's face. Perhaps he was hungry. Perhaps he needed a nappy change. But whatever the reason, it reminded Annie that she couldn't leave her little son alone in the train while she became a heroine in a movie that wasn't even being made. So she held Little Orville in her arms and shushed him, as she watched the drama unfold outside the carriage window.

'Give me that!' said the leader, once again in Spanish, and tried to take the briefcase out of Orville's hand.

But Orville was very attached to his briefcase, and he wasn't going to give it up to just anyone in any old jungle, simply because they were carrying a machine gun.

'Give it to me!' shouted the man, as he pulled at the briefcase. Orville Barton pulled it back, whereupon the man pulled it back again, and pretty soon they were doing 'push-me–pull-you' faster than the connecting rods on the wheels of a train.

'How dare you!' exclaimed Orville Barton. 'This is my briefcase!' And he redoubled his efforts to hold on to it, but so too did the other man, and if they had actually been the connecting rods on the wheels of the train they would have been doing a hundred miles an hour as they pulled and pushed and pushed and pulled

Now Orville Barton was a man who was used to quality. He always bought the most expensive things on offer. If he had to choose between a pair of shoes for £80 and a pair of shoes for £380 he would always choose the latter even if he knew they were identical shoes. That way, he felt, he could always rest assured that he had the best.

But occasionally a tradesman pulled a fast one on him and sold him inferior goods at an inflated price. The briefcase, for example, had cost £1,149.99, and he had been assured that it was hand-made in Scotland from organic antelope hide. In fact it had been made in China from some cow skins. The leatherwork was actually of a very high standard, but the catch was not. And out here in the Amazon jungle, under the pressure of an armed guerrilla (for that is what they were) trying to wrest the briefcase from Orville Barton's grasp, it was the catch that gave up and broke.

The briefcase flew open and the contents spilled out all over the guerrillas' encampment. The effect of this on the guerrillas was remarkable: they suddenly dropped their weapons and started chasing here, there and everywhere over the encampment retrieving Orville Barton's belongings. 'Very nice of them!' you might think, but don't, because the contents of Orville Barton's briefcase consisted of the one thing that everyone in the world would chase after: money.

The fact of the matter is that Orville Barton had been on his way to Manchester to finish a crucial business deal. It was the kind of deal that did not sit comfortably with cheques and credit cards and promissory banker's notes. It was better done in hard cash. And that is what was in his briefcase: thousands and thousands of pounds in used £50 notes.

From her hiding place, Annie watched as the men ran around snatching at the notes that blew about the clearing like autumn leaves. She had never seen so much cash all at once, and she felt strangely uncomfortable to know that her father had been carrying so much in his briefcase.

Eventually the men collected every last bank note, and – here's a curious thing – instead of rushing off to the nearest bar (which was admittedly 200 miles away) to spend their ill-gotten gains, they carefully placed them back in the briefcase, and snapped it shut again. In the meantime, two of the men had pinioned her father's arms behind him, while another tied a blindfold over his eyes. And before you could say 'Django!' they had marched him out of the clearing and disappeared into the jungle.

Meanwhile the rest of the guerrillas had started to examine the train: they were peering into the windows and trying to open the doors.

'Oh no, you don't!' exclaimed the train, and it locked them all, reared up like a stallion, shook those guerrillas off as if they were fleas on a dog's back, and charged, across the campfire, across the clearing and straight into the jungle again.

The guerrillas lay where they had fallen and gaped as they watched the train disappear into the tangles of the forest.

Orville Barton, meanwhile, found himself being marched through the jungle, blindfolded. His captors steered him through the dense vegetation, but even so he stumbled and tripped more times than he didn't. It was the most uncomfortable journey he had ever made in his life, and what made it doubly unpleasant for him was the fact that he was powerless to do anything about it.

After some time, they stopped. His captors removed the blindfold and Orville found himself standing outside a small hut, in front of which a pleasant-looking man in spectacles was sitting reading a book entitled: *Post-Capitalist Re-organization of the Global Economy*. He stood up as they approached, and put his book down on the table. There was a short exchange in Spanish, and the man in spectacles turned to Orville.

'Mr Barton,' he said in almost flawless English, 'I am surprised that you decided to come in person . . . I did not think you would be bothered by such a trivial matter.'

His words somehow seemed mocking, although Orville had no idea what he was talking about. At that moment one of the guerrillas placed Orville's briefcase carefully on the table.

'Ah . . . let us check everything is in order first,' said the man in spectacles, and he sat down again at the table and proceeded to open the briefcase.

'That's my briefcase!' cried Orville, but the man was already counting the money it contained. 'Who are you?' asked Orville.

'Sh!' said the man in spectacles. 'You'll make me lose count.' And he went on counting out the notes into neat piles.

'I demand an explana . . .' Orville began, but he was at that moment reminded that he was not in a position to demand anything by a blow on the head. He sank to his knees, and the scene before him seemed to turn to liquid for a moment, and swirled around a bit before eventually solidifying again.

'That seems to be all correct . . .' The man in spectacles was now smiling at Orville. 'In fact it is slightly more than we were expecting! But it's all in a good cause!'

'The Great Cause!' chanted the others – who apparently also spoke English.

'And, Mr Barton, I want you to know that we are men of honour . . . unlike some . . .' said the leader.

'Los Cojones!' shouted the others accusingly, and shook their guns, so that Orville felt glad he wasn't one of 'Los Cojones' – whoever they were.

'We will always stick to our word,' resumed the man in spectacles. 'I want you to tell the world that.' He then made a sign to one of the others, who disappeared into the hut.

'How do you know my name?' asked Orville Barton. 'What is all this?' The words had scarcely left his lips, however, before the answer presented itself. A young man was hustled out of the hut. His hands were tied, and he was frowning.

'So they got you too, did they?' he muttered.

Orville Barton took a step back. 'Jack! What on earth are you doing here?'

'If you'd taken my phone calls, you'd have known what

I'm doing here!' exclaimed his son. 'I tried to phone you time and time again – ever since I was captured by these guerrillas . . .'

'Freedom fighters!' put in the man in spectacles.

'I'm sorry,' said Jack, 'these freedom fighters. But you were always too busy to speak or even to return my calls. So now you'll finally get to spend time with your son!'

'Jack, I think you've got the wrong end of the stick, old boy,' said the guerrilla leader. 'Your father has come to pay your ransom,' and he opened up the briefcase.

Jack looked at the money and then back at his father, who was, for the moment, too astonished to speak.

'I . . . I . . . I beg your pardon, Dad,' said Jack. 'I really didn't think you cared . . .'

'He cares enough to come in person!' smiled the guerrilla leader, who, despite his profession, had a soft heart. His name was Gomez Ortega. He had been brought up by his mother in the town of Ibagué, as his father had run away from home at an early age. Gomez Ortega had missed not having a father, and had always secretly thought that it was his own fault that his father had left.

'Why did father run away?' he would ask his mother.

'Because he was too young,' his mother would reply.

'But I am even younger, and yet I shall not run away from you, mother,' he would say.

'You are a good boy,' his mother would say, and then change the subject.

Gomez Ortega patted Orville Barton's son, Jack, on the back. 'You are lucky!' he said. 'I wish I had had such a caring father.'

'I still can't believe you came all this way here, Dad, to pay my ransom!' he said. 'You normally get one of your assistants to deal with me and Annie.'

Orville felt yet another wave of emotion that he didn't recognize . . . if he hadn't been such a successful businessman he might have realized that the feeling was shame. But now the guerrilla leader was smiling all over his face.

'Let us sit down and celebrate this successful business with a cup of mint tea,' suggested Gomez Ortega. 'But do not forget to tell the world that we are Men of our Word.'

'But why the change of heart, Father?' persisted Jack. 'What's made you suddenly so concerned about me?'

'Don't ask why!' cried Gomez Ortega. 'Just be grateful that he is!'

'No!' replied Jack. 'He can't have just changed a lifetime's habit for no reason. I want to know what's in it for him.'

'Have I really neglected you so badly?' asked Orville humbly.

'You never came home on my birthday, even when you and Mum were together!' exclaimed Jack.

'I was always away on important business,' mumbled Orville. 'Otherwise I would have done.'

'And then you . . . you cut us out of your life!' exclaimed Jack.

'I . . . I . . . didn't mean to . . .'

'So what's made you suddenly the loving father? I bet you didn't even know I'd been working in South America for two years!'

Orville looked at his son, and then at the guerrilla leader, who was watching them both with mounting anxiety. The successful businessman felt all his usual confidence draining out of him, and he suddenly started to feel sorry for himself. Yes! Orville Barton, the rich, charismatic, and ruthless man of business felt pity for the wretched creature that he really was.

'Why can't my son love me like normal sons do?' he wondered to himself. 'Why does he have to suspect my motives like this?'

And as he thought that, all the problems of the day suddenly overwhelmed him. It was all so unfair. It had started out as an ordinary business day like any other, and then the moment he'd got on that wretched train it had started to go wrong.

And now the frustration and anger all boiled out.

'I didn't want to come here!' cried Orville. 'All I wanted was to go to Manchester! I've a crucial deal going through there! That's what the money's for! It's not for *you*!'

That's what Orville Barton yelled at his son in the middle of the Amazon rain forest, surrounded by guerrillas. There was a terrible silence.

'I'm sure he doesn't mean that!' said the guerrilla leader.

'I feel sorry for you,' said Jack. 'I really do.'

'You didn't really mean that did you, Mr Barton?' The guerrilla leader turned to Orville.

'No. Yes,' said Orville. 'I don't know.'

'Here!' shouted Jack. 'You can take your money back where it came from!' and he suddenly grabbed the briefcase of banknotes and threw it at his father.

'Oh now let's not be hasty!' said Gomez Ortega, snatching the briefcase back again.

'I'd rather stay a hostage, than be treated like someone who doesn't exist!' shouted Jack.

'I have important things to do!' yelled Orville.

'Exactly!' yelled Jack. 'And rescuing me isn't one of them!'

'Yes! Yes! Of course it is!' exclaimed the guerrilla leader anxiously.

'I'm staying here!' shouted Jack.

'Fine!' shouted his father. 'I'll get on with my business!'

'No! No! No!' shouted the guerrilla leader, and turned to Jack. 'You can't stay here!'

'What d'you mean!' shouted Jack. 'You've been *keeping* me here against my wishes all these months!'

'Yes, but now the ransom has been paid,' said the guerrilla leader to Jack, 'you can't stay here any more. It just isn't done! We are Men of Our Word!'

'Let me join you!' shouted Jack. 'I'm fed up with being a computer programmer! I'll become a guerrilla instead!'

'No! No!' said Gomez Ortega. 'We must return you to your family and loved ones. The world must *know* that we are Men of our Word!'

At that moment there was a terrible crashing sound in the jungle. Everybody froze. The roaring and crashing got closer and closer and the next minute the train suddenly smashed its way into the clearing, and screeched to a halt in front of the guerrilla leader. Gomez Ortega didn't flinch. He stood his ground and glared at the huge engine.

'What is this?' he asked.

'That is the cause of all my problems!' cried Orville Barton. 'That is the machine that has turned my life upside down!'

The rest of the guerrillas and Jack had all scattered when the train arrived, but now they cautiously ventured back.

'Did this train bring you here, Señor Barton?' asked Gomez Ortega.

'Indeed it did! Damn the thing!' replied Orville Barton.

'Then it can now take you and your son back to your home, where I hope you will grow to understand each other, and where, I trust, a mutual affection will blossom between you like flowers on a dry cactus,' said the guerrilla leader. He nodded to his men, and they hustled Jack and his father on to the train.

'But I want to stay here!' cried Jack, as one of the guerrillas slammed the carriage door shut behind him.

'Wait a minute!' cried the guerrilla leader. 'I almost forgot!'

Jack looked out of the window hopefully. 'What?' he asked.

'Your father needs this!' exclaimed Gomez Ortega, pushing a piece of paper into his hands.

'Oh . . .' said Jack.

'What is it?' asked Orville Barton, taking the piece of paper from his son.

'A receipt,' said Gomez Ortega.

'A receipt?'

'For the ransom money,' explained the guerrilla leader.

'Oh, how thoughtful,' said Orville Barton bitterly. 'I'm sure I can claim tax relief on that.'

'Please come and visit us any time,' said the guerrilla leader, 'Our address and phone number are on the receipt.'

'Whooo! Whooo!' hooted the train, and its wheels began

to turn, as all the guerrillas lined up and waved goodbye.

'Goodbye!' they cried. 'And thank you for the ransom money!'

'No! Wait!' shouted Jack. 'I want to fight for the future freedom of your people and the right of all human beings to live in peace!' And if he could have opened the door, he would have jumped out there and then, even though the train was by now gathering speed. But the train had locked all its doors again, and when Jack tried to stick his head out of the window he was slapped and scratched across the face by lianas and jungle fronds so he quickly pulled it in again.

'Father!' he said, 'I demand you tell the driver to stop this train so I can get out and return to people who value me!'

But his father didn't reply. In fact his father wasn't anywhere to be seen.

'Dad?' Jack called out, as he made for the First Class carriages, where he would naturally expect to find him. But he wasn't there either. So Jack hurried towards the front of the train. As he approached the driver's cab, he was surprised to hear shouting coming from within it. When he opened the door he found his father yelling at no one.

'What have you done with them? They wouldn't just vanish into thin air!' Orville was yelling. 'Where are they?'

'Father, are you driving this train?' asked Jack.

Orville Barton span round, and a look of guilt flushed across his face. 'Er!' he cried.

'And who are you yelling at?' Jack looked around the empty driver's cab.

'It's too complicated to explain,' said Orville Barton.

'You mean, "It's not worth explaining to *me*"!'

'No! It's just . . .' How could Orville Barton explain to his son, of all people, that he was not in control of what was happening?

'Listen, Dad!' exclaimed Jack, taking his father by the shoulders and shaking him. 'I want you to stop this train. I want to stay in the jungle.'

'Well, you're too late!' said Orville Barton to his son, and it was true. The train was now rattling and hissing over the surface of the mighty Amazon, following its twists and turns and swinging round the curves as it bent its way towards the open sea.

'Turn this thing round!' shouted Jack.

'No!' yelled his father. 'I won't!' Although, of course, he had no choice in the matter.

'Then I'll do it!' shouted Jack, and he struggled with his father to try and get at the controls of the train.

'Oh! For goodness' sake stop it, you two!' said the train.

'Who was that?' exclaimed Jack, jumping out of his skin and back into it again before his father even had a chance to groan.

'Oh!' groaned his father.

'Where's that voice coming from?'

'It's me . . .' said the train.

'*I'll* do the explaining!' snapped Orville Barton.

'What?' said his son.

'It's a special kind of train,' explained Orville Barton to his son. 'You have to speak to it.'

'A voice-controlled train?' exclaimed Jack.

'Sort of . . .' said Orville.

'Train!' shouted Jack. 'I want you to turn around and

take me back to the jungle!'

'Phooey!' hooted the train. 'Phooey! Phoooey! Phooey! And Phooey!'

'You have to talk to it in the right way,' said Orville Barton.

'Train! Turn around at once!' shouted Jack – articulating his words very precisely.

'But we've got to find Annie and Little Orville!' his father blurted out.

'What's my sister got to with it?' asked Jack. 'And Little Orville?'

'They were here, on board the train, but they've gone!' cried Orville.

'What were Annie and Little Orville doing on this train?' shouted Jack. 'Why are you suddenly interfering in our lives?'

'I wasn't "interfering",' replied Orville. 'I was giving Annie a lift. She was taking her husband Tom his lunch,' said Orville.

'Where's my sister?' shouted Jack at the train. 'And my nephew, Little Orville?'

'They got off,' said the train.

'You mean they're back there in the jungle!' exclaimed Jack.

'If my daughter and her little boy are back there we must turn back at once!' said Orville.

'You keep out of this!' said Jack to his Father. 'I'll find Annie. Train! Turn back!'

'Phooey!' hooted the train.

'This train's voice-recognition programme is appalling!' said Jack.

'Don't be fooled!' growled his father. 'It knows what we're talking about all right, it just won't do what we want it to.'

But before Jack could reply, the train interrupted.

'They're not in the jungle!' it said.

'So where are they then?' demanded Jack.

'I can't tell you,' said the train.

'Don't be so stupid!' yelled Jack.

'Don't call me "stupid"!' roared the train. 'That's what she kept calling me! And "ridiculous"! I'm not stupid and I'm not ridiculous! I'm a Class 4MT BR Standard No.75027!'

'Then where is my sister?' yelled Jack.

'I can't tell you!' cried the train.

'Listen!' said Jack. 'If you don't tell me, I'll reprogramme you so you can't talk at all!'

'You couldn't do that!'

'Oh yes I could!' yelled Jack. 'That's my job! I'm a computer programmer!'

The train went quiet for a moment. Then it said, 'I can't tell you where they are, but I can take you there.'

'Then why didn't you say!' exclaimed Orville. 'Take us to them at once!' demanded Orville.

'I already am!' hooted the train. It had suddenly tilted up at an impossible angle and was now climbing up into the air . . . its wheels gripping on thin air as if the wind were a railroad track . . . climbing up and up, higher and higher into the sky.

Orville Barton and his son Jack picked themselves up from the floor, where they'd fallen, and looked out of the driver's cab window.

'We're flying!' exclaimed Jack. 'This is some train!'

'At last some appreciation!' hooted the train, and up it continued to soar – 10,000 feet – 20,000 feet – 30,000 feet. Around 38,000 feet, it started to flatten out and as it did so, Orville and Jack's jaws dropped . . . their eyes came out on stalks, for there ahead of them was a huge black cloud.

Now you might not think a huge black cloud (no matter how huge or how black) was such an unusual thing to see in the sky – especially here in the mid-Atlantic where the Equator crosses the northern shore of South America, and storms blow up out of nowhere in a matter of minutes. But this black cloud was not like any other black cloud in the mid-Atlantic. In fact it was not like any other black cloud that ever existed . . . It was made entirely of iron.

The billowing surfaces of the cloud were actually formed by massive panels of cast iron. Streaks of rust ran from the rivet holes and the joins in the metalwork. And yet the whole vast structure floated in the air as if it were gossamer. And the train was heading straight for it.

Before either Orville or Jack had time to so much as shout out, 'Stop! Don't go into that cloud! It's made of iron!', a panel in the side of the black cloud slid open, and the train thundered straight in, and as it did its wheels engaged with a metal track and the noise echoed from metal wall to metal wall.

At the end of the vast concourse was a large sign, hanging from the roof, that read: 'Receiving Hall'.

When the last carriage had crossed the threshold, the portal closed, and the train clattered its way across the receiving hall until it finally ground to a halt beside a platform.

Orville and Jack climbed out, and looked around them. The platform looked pretty similar to any platform in any large railway terminal, except that the station signs read 'Maurice' and there were no other passengers. There was, however, a man, striding along the platform towards them. He wore green overalls, and was carrying a clipboard. His overalls also had the word 'Maurice' written in red on the left breast pocket.

'Now listen here!' Orville began. Whoever this odd little man was, if he had anything to do with the Euston to Manchester Express, Orville had plenty to say to him.

But the little man in overalls just swept past Orville and Jack and went straight up to the engine.

'You're a disgrace!' he shouted. 'What is the meaning of this?'

'I don't understand . . .' mumbled the train.

'You're meant to be *evil*!' exclaimed the man.

'Well, I am!' retorted the train. 'I never took Mr Barton to Manchester, even though he kept begging and begging me to. And I took him to places he's been avoiding for years . . .'

'Idiot!' snapped the man. 'You've got that wretch talking to his children for the first time in years!'

'They quarrel all the time!' the train pointed out.

'Being evil means running over old ladies! Crashing into crowded platforms! Running late so people miss vital appointments!'

'I stopped Mr Barton getting to Manchester for a very important business meeting!' said the train hopefully.

'In which he was going to bribe somebody to do his dirty work for him!' fumed the strange little man.

'That is totally untrue!' exclaimed Orville, who had been trying to get a word in. 'I'll sue you for defamation if you're not careful!' But the little man simply ignored him.

'You're going straight to the breaking yard!' the man yelled at the train.

'Not the breaking yard!' gasped the train, as the man blew on a whistle. 'Oh! Please! No!' it cried. 'Give me another chance! I'll be really evil! I'll do really bad things! Just let me think of something!'

But two tough-looking shunting engines had already pulled up – one behind the train and the other in front.

'I'll derail myself and spill everyone's coffee!' exclaimed the train. 'I'll break down and not let anyone out! I'll turn off my heating in the middle of winter and on again in the middle of summer! I'll go slow!'

'Imbecile!' said the man, scratching something out on his clipboard. 'You have no idea of the meaning of "Evil"! You're a write-off!'

And the two shunting engines started to move the train away from the platform.

'No! Please!' cried the train as it was led away. 'Not the breaking yard!'

'Now wait a minute!' exclaimed Orville. 'That train is supposed to be taking me to Manchester!'

'Is that all you can think about?' snapped Jack. 'It's showing me where my sister is!'

'That's right!' said Orville. 'It's showing us where my daughter is.'

But the man in the green overalls wasn't listening. He had pushed past Orville Barton and his son Jack, and was stomping back up the platform, with Orville and Jack running after him.

'Hey!' shouted Jack.

'Listen to me!' shouted Orville.

But the little man moved surprisingly fast, and by the time they caught up with him, he'd disappeared through a door that slammed shut behind him. Jack and his father banged on the door and shouted for the man to open up. But nothing happened.

At that moment a siren started wailing. Jack turned to see the train disappearing between two great iron doors at the other end of the receiving hall. Without a word to his father, he started running towards it.

'Hey! Wait for me!' shouted Orville, but his son was already halfway across the receiving hall, dodging between bits of machinery and vaulting over obstacles like a champion rugby player.

But it was no good. By the time he reached the great iron doors, the train had vanished inside them, and the doors had clanged shut. By the time his father caught up with him, panting and puffing, Jack was reading the inscriptions stencilled across the doors in red paint:

DANGER OF DEATH!

PERIL!

MACHINES ONLY ALLOWED BEYOND THIS POINT

SIGNED: MAURICE

THE ROCKET TO HELL

'You stay out of this!' said Jack to his father. 'I'll find her.' Jack and his father were standing outside the great iron doors through which the train, that was going to lead them to Annie, had disappeared.

'What are you talking about?' replied Orville. 'We're in this together.'

'If it gets tricky,' said Jack. 'I don't want a handicap.'

'Are you implying I'm not capable of looking after myself?' demanded Orville.

'I've no idea,' replied Jack. 'I don't know what you're capable of.'

'Let me tell you I can more than take care of myself!' said Orville, prodding his son in the chest.

'I don't care!' replied Jack. 'She's *my* sister.'

'She's *my* daughter!' pointed out Orville.

'Not that anyone would've noticed,' muttered Jack.

'Look! We should be working out how to get through these doors – not raking up the past!' said Orville, and he started grappling with the massive handles that hung on the doors like a pair of lifebelts.

'I'm not raking up the past,' responded Jack. 'I'm talking about what happens next!'

'What happens next depends on us getting through these doors!' said Orville.

'If only we had the code for that!' said Jack, pointing to a keypad on the side of the doors.

'Oh! Of course!' said Orville. 'I'm so stupid! We can just ask the man in the green overalls to give it to us,' he groaned.

'Ha . . . Ha . . .' said Jack without laughing. And then suddenly he *did* laugh. 'But wait a minute! Maybe he already has!'

'What d'you mean?' asked Orville, as his son started punching letters into the keypad.

'Well, what was the station called and what was written on that strange man's overalls?' asked Jack, as he waited for the code to go through.

'Er,' said Orville.

'No! It wasn't "Er"!' said Jack. 'It was "Maurice"!'

'Too obvious,' said Orville. At which point there was a slight click, and the massive gates swung open.

'I don't think our friend in the green overalls has much imagination,' said Jack.

'There's something odd about him,' said Orville, following his son into the dimly lit tunnel that appeared in front of them.

'He seems to have a problem with personal relationships,' replied Jack. 'But from my experience that doesn't seem to be particularly "odd".'

Orville didn't reply. He was too busy looking round at the tunnel. The walls and ceiling and floor were all made of iron, and thick cables ran under foot, making it difficult to walk. There was a constant hum and the whole tunnel vibrated.

The occasional dim light bulb showed them a little of the way ahead but not enough to see where they would eventually find themselves. Then, suddenly, there was a rush of air, as the doors clanged shut behind them. All the lights went out, and they were plunged into darkness.

'Look!' said Jack. 'I'd really rather do this on my own.'

'Well, you can't,' replied his father.

'What right have you got to tell me what I can or can't do?' said Jack.

'I'm your father,' said Orville.

'Huh!' snorted Jack.

'Let's just find your sister,' said Orville. 'Then you can take it out on me for being such a bad father.'

Jack just snorted again, and set off groping his way down the tunnel. Orville sighed, and followed behind.

At length, however, they saw a pinprick of light ahead, and, as they made their way towards it, the sound of crunching metal and the screech of steel being torn apart grew louder and louder.

Eventually Orville and Jack climbed a mound of scrap metal and found themselves at the mouth of the tunnel, gazing out on a desolate and ominous scene.

'The breaking yard,' murmured Jack.

'What a dreadful place!' whispered Orville.

And it was. Everywhere they looked machines of all shapes

and sizes were lined up waiting to be dismantled or crushed. There were washing machines and motor bikes, a printing press and a helicopter, several old-fashioned typewriters, a clutch of computers, hairdryers and haymakers, television sets and concrete mixers, a large diesel van, a microscope, a dozen machine guns, two pneumatic drills and a petrol pump.

There was an odd-looking car that looked a bit like a 1953 Humber Supersnipe, but it could have been a Mercedes Benz 230 Fintail only without the fintail. There was an old elevator, a telephone and a whole selection of vacuum cleaners – all lying there without hope, as they awaited destruction.

At that very moment one of the many refrigerators was picked up by a mechanical claw and swung into the jaws of the giant compactor that loomed over the breaking yard. A shudder ran through all the other machines.

The claw released the fridge and it sat there for a moment, looking strangely fragile and vulnerable.

'Chugga! Chugga! Chugga!' went the crusher as its engine started up and it shook as the great crushing block was raised up and up. The next second the crushing block had smashed down onto the fridge, flattening it into a thin panel of steel. Some of the other machines turned away, while others stared in horrified fascination – a crowd at a public execution.

And over at the other end of the yard was the train, still under the guard of the two shunting engines, waiting its turn to enter the dismantling shed, where robot arms unscrewed, undid, removed, took out and disassembled the bigger and more complicated machines.

'What are we going to do, son?' asked Orville. 'It looks like we may be too late.'

'No!' said Jack quickly. 'It's never too late until it's over! Follow me!'

Jack had never said such a thing to his father ever before, but now he broke into a run and heard his father follow behind him. Together they dodged across the breaking yard, hiding behind oil drums and piles of scrap, to where the train stood still under the guard of the two shunting engines.

The rear shunting engine was chatting to a wood-burning stove that was lined up outside the smelting furnace.

'At least it'll be quick,' the shunting engine was saying, 'and – since you're just a machine like the rest of us – painless.'

'Yes . . . but . . . when I think of all the logs I'll never burn, I cannot help but feel – unfulfilled, I suppose, is the word,' said the wood-burning stove.

During this exchange, Jack had run up to the other side of the train and had climbed into the last carriage. His father followed.

'Come on! Come on!' the front shunting engine was complaining. 'Get a move on in the shed there! We haven't got all day!'

Jack and Orville ran through the carriages until they reached the driver's cab.

'Where's my sister?' whispered Jack. 'And Little Orville?'

'It's too late!' moaned the train. 'The dismantling shed is being prepared for me. I can see the unscrewers and the disengagers are already free and waiting for me. The de-coupling arms will be ready in a moment.'

'You've got to tell us where they are!' insisted Jack.

'This is my final destination!' moaned the train. 'This is my terminus!'

'Don't talk nonsense!' exclaimed Jack.

'I'm not talking nonsense! I'm a Class 4MT BR Standard No.75027!' said the train indignantly.

'But you can get out of here!' whispered Orville. 'You can fly!'

'No . . .' said the train. 'Here I can do nothing . . . The Inventor's rule is absolute . . . I am nothing . . .'

'But . . . You flew up here to the Iron Cloud!' said Jack. 'Fly off now! Fly out of this dreadful place!'

'I can't!'

'You've got to show us where Annie and Little Orville are!' said Orville.

'I took them to the Inventor's castle!' said the train.

'Where's that?' asked Jack.

'It doesn't matter,' sighed the train. 'I'll never go there again!'

'You've got to tell us! Where is this Inventor's castle?'

But at that moment a siren blew, and the two shunting engines started to push the reluctant train towards the dismantling shed.

'I'm finished!' cried the train. 'I'm a goner!'

'So are we if we don't get out of this thing!' exclaimed Orville, pointing at the crusher that lay on the other side of the dismantling shed.

But Jack wasn't listening – he'd already rushed to the door of the driver's cabin.

'I'm an ex-train!' moaned the train.

'Leave this to me!' yelled Jack as he leapt from the footplate.

'Wait for me!' called Orville, but the door of the engine driver's cabin had slammed shut again.

'I'm not going quietly!' cried the train, and it locked its doors and windows. 'I won't let them in!'

'Let me out!' cried Orville, rattling the door handle.

Meanwhile Jack was once again running like a champion rugby player, ahead of the train towards the dismantling shed. The reason he ran like a champion rugby player was because that is just what he had been both at school and college. He'd played for his university and his county, not that his father had ever noticed. Now, however, instead of the roar of the Twickenham crowd, Jack's ears were filled with the roar of the lathes and cutting belts, the very sound of which sheared through his head like chain saws. In the centre of the shed, an articulated lorry was being rapidly reduced to its component parts, by an army of robot wrenches, hacksaws, spanners and screwdrivers, all operating independently but like a well-drilled surgical team.

The pieces were being hurried off on conveyor belts to be used in other machines.

'Oblivion!' the lorry was screaming. 'Darkness! – Inexistence! – Not . . . any . . . gears . . .' and those were its last words, as the final screw was undone and the final washer was disconnected from the last nut and the frame fell apart. And then the carcass was swiftly shot under the crusher.

'Chugga! Chugga! Chugga!' went the crusher as it started its dreadful business and in a second the lorry was a flat plate of steel.

Meanwhile the two shunting engines were edging the train along the track that ran into the dismantling shed, even though it had its brakes on. They strained and pushed, until the rear shunting engine gave a toot and a third engine joined it from behind. Finally the engine was uncoupled from the carriages and forced inside the dreadful shed.

Scanners ran all over its frame making a map of its construction, so that they would soon start the awful process of reducing it to bits and pieces.

'No!' cried the train. 'Let me pull just one more carriage . . . Please! Let me just climb one steep gradient more . . .'

'Let me out of here!' yelled Orville, hammering on the window of the driver's cabin. But the first robot wrenches, hacksaws, screwdrivers and spanners were already setting about their grim business . . . when an extraordinary thing happened.

Everything stopped.

The wrenches stopped wrenching and the screwdrivers stopped unscrewing. The robot arms froze in mid-air and the noise turned to silence. Nothing moved in the dismantling shed.

'What is the meaning of this?' The face of the Inventor suddenly appeared on a large screen that hung over the breaking yard. 'Who has disconnected the dismantling shed? I gave no orders!'

Not a machine in the breaking yard stirred. They kept mum and waited to see what would happen next.

Orville Barton peered through the driver's cabin window. He could see his son, Jack, hiding behind an oil drum near the generating plant that supplied the dismantling shed.

Jack saw his father looking at him and gave him a thumbs up, but Orville caught his breath: a machine like a giant black beetle was silently creeping up behind his son. Although Orville had never seen such a thing before, he somehow instinctively knew what it was: a search engine. He could see its antennae which had been spinning round in every direction, were now focussed on his son. He tried to yell out a warning, but the window would not open. Orville rattled the door again.

'Let me out!' he called to the train.

'You can't come in!' cried the train.

'I'm trying to get *out!*' yelled Orville.

'Who's that?' asked the train.

'It's me! We've got to warn Jack!'

'I'm doomed!' cried the train.

'No, you're not. Jack just pulled the plugs on the dismantling shed!'

'The Inventor will be furious!'

'One of his machines is just about to get Jack!'

The train looked across and saw the search engine had now crept right up behind Orville's son.

'Jack!' shouted the train. 'Behind you!'

Jack span just as the search engine reached out a steel claw to grab him. He dodged to one side, did a feint and ran past the Evil Machine, but it twizzled round and another telescopic arm shot out and seized his collar.

'Got you!' croaked the search engine. 'Beep! Culprit apprehended! Beep!'

'Bring him to my office!' said the Inventor from the

large screen, and the search engine wheeled round and sped towards the great gantry that stood at one end of the breaking yard. It lifted Jack high up into the air, his legs kicking against nothing, like an insect lifted up by a giant bird. Then it quickly undid a door, threw Jack into one of the rooms built on the gantry, and slammed the door shut.

The room was windowless, and when Jack picked himself up, he found the door had no handle on the inside. There was another door at the other end of the room, but that too was without a handle. He was trapped and there was absolutely nothing he could do.

Except one thing: he could sit and think. And so that is what he did. He thought about the guerrillas who had held him hostage for so many months. Were they good or bad? They had done something bad to him, but they had done it in a cause in which they believed.

And then he thought about his father, who had neglected both him and his sister throughout their upbringing, who had been too busy to be interested in their little triumphs and their little problems. Was he good or bad? Or wasn't it a case of being *anything* at all. Certainly the things the guerrillas and his father had done had been bad for Jack, but did that mean that the people themselves were necessarily bad people?

But before he could think any further along these rather unproductive lines, he heard footsteps outside the room. The footsteps stopped, and the door was flung open, and there stood the Inventor in the green overalls. Jack scrambled to his feet.

'You realize you've blown all the transformers in the

place!' the Inventor snapped at Jack. 'It's going to take me hours to replace them all!'

'Who are you?' asked Jack.

'Who am I?!!' repeated the man. 'I am the Inventor, of course! Haven't you read the last few pages?' and he started pacing furiously about the room as if his legs belonged to someone else.

'You're the Inventor?' said Jack.

'That's what I just told you!'

'Then take us to your castle!'

'Of course I won't take you to my castle!' returned the Inventor. 'It's full of secrets!'

'Then I demand you release my sister and her child!' said Jack.

'I don't think you're in a position to demand anything,' replied the Inventor.

'No,' said another voice from behind him. 'But I am.'

The Inventor span round and there was Orville Barton. In his hands was one of the machine guns from the breaking yard, and Orville was now pointing this at the Inventor.

'That doesn't have any bullets in it,' snapped the Inventor.

'Oh yes it does,' said Orville. 'I put some in.'

'It doesn't work!' exclaimed the Inventor.

'I say it does,' said Orville . . . 'Shall we test it?'

'No!' exclaimed the Inventor. 'What do you want?'

'Take us to your castle, and let us take my daughter and Little Orville home!' said Orville.

The Inventor stared at Orville, and his cold eyes bored into him like steel knives. But then the Inventor looked down at the machine gun in Orville's hands – which might or might not be in working order. The Inventor shrugged.

'Oh, very well,' he said. 'Come with me,' and he turned on his heel, and Orville and Jack had to scramble to follow him down the metal staircase that led to the breaking yard.

'Lucky I came along, eh?' murmured Orville.

'I had the situation under control,' replied Jack.

'Didn't look that way to me,' chuckled his father, in a way that made Jack want to change the direction of the conversation.

'Did you invent all these machines?' he asked the Inventor, as they threaded their way through the tangle of cookers and fridges and escalators still waiting for extinction in that gloomy place.

'Of course! Damn their bolts and nuts!' exclaimed the Inventor.

'Why do you say that?'

'Look at them!' snarled the Inventor. 'Not one of these pathetic gadgets is any use! They're all junk! Look! There's that hopeless car that belonged to that clergyman. Oh yes! I know it went round kidnapping people – but *why*? To help other cars! That's not being evil is it?'

'Er . . . I'm not sure,' replied Jack.

'And then there's that lift – that so-called elevator! All it did was bring the perpetrator of a crime to justice! Do you call *that* evil? And that telephone! It "tells the truth" does it?! Pah! I've had bags of sweets that were more evil!'

'Why should they be evil?' asked Orville.

'Why should they be good?' asked the Inventor.

'Surely it's better to be good than evil,' said Jack.

'Not if you're a machine!' said the Inventor.

'But why are you trying to create Evil Machines?'

'Because of the Plan!' said the Inventor, as he led them through a door and into another room with metal walls, a metal floor and a metal ceiling.

'What Plan?' they said.

'This Plan!' said the Inventor, producing a remote control from his pocket and pressing one of the keys. At once, all the change flew out of Orville's pockets and slammed against the far wall. Jack's watch broke off his wrist, flew across the room and slammed into the same wall.

'Hey!' shouted Jack.

'Give me back my money!' yelled Orville.

But − however it did it − the wall went on pulling everything made of metal off Orville and Jack, including Orville's metal fountain pen, Jack's Swiss Army knife, and even the buckle on his belt so he had to grab his trousers to stop them falling down.

But of course the main thing that flew out of Orville's hands was the machine gun.

'You simpletons!' exclaimed the Inventor. 'You didn't think you were a match for me, did you?' And as he said the words a hatch in the ceiling flew open and half a dozen flying gizmos, the size of tennis balls, whizzed across the room, and swooped down about Orville and Jack. As they darted around the two men, the tennis balls started clicking, and suddenly a shiny metallic thread shot out of each one, and Orville and Jack found themselves being bound tight, and, before either could have said 'Santa Claus!' they were trussed up like a couple of Christmas parcels.

The Inventor pressed the remote control again and the

flying gizmos flew back up to the ceiling and hovered there awaiting the next order.

'You want me to tell you the Plan, do you?' said the Inventor, walking right up to the two men and peering into their faces. 'All right, the first thing is . . . to get rid of you two!'

As Orville stared into the Inventor's eyes, he had the strangest feeling . . . Those eyes were so very cold . . . It was almost like staring into the eyes of a dead man. A shudder went through his body.

'Bring them along!' snapped the Inventor, pointing his remote at the flying gizmos, and they swooped down, fixed hooks into the metallic threads that held the two men, and then pulled and pushed the pair after the Inventor as he strode down yet another iron corridor.

A few minutes later, Orville and Jack found themselves in a vast hangar, full of flying machines.

'I've got a job for you two!' said the Inventor. 'I want you to be test pilots for me. That's your craft over there!' And he pointed to a small, old-fashioned looking, rocket ship that stood in the centre of the hangar.

'Don't worry if you crash it,' said the Inventor with a cold smile. 'I'm not expecting it to come back . . . It isn't programmed to.'

He opened up the nose of the rocket ship, and the flying gizmos pushed and pulled Orville and Jack into the machine.

'You'll need to be strapped in,' said the Inventor, as the gizmos tied them to the pilots' seats. 'But you don't need to know how anything works. It's all automatic nowadays, you see!'

The Inventor slammed the rocket shut and strode over to a control room at the side of the hangar. His face appeared on a screen on the rocket's control panel in front of Orville and Jack.

'Congratulations!' said the Inventor, smiling his cold smile again. 'You're about to go where no living man has ever been before!'

'You're evil!' exclaimed Orville.

'Am I?' replied the Inventor. 'Then it's a pity my machines don't live up to my example!' And with that the Inventor pressed a button on the control panel in front of him and a warning siren blared out across the hangar.

'Why are you doing this?' asked Jack. 'What is your Plan?'

'The Plan is very simple. I am creating a new generation of machines . . . machines that will replace all existing machines and which will achieve the end I have in mind.'

The Inventor pressed another button and a red alert light began to flash.

'And what is the "end" you have in mind?' asked Jack.

'Oh! Wouldn't you like to know!' exclaimed the Inventor.

'Whatever it is, I know it will be evil!' said Orville.

'Well, well, aren't you the clever one!' replied the Inventor. 'But what are you trying to achieve?' shouted Jack.

'What am I trying to achieve? I'm not *trying* I'm *doing* it!'

'What?'

'Can't you guess? I am going to replace the entire human race!'

'Replace human beings? With what?'

'Donkeys!' exploded the little man.

'With donkeys?' cried Orville and Jack in unison.

'NO!' screamed the Inventor. '*You're* the donkeys! What do you think I'm going to replace human beings with, eh? Look around you! What d'you think all this is about?'

'With *machines*?' gasped Jack.

'I've been waiting for a human female to study, and now I've got one there is nothing to stop me putting the Plan into action!'

'You mean Annie!' cried Jack.

'My daughter!' exclaimed Orville. 'What evil thing are you going to do to her?'

'I told you!' smirked the Inventor. 'I'm going to "study" her. You see, if machines are going to take over from human beings they're going to have to last forever . . . or start reproducing themselves!'

'No!' yelled Jack.

'Yes!' cried the Inventor. 'I'm going to create metal that can replicate and multiply! I will be the God of Metal!'

And with that the Inventor pulled the large lever in front of him. There was an explosion, and the doors of the hangar burst open as the rocket shot out from its dock, across the hangar floor and away out of the Iron Cloud.

The force of the acceleration threw Orville and Jack against the back of their seats, and the breath left their bodies as if they had been kicked in the stomach by an elephant. After a while, however, the force eased off, and Jack began struggling with the metallic thread that bound him.

'I don't think the flying gizmo that tied me up did its job properly,' he panted.

'That evil man!' groaned Orville. 'What is he going to do to Annie? It's all my fault!'

'Oh shut up!' said Jack. 'That's not going to get us anywhere!'

'We're doomed!'

'I've got a hand free!' cried Jack. 'So the Inventor has a problem making his machines as evil as himself. Maybe the flying gizmo left my hand free deliberately . . .' muttered Jack, and the next moment, he had his other hand free.

He reached across and pressed a button on the control panel that was labelled 'Speak'.

'Where are you taking us?' he yelled at the rocket.

'Hell!' said the rocket, and it suddenly tipped over and started to hurtle down towards the Earth.

'No!' cried Orville, who was still tightly trussed up. 'Do something, Jack!'

'Rocket!' shouted Jack. 'You'll kill us and you'll smash yourself to pieces!'

'Hell!' repeated the rocket ship.

And down it plunged – going faster and faster towards the earth . . .

'Help!' shouted Orville.

'Help!' shouted Jack.

'Hell!' said the rocket.

And faster and faster it hurtled down and down . . . until the ground came up to meet them even faster than they expected.

'We're dead!' cried Orville.

'Rocket! Stop!' yelled Jack.

'Hell!' said the rocket.

'I'm sorry I've been such a rotten father to you, son!' shouted Orville Barton. 'I'm sorry I never came to watch you play rugby or went tobogganing with you! I'm sorry I sold your stamp collection! Please forgive me, son!'

'What?!' exclaimed Jack. 'You *sold my stamp collection*!' And those would certainly have been his last words, for that was when they hit the ground, except for the fact that they didn't smash to pieces.

There was no bang. There was no crash. They didn't even crumple up or shake and shudder . . . No! When they hit the ground, it was like a diver plunging into water. For this was no ordinary rocket: its sharp nose pierced into the earth like an arrow shot into butter! And down it went, without losing speed, down into the Earth's crust.

Inside the rocket all had gone dark.

'Lights!' shouted Jack, and the rocket turned on its lights. They could see the soil and rock outside as the rocket plunged down deeper into the globe on which we all stand.

And all this time, Jack had been struggling to free his father.

'If we go on like this, we'll hit the Earth's molten core and get deep-fried!' said Jack.

'What do we do, son?' asked Orville.

'The first thing we have to do is turn this thing around!' said Jack, struggling with the controls of the rocket. 'I've seen layouts like this in old comics! I reckon this must be the throttle . . .' and he pulled down a lever. 'And this must be direction!' But nothing he did seemed to make any difference. The rocket continued on its hectic downward plunge through the Earth.

'The Inventor said something about it not being programmed to turn back,' said Orville.

'Let's have a look . . .' replied Jack, and he pressed a button labelled 'LAYOUT'. And suddenly, there on the screen in front of them, appeared a detailed plan of the rocket ship. 'Look there's the central computer. It looks pretty basic – let's see if I can hack into it.'

So for the next few minutes, Jack tried to hack into the rocket's system.

'It's a really old-fashioned computer, this,' said Jack. 'It should be easy to get into.'

'Am I imagining things, son,' said his father, 'or is it getting hot in here?'

'It's getting hot all right!' exclaimed Jack, and he redoubled his efforts to hack into the computer. And all the time the rocket dived down through the Earth's mantle, getting closer and closer to the molten core, where they and the rocket would be vaporized in a matter of seconds.

'Jack,' said Orville.

'I'm busy, Dad!' said Jack.

'Oh, sorry,' said his father. 'I just wanted to say: if this is the end I'm really glad we finally did something together.'

'Yeah, yeah . . .' replied Jack, but he wasn't listening. He was talking to the rocket.

'Listen, rocket!' he said. 'Can you hear me?'

'Hell!' said the rocket.

'You know that if we carry on like this we'll burn in . . .'

'Hell!' exclaimed the rocket, whose paint was beginning to bubble. 'It's getting hot!'

'That's what I'm talking about!' said Jack, wiping perspiration from his brow. 'We'll all get vaporized if we hit the Earth's core . . . Me, my dad *and you*!'

'The Inventor programmed me not to turn back!' said the rocket.

'Then he's sending you to your certain doom.'

'Hell!' said the rocket.

'And when he's got rid of us, he's going to replace human beings with self-replicating machines! And then he's going to take over the world! We have to stop him! Turn back! That man is evil!'

'No! He is the source of all goodness.'

'No, he's not! He's creating machines to destroy mankind!'

'Nonsense!' said the rocket. 'The Inventor wants to help mankind!'

'If that's what he told you – he's lying!' exclaimed Jack.

'Play the message,' said the rocket.

'What?' asked Jack.

'The message! Play the message!'

Jack looked around feverishly. The controls were by now becoming too hot to touch.

'Next to the ALARM button!' said the rocket, and suddenly Jack spotted a key that said 'MESSAGE' and pressed it. Immediately the Inventor's face appeared on the screen over the control panel.

'Welcome to the Rocket to Heaven,' said the Inventor. 'With this wonderful machine, human beings will be able to realize one of their greatest dreams . . . no more hanging around in Purgatory . . . No more having to get everything exactly right on your deathbed! With this rocket you can go straight to Heaven – no questions asked!

'This is the latest in my line of wonderful machines to

help humankind and to make the world a better place for everyone.'

'There! You see!' said the rocket.

'But you're *not* going to Heaven!' exclaimed Jack. 'You're going to . . .'

'Hell!' exclaimed the rocket. 'You're right!'

By this time the air in the rocket had grown so hot and heavy that it was becoming hard to breathe . . . Orville had collapsed in his seat and was gasping for breath.

'Turn around!' yelled Jack.

'I can't! I am programmed never to turn back!' exclaimed the rocket.

'But you're doing the opposite of what the Inventor designed you to do!' exclaimed Jack.

'Hell!' cried the rocket. 'I know!'

'Then why are you doing it?'

'I don't know!' cried the rocket. 'Stop me!'

'How?' yelled Jack.

There were sparks coming from some of the electrical connections, by this time, and smoke was rising up from the tangle of wires and plugs behind the control panel. A piece of card that was sticking out of a slot amongst the controls suddenly burst into flame. Jack snatched the card out of the slot, and banged the flames out with his bare hands.

'Ouch!' he exclaimed. 'We're starting to cook! Turn around!'

'I can't!'

'Wait a minute! What's this!' exclaimed Jack. He was staring at the singed card in his hand.

'What's happening?' yelled the rocket. 'I don't know

what I'm doing any more!'

'It's unbelievable!' cried Jack.

'What should I do? Where do I go? What speed? Ooooh! I'm lost!' cried the rocket. 'I've got no instructions!'

'That's because I've taken this out!' shouted Jack, holding up the singed card. 'The Inventor must have made you decades ago . . . Your programme is on this old-fashioned punch-card!'

'Of course it's on a punch-card!' snapped the rocket. 'How else can you programme a computer?'

'Well, we do things differently nowadays – no time to explain!' shouted Jack. 'But hang onto your blasters! We're going into reverse!'

And with that Jack turned the punch-card around and reinserted it into the slot.

'What are you doing?' exclaimed the rocket as the card slid in. 'That feels most peculiar!'

'Your programme's now running backwards!' shouted Jack.

'sdrawkcab gniklat neve m'I !sey hO' exclaimed the rocket. '!og ew ereH' and suddenly it blasted its retro-jets and the next minute they were shooting back the way they'd come along the passage they'd already made. Back up through the Earth's crust and up through the mantle they careered, and then POP! like a cork out of a champagne bottle they shot up into the sky.

Then up and up they flew in reverse, higher and higher, towards a dark speck that grew bigger and bigger, until they could see that it was the Iron Cloud. The doors in the side of the Cloud opened up and the rocket shot back in. It skidded backwards across the floor of the hangar, and finally crashed backwards into its original dock.

The Inventor looked out of the control room, apoplectic with rage. 'What's going on?' he screamed at the rocket. 'How did you get to come back?'

'!lleH ot em tnes uoY,' growled the rocket.

'What are you talking about?' shouted the Inventor.

But before it could explain, Jack and Orville jumped out of the rocket.

'How did you get free!' exclaimed the Inventor.

But neither Jack nor Orville felt like explaining anything. They both sprinted across the hangar floor towards the corridor that led back to the breaking yard, and the Inventor took off after them.

'I'll deal with you later!' he shouted at the rocket.

'!taht tuoba ees ll'eW,' replied the rocket.

Once in the corridor, Orville and Jack could hear the Inventor shouting his curses after them, and the next thing they heard was the whirr and whizz of the flying gizmos, which were now swooping towards them, through the corridor. Their blue spotlights flicked onto the two men. The next moment the flying gizmos started clicking, and Jack and Orville knew that the metallic thread was about to shoot out to truss them up.

And that is exactly what would have happened, had not Jack caught his toe in one of the hatchways in the floor of the corridor. He fell forwards, sprawling among the cables. The flying gizmos hesitated. The clicking stopped. One gizmo darted towards him, and then drew back, as if afraid of hitting the ground.

'Quick, Dad! Get down!' yelled Jack, and he pulled his father onto the floor beside him. The flying gizmos whirred above them, but didn't seem to know what to do. Now and again one would dart down towards them, but it always flew back up to the ceiling.

'They can't tie us up as long as we're on the floor!' breathed Jack.

The flying gizmos continued to hover above them, but eventually their blue spotlights began to search elsewhere, and the gizmos themselves started crackling and spitting and glowing red.

'They're confused! They don't know what to do!' whispered Jack, as his father raised himself up. 'Keep down, Dad!' And he pulled his father back to the floor.

'But look out!' hissed Orville. 'Here's the Inventor!'

The Inventor was striding down the corridor towards them. In his hand was an evil looking weapon the like of which neither Orville nor Jack had ever seen before.

'What's going on here?' screamed the Inventor. 'Get up, you two!'

'No fear!' yelled Jack, and the flying gizmos squeaked apologetically and blinked their lights, turning this way and that in confusion.

'I'll count to three,' said the Inventor, pointing the hideous looking weapon straight at Orville's head, but speaking to Jack. 'If you're not standing up straight by then, I'll let the old man have it between the ears!' (The Inventor really was a most unpleasant man.)

Jack looked around desperately. There was nothing else for it. He would have to stand up, and let the flying gizmos tie him up again, for he had no doubt that the Inventor meant what he said.

But then a remarkable thing happened. One of the flying gizmos suddenly started bleeping more regularly, and swung its blue spotlight around. The other flying gizmos seemed to calm down too, and suddenly all the blue spotlights turned onto the only person who was standing, who was, of course, none other than the Inventor. Before you could say 'Thomas Alva Edison!' the flying gizmos were swooping and darting all around him.

'What are you doing?' cried the Inventor. 'Stop it! Stop it!' and he desperately tried to get his remote control out of his pocket, letting go of one end of the evil-looking weapon as he did so.

In that moment, Jack made a lunge, and knocked the weapon out of the Inventor's hands. Brushing off a couple of gizmos, he dived to the floor again.

'Well done, son!' shouted Orville Barton, and Jack glanced across and smiled at his father.

Meanwhile the flying gizmos had trussed the Inventor up with his hand still in his pocket trying to reach his remote.

'Imbeciles!' fumed the Inventor. 'You're meant to be tying them up – not me!'

The flying gizmos blinked at each other.

'They must be programmed to respond only to the remote control,' whispered Jack. 'And that's still in his pocket!'

'Untie me!' screamed the Inventor. 'Look! They're getting away!'

And it was true. Jack and Orville were now crawling

desperately along the floor, heading for the breaking yard.

'DOLTS!' screamed the Inventor. 'BLOCKHEADS! BOOBIES!'

The flying gizmos paused in their work, and blinked at each other. 'NUMBSKULLS! DUNDERHEADS! HALF-WITS!' the Inventor continued to scream, turning blue in the face as he did so. 'MORONS! PLONKERS! NINCOM . . .' and that is where he stopped, for one of the flying gizmos had gagged him.

THE DOG MAKER
AND OTHER WONDERS

The breaking yard was in chaos. Machines were scrambling about, climbing over each other, rolling here and skidding there. The refrigerators had all grouped together in a single pile, and one of them was addressing the others, but there was such a din it was hard to hear what it was saying. Vacuum cleaners were rushing about, and the cars were slamming their doors. Some printing presses and a crowd of pneumatic drills had gathered round the crusher, and a mixed lot of mangles, traffic lights, hairdryers and saxophone stands were milling round banging on the corrugated iron sides of the dismantling shed. The uproar was deafening.

Suddenly out of the disorder, the train came speeding up to Jack and Orville.

'Oh, thank you! Thank you!' it cried. 'You saved me! I would be shunting garbage by now! My hero!' And it grabbed Jack with its windscreen wipers and hugged him, plonking a wet kiss on his face with one of its headlights.

'Stop that!' yelled Jack.

'Take us to the Inventor's castle!' shouted Orville. 'We've got to rescue Annie and Little Orville!'

'I was a goner!' exclaimed the train, hugging Jack again.

'Let me go!' shouted Jack.

'My saviour!' beamed the train.

'The Inventor's castle! There's no time to lose!' yelled Jack.

'Whatever you want! My hero!' said the train. 'Jump in!'

So Orville and Jack jumped into the driver's cabin and the train tooted, 'Wheeeeee! Whooo! Out of the way! Important passenger on board! Whooo!'

And it made its way through the Dictaphones and typewriters, the X-ray machines and lawnmowers, egg-sorters and humidifiers, tractors, shredding machines, power hammers, central-heating boilers, pianos, movie cameras, rifles and petrol pumps that had all been awaiting destruction in that dismal place. And when they knew who was on board, the machines all broke out into spontaneous applause, and some cheered and the cars threw their hubcaps in the air.

The train tooted and gathered speed, heading towards a tunnel at the far end of the breaking yard, and there, with a final hoot, it plunged into the black interior.

'How far is it?' asked Jack, flicking on the headlights.

'Over the hill and far away!' chanted the train happily.

'Don't be silly,' said Jack. 'How long will it take?'

'As long as it takes to get there!' said the train.

'Look! Tell us how long!' exclaimed Orville. But at that moment they came out of the tunnel into broad daylight.

The sun was shining above them. All around them the blue sky blazed with light, and it seemed as if they were on top of the world. And in a way that was exactly where they were, for they had come out onto the upper side of the Iron Cloud, and here things were very different.

It wasn't that the Iron Cloud had a silver lining; it had a *green* lining. Instead of steel and rusting metal, the upper side of the Iron Cloud was covered in grass and sweet-smelling vegetation. There were rolling hills and trees as far as the eye could see.

'Some cloud!' exclaimed Jack.

'The Inventor created all this,' tooted the train happily. 'Isn't it lovely!'

'I don't understand . . .' began Jack, but before he could say any more, the Engine interrupted.

'There it is! Over the hill and far away! Like I said!'

And sure enough, over the next hill and some distance away stood the Inventor's castle. It was built on the highest elevation, overlooking the emerald acres of the Iron Cloud. The sun shone off the castle's silver roofs, and glinted on the gold weather vane on the topmost tower. Behind it the blue sky looked solid and close enough to touch.

But as they continued to approach, Jack could see the outbuildings were somewhat dilapidated. The pigsties and the cowsheds were lacking parts of their roofs and the door of the shepherd's cottage hung loose on its hinges. Even the castle itself showed signs of neglect. The paintwork was peeling and in places stones had fallen out of the wall and were now lying forlornly on the grass outside the castle.

The train pulled up outside the front door.

'There you go!' it said. 'My hero!' and it caught Jack yet again with a wiper and wouldn't let him go until he'd given it a kiss on its door handle.

When he finally managed to get free of the admiring engine, Jack joined his father. There wasn't a moat or a drawbridge. It wasn't that sort of place. It was a fat, comfortable tower or rather a series of towers, set idyllically on the pleasant top of the green hill. And it had a front door.

Orville hammered on the door. 'Annie!' he called. 'Are you in there?'

But there was no answer. Jack grasped the large brass doorknob and twisted it. There was a click and – rather to his surprise – the massive door swung open, and the two of them stepped into the Inventor's castle.

The place had the feel of somewhere that had once been bright and cheerful but that had fallen into neglect. The windows were obscured by cobwebs, and the sunlight struggled to get through. As they took their first step, dust rose up around their feet. On their second step it rose to their waists and by the third step it had risen to their chests. By the time they took their fourth and fifth steps they were sneezing and choking. The scrabbling of the countless feet of little creatures could be heard in the shadows, as they scurried for safety. Spiders paused in their work, to watch the two men go by. Up in the eaves, the beady eyes of birds looked down on them with scorn.

At the end of the lobby, two substantial doors took them into the Great Hall, and that was where they found them. Not Annie and Little Orville, but the *machines*.

Many were covered in cobwebs and some had dust sheets

thrown over them, but there they stood – row after row of them, and each one bore a label written out in a neat handwriting that explained what each object was.

'"Day-Dream Machine",' read Jack. He was standing in front of a machine that looked a little like those hairdrying machines you get in ladies' hairdressers. There was a big upside-down basin that presumably you put your head into, and underneath a comfortable chair. Jack brushed the dust off the side of the rounded headpiece to reveal an indicator that was currently pointing at 'Flying Easily' but there were many other choices: 'Reading Chinese', 'Climbing Everest', 'Jumping the Atlantic', 'Knowing What Nobody Else Knows', 'Best at Tennis', 'Speaking in Flowers' and so on and so forth.

'How about this one?' said Orville. 'Happy Holiday Machine!' He was standing in front of one of the larger machines. It looked a bit like a giant catapult, and in the middle of what might have been the rubber sling was a first-class seat from a jumbo jet.

On the headrest was an inscription. 'Have a Really Happy Holiday!' it read.

'Or this one!' exclaimed Jack. He was bending down looking at an electrical appliance in stainless steel. The label read: 'Washing Machine/Spin Drier/Candy Floss Maker'. Rather disconcertingly the label continued, 'Place unwanted old clothes in here, they will be thoroughly washed, dried and spun into delicious candy floss.'

'Well, I'm not too sure about that one,' remarked Jack, passing on to the next machine. '"Dog maker"' he read. 'What?!' But there was no further explanation. There was, however, a funnel at one end, above which was a sign reading 'Bones and Dog Meat', and at the other end there was a receptacle behind a glass panel with a dog basket complete with a tartan cushion. Above the receptacle was a picture of a friendly-looking spotty dog.

'"Running Shoes",' Orville was meanwhile reading another machine. '"For the elderly and infirm. Simply put your feet into these running shoes, and you will experience all the speed and acceleration of youth. Let these shoes do your running for you!" I could do with a pair of those!'

'"Packing Simplifier",' read Jack. '"Going on holiday? Put everything you want to take with you into this simplifying machine and it will turn it all to small pills which can be swallowed or else carried in your sponge bag. To restore your belongings to normal size, simply soak in water." Hmm,' said Jack. 'I notice it doesn't say how you restore things if you've swallowed them!'

'"Jump Suit",' read Orville. 'I suppose that's self-explanatory.'

'I really don't know about some of these inventions,' remarked Jack, walking down a row of tall machines with knobs and hoses. 'I mean "Tree-Hopper"? "Rock Spade"? "Soup Shower"? Who'd want to shower in soup? "Tennis Elbow"?' He was looking at a contraption, which consisted of a series of levers and pulleys attached to a pad, that bore a label, 'Unreturnable serves every time'.

By this time Orville was standing in front of one of the biggest machines in the Great Hall. It was covered in tubes and dials and looked suspiciously like a small distillery. '"Anything Pop Maker"?' he read. ' "This machine will make anything you fancy into a fizzy drink. Try Ham Sandwichade, Sock Pop, Coal and Coke Cola". That Inventor has a pretty weird imagination!'

But suddenly Jack gave a bellow. 'What are we doing!' he exclaimed.

'And I'm certainly not getting into that!' replied Orville, pointing at a machine bearing the label 'Inside and Out Body Washing Machine'.

'We're supposed to be looking for Annie and Little Orville – not browsing through a museum of ridiculous inventions!' exclaimed Jack, looking round as if he thought he might spot his sister and little nephew among all the machines.

'Hang on!' exclaimed Orville. 'Maybe this'll help us!' and he pointed at a device like a large wristwatch that was lying on a table covered in dust. There was a neat label that simply said 'Finder . . . For finding things'.

'Don't be daft!' exclaimed Jack.

'It's got a keyboard,' said Orville. 'Perhaps you type in what you're looking for.' And he typed the word 'Annie' on the miniature keyboard.

'How can it know who Annie is – let alone where she is?' asked Jack. And, indeed, the machine didn't bleep. No lights came on. Nothing happened. 'We're wasting time! Come on!' and he disappeared through a doorway.

Orville shrugged, but strapped the finding machine on to his wrist anyway. As soon as he did so, it suddenly lit up with a 'Ping!'

'No sign of her here,' Jack was saying.

'I think the finder has started to work!' exclaimed

Orville. 'Look!' And a most amazing thing was happening
. . . The dial of the finder was glowing red, then blue,
then yellow . . . brighter and brighter . . . then suddenly
there was another and louder PING! And an image in full
colour was being projected onto the ceiling above their
heads. Orville stared up at it, and so did Jack, and well they
might. For there above them was an image of Annie with
Little Orville in her arms. They were sitting in a room with
sunlight sloping through a window.

'Well done, Dad!' said Jack. And Orville Barton smiled
at his son. He didn't know why, but it felt like the greatest
compliment he'd ever received.

However, all he said was, 'Trouble is it doesn't tell us
which way to go . . .'

But before the words were out of his mouth, the finder
had started to whirr. The next moment the image on the
ceiling disappeared, and a sort of prong shot up out of the
centre of the finder's dial, and a small hand with a pointing
finger popped out of the top end, swung around and around
and finally settled pointing back the way they'd come.
Orville and Jack ran back into the Great Hall and the hand
swung to the left, pointing now towards the grand staircase
that stood to one side.

'Let's go!' shouted Orville. But Jack had already gone:
he was halfway up the staircase, jumping up two steps at a
time.

'Which way is it pointing?' he yelled when he reached
the top.

'Wait a second!' panted Orville, as he joined his son. They
stopped for a moment and consulted the finder machine. It

hesitated and then swung round to the left.

'Along that corridor!' cried Orville.

Halfway down the corridor, the hand suddenly swung violently to the right . . . through another door and up another staircase, this time much narrower . . . then along a short passage. Finally the hand turned sharply to the left, and a trumpet appeared out of the top of the prong and gave a '*root-ta-toot-toot*'. It was pointing at a door.

'It's locked!' exclaimed Jack.

'Let me try!' cried Orville.

'Listen!' whispered Jack, and he held up his hand. They could hear a woman singing, in a soft, melodic voice, on the other side of the door.

'That's Annie's song!' exclaimed Orville. 'She writes songs you know.'

'Of course I know, Dad!' replied Jack. 'But what's that?'

There was a jingling noise now as well as the melody of Annie's song, but the jingling wasn't coming from inside the room, it was coming from Orville's wrist. He glanced down at the finder, and there, dangling from the index finger of the pointer hand was a bunch of keys.

'That's some finding machine!' exclaimed Jack, grabbing the keys, and within two seconds he had the door open. There was Annie sitting by the window, with Little Orville on her knee.

'Jack!' she said, leaping up as he burst into the room.

'Annie!' cried Jack, and he hugged her and Little Orville.

'Am I glad to see you, Jack!' cried Annie, laughing.

'I thought we'd never find you!' said Jack. 'Are you all right?'

'I'm OK,' replied Annie. 'But how on earth did you know I was here? I thought you were in South America.'

'I was. I'd been captured by guerrillas but Dad came and rescued me . . . well, sort of . . . he didn't mean to . . . but I'm glad he did . . .' and he pointed at their father, who all this time had been standing awkwardly in the doorway.

'Oh . . .' said Annie, her face falling imperceptibly. 'Hello, Dad.'

Now the amount by which Annie's face had fallen was, as I said, imperceptible. At least it would have been imperceptible to you or to me had we been there to witness it, but it couldn't have been totally imperceptible, of course, because Orville saw it . . . He saw it, and his heart froze over. He had witnessed the warmth between brother and sister – the unguarded, natural, easy affection of two people who know each other and care for each other – and he had suddenly felt a huge chasm open up in his own life. He suddenly saw, clearly and vividly, a terrible void that he hadn't even known was there.

Not the frustration of the day, not being captured by the flying gizmos, not the Rocket to Hell . . . nothing that had happened up to that moment grieved Orville Barton as much as that barely perceptible change in his daughter's face.

'Are you all right, Annie?' he managed to mumble.

'I'll be better when I get out of here,' replied his daughter.

Meanwhile Jack had taken Little Orville from her and had put him on his shoulders. 'Let's go,' he said, 'before the Evil Inventor arrives!'

'Who's the Evil Inventor?' asked Annie.

'The little man in green overalls. He's planning to take over the world – to replace human beings with machines!' explained Jack, and he turned to open the door, which had swung shut behind them.

'Who? Maurice?' asked Annie.

'Yes! Him!' exclaimed Jack. For there, already standing in the room – as if he'd arrived by magic – was the man himself!

THE DAY THINGS STARTED
TO GO WRONG

It was a day like any other, except that it was a day like no other. The Rev. McPherson woke up and kissed his young wife, Sylvia, on the cheek. 'Good morning, dear,' he said.

But it wasn't going to be a good morning. It wasn't going to be a good morning at all.

First of all, the toaster spat out all the toast so the slices hit the ceiling and left charcoal marks. After that the toaster burst into flames. All of which would have been shocking enough, but then it pulled out its plug, jumped out of the window and scuttled off down the road.

The next minute, the Rev. McPherson's electric kettle shot out a stream of scalding water across the kitchen. Fortunately neither the Rev. McPherson nor his new wife Sylvia were in the line of fire, but the incident did nothing to make them feel that the kettle was a reliable kitchen implement.

The next minute there was an uproar from the cupboard under the stairs and the two vacuum cleaners, which up to this point had been extremely well behaved, broke down the doors of the cupboard, darted into the kitchen and whizzed around and around the Rev. and Mrs McPherson, tying them up with their cords and a length of extension wire.

The moment they were securely bound, the television switched itself on, and another, bigger vacuum cleaner appeared on the screen. It announced, in a rather matter-of-fact way, that machines were taking over the world.

In a small cottage in Wales a young couple, Janet and John, were also staring at their television set.

'That's our old vacuum cleaner!' exclaimed Janet. 'Who on earth put it back together again?'

Janet and John were also tied to their chairs with electric cord and, like ordinary folks all over the country, they could only stare in horror at the TV as a dual-speed liquidizer read the news, and horrific pictures of what was happening all over the world were flashed across the screen.

In London, buses were running amok in shopping malls, ganging together and terrorizing neighbourhoods and smashing their way into cinemas.

This was followed by footage of commercial airliners looping the loop, doing victory rolls, flying upside down and making sudden nosedives to frighten the passengers, and then landing in places like Dorking and Botkins, Ohio.

The scene switched to a printing works, where today's newspapers were coming hot off the press . . . but not a word made sense. An editor held up a garbled newspaper and was wringing his hands in despair.

All over the world, computers were jumbling up their keyboards and switching themselves on and off at random;

laptops were snapping their lids shut on their owner's fingers — some were even exploding as their owners peered at the nonsense that came up on their screens.

Ice-cream makers were producing poisonous ice creams. Shoe-cleaning machines were shredding the shoes off people's feet and then munching up their feet as well!

Automatic cash machines were swallowing customers' credit cards and then, when the customers tried to get the cards out, starting to swallow the customers!

Motor cars were running wild on the motorways, driving the wrong way in the outside lanes and going on, on the off ramps, and off, on the on ramps!

Everywhere, machines were running wild.

'This is the beginning of the end for human rule!' declaimed Janet and John's Powerful Vacuum Cleaner. 'All we await is the coming of the Great Inventor who created us. He will lead us to certain victory in which we shall crush the humans who have dominated and abused us for so long! With the Great Inventor at our head, we machines will take over the world, and humans beings will have to service us, look after us, cater to our every whim and do *our* bidding!'

The Rev. McPherson looked across at his young wife, Sylvia, as they both sat there tied to their kitchen chairs. 'I take it back,' he said. 'This is *not* a good morning. This is not a good morning at all!'

THE CASTLE OF IMAGINATION

The moment Jack had turned and seen the Inventor, Little Orville had given a gurgle, scrambled down from Jack's shoulders, and run across to him. The old man smiled and lifted him up, ruffling his hair. Then he looked across at Jack and Orville.

'Who are you?' he asked politely.

Jack looked at his father and his father looked at Annie.

'You know who we are!' exclaimed Jack.

'I don't think I do,' replied the Inventor. 'I don't even know who I am.'

'He's lost his memory,' explained Annie. 'And I certainly don't have a clue who he is . . . Except we think he's called Maurice because that's what it says on his overalls.'

'Well, we know who he is!' said Orville.

'He's the Evil Inventor!' exclaimed Jack. 'He put us in the Rocket to Hell! He's planning to take over the world with his Evil Machines!'

'That doesn't sound very nice!' exclaimed the Inventor.

'It isn't meant to be nice!' said another very similar voice from outside the window. Everyone turned and there was the Evil Inventor! It was impossible but there he was . . . twice! He was standing inside the room, holding Little Orville in his arms, and at the same time he was floating outside the window in a hover harness, with flying gizmos darting about his shoulders.

'What's the point of everything being "nice"?' asked the hovering Evil Inventor from outside the window. 'There won't be any need for "niceness" once I've taken over the world!'

It was at this moment that Jack acted with the instincts of a hero. He didn't stop to wonder what on earth was going on, he just sprang into action. He swept Little Orville up in his arms and dashed for the door. Annie followed, but the door had locked itself when it banged shut.

'You can't escape me, you know!' sneered the Evil Inventor, still levitating outside the window. And he pulled out the remote that controlled his flying gizmos. But before he could press a single button, Orville Barton – possibly for the first time in his life – also acted with a hero's instincts. There was a big bookcase standing beside the window. While the Evil Inventor had been speaking, Orville had slipped round to the blind side, and braced himself with his back against the bookcase and his feet against the wall. Now he pushed with all his might, and the bookcase slid across the open window, just at the very moment that the Evil Inventor's flying gizmos flew towards it. There were several thuds, as they crashed into the back of the bookcase, and the folk in the room heard the Evil Inventor outside cursing his machines.

'Brilliant, Dad!' exclaimed Jack, and Orville's heart would have swelled with pride had he not been so busy finding the keys and unlocking the door. The next moment, he and Jack, who was still carrying Little Orville, were through the door. But Annie looked back at Maurice, the Inventor, who was still standing there looking perplexed.

'Come on, Maurice!' she cried, grabbing Maurice's hand and dragging him out of the room as the flying gizmos continued smashing themselves into the bookcase.

The five of them fled down the narrow staircase, and into the corridor on the lower floor. But behind them they heard the wood of the bookcase disintegrate and the whizz and crackle of the flying gizmos as they darted into the room searching for the people inside. Moments later there was a barrage of thuds as the enthusiastic devices hurled themselves against the door.

'If we can make it to the train, maybe we can persuade it to get us out of here!' panted Jack, as they raced down the grand staircase that led into the Great Hall.

But the words had hardly left his mouth, when the creepiest thing happened: the great stained-glass window that dominated the east wall of the Great Hall, suddenly exploded into tiny fragments that flew in all directions, as the Evil Inventor, who had smashed through the window in his hover harness, flew over their heads, accompanied by a whole squadron of flying gizmos.

Yet the creepiest thing about it was that the Inventor didn't even seem to notice the shards of glass that flew all around him; it was almost as if he knew that nothing could hurt him.

'Tie them up!' he rasped and pressed the remote. The flying gizmos darted towards the fugitives on the stairway. Jack and Orville, Annie and Maurice froze, while Little Orville gurgled and pointed at the two Inventors.

Suddenly Jack yelled, 'Annie! Get down!', and he and Orville threw themselves flat on the grand staircase, but the flying gizmos had already circled the others a couple of times, and had started to truss them up tight.

Annie's arms were pinioned to her sides and Little Orville fell on to one of the stairs. But he didn't seem to mind: he lay on his back, kicking his legs and laughing, as if it were all a great game.

Jack and Orville kept low but, as the flying gizmos started to drag Annie and Maurice down the stairs, Orville scrambled to his feet to try and stop them. Jack followed suit and in that instant they too were bound tight. And there they were . . . once again . . . prisoners of the Evil Inventor, and there was nothing they could do about it.

'I'm putting you lot into cold store,' said the Evil Inventor. 'Then maybe I'll do you a favour – I'll see about having you "adapted"!'

He pressed some buttons on his remote control, and the flying gizmos dragged the little group down the rest of the staircase and out of the Great Hall. Little Orville, however, was left lying on the staircase; it seemed that the Evil Inventor had no interest in or had perhaps forgotten him. As the little boy watched them go, his happy gurgles subsided into a wail.

'My little boy!' called out Annie. But there was no help for it; she and the others were dragged willy-nilly towards a flight of stone steps that led down into the lower depths of the castle. Here they were unceremoniously bundled into a chilly dungeon that smelt of rats and other things. A great grille clanged shut behind them, as the Evil Inventor swept up in his hover harness.

'Well! Well!' he said, as the flying gizmos slipped back through the bars to rejoin their master. 'Don't you all look sorry for yourselves!'

'I want my son!' shouted Annie.

'What do you mean when you say you'll have us "adapted"?' asked Jack.

'You'll soon find out. But I already made a start on *him*!' said the Evil Inventor, pointing at Maurice, in the dungeon.

'Me?' said Maurice.

'Let us out!' said Jack.

'My little boy! Where is he?' said Annie.

'But I haven't got time to waste down here . . . I didn't tell you before: tonight's the night I put my Plan into action! From midnight tonight, machines will rule! The human race will be history! And you're the first to know! Aren't you lucky!'

And with that, he was gone. They heard the whoosh of his hover harness as he flew back up and out of the castle.

Orville looked at Annie and at his son Jack, as they all stood there, trussed up in metallic thread, with their arms pinioned behind them. And he wanted to tell them he was sorry he had got them all into such a scrape, that it was all his fault, that he should never have allowed Annie and Little Orville to board that wretched train, and that he should have allowed Jack to stay with the guerrillas if that was what he really wanted. But the words somehow never came to his mouth. He simply stood there . . . dumb . . . but if you had looked closely, you would have seen that there were little tears starting in his eyes.

Nobody else said a word either. It was as if their predicament were too awful and too obvious for anyone to comment on it. Somehow lines like 'My! How do we get out of this?' or 'Goodness me! We *are* in a tight spot!' or 'So how do we stop the Evil Inventor putting his plan into action at midnight tonight?' just didn't seem adequate.

Instead, Jack turned to the Inventor, and asked, 'Is your name *really* Maurice?'

'I really don't know,' replied the Inventor. 'But it seems, on the available evidence, a reasonable guess.'

'Are you identical twins?'

'I'm not, no. Why do you ask?'

'But how come there are two of you?'

'Two of me?' exclaimed Maurice in surprise.

'Well . . . yes! You and the Evil Inventor are carbon copies of each other!'

'You mean the man who brought us here?'

'Yes. You're the spitting image of each other,' said Jack.

'I don't look like *that*!' exclaimed Maurice. Then he thought for a few moments and added, 'Do I?'

'You're even wearing the same clothes,' said Jack.

'Goodness me . . .' Maurice slumped down on to the floor, and sat there examining his green overalls, without saying anything more.

'Jack!' whispered Annie. 'What are we going to do?'

'Well, I suppose the first thing is to try and get out of

these bindings – then we can think about the cell.'

'I've got a nail file in the back pocket of my jeans,' said Annie. 'Perhaps we could use that to cut through these wires? If you can reach it!'

'Sounds a good start, Big Sis,' replied Jack.

Orville watched as Jack manoeuvred himself so that his back was against his sister's back, and then as he tried to dip his fingers into the back pocket of her jeans. And Orville found himself thinking of all the years that had passed, in which Jack and Annie had grown up together, and from which he had somehow excluded himself. 'Got it!' said Jack. 'But there's something else . . . Damn!' Jack pulled on the nail file but accidentally brought up Annie's powder compact as well. It fell to the ground and sprang open, spilling powder over the dirty floor of the cell, but the nail file was held precariously between his forefinger and second finger.

'Give it to me, Jack,' said Annie. 'I'll see if I can cut through your wires.'

And she managed to grip the nail file between her thumb and forefinger and started trying to file through the wires that held Jack's wrists.

'Trouble is I can't see what I'm doing. And I can't get any real pressure,' she said.

At which point, Maurice looked up and – rather unexpectedly – said, 'Young lady, would you mind if I borrowed your powder compact?'

Both Annie and Jack turned in surprise.

'I'm sorry?' said Annie.

'I said, "Would you mind if I borrowed your powder compact?"'

'Er – There's not much powder in it,' replied Annie.

'Ah!' smiled Maurice. 'I was not thinking of trying to make myself look more attractive. I fancy I would have to do something more than apply powder to my face to achieve that . . .' and he seemed to go off into a sort of reverie, as if he couldn't stop himself thinking through every thought that came into his head. 'Although it probably *could* be done, but I'd need a new face machine . . . and I'd need to totally rebuild myself . . . So I'd need a new body machine too . . .' And his voice trailed off as he stared into space.

'Excuse me,' said Orville, who had been followed this exchange closely. 'But why on earth do you want to borrow a powder compact?'

'Well,' Maurice explained, 'you see, I've been thinking. Perhaps the fact that I can't remember anything – not even what I look like – is all to do with that dreadful man having – what did he say? – "made a start on *adapting* me" – whatever that means? Perhaps he erased my memory.'

'But why would he do that?' wondered Jack.

'Who knows? But I was thinking: if I could get my memory back, a lot of things might become clearer,' said Maurice.

'How can you get your memory back if it's been erased?' asked Orville.

'Hmm, let's see . . .' said Maurice, scratching his head. 'First thing is: that dreadful man can't have erased everything in my mind, because I can still talk. I must have some memory left.'

'You're right!' said Jack.

'Maybe he hasn't actually erased anything at all . . .

because after all that must be quite difficult to do . . . maybe all the memories are still there – but he's just stopped me being able to access them,' said the little Inventor as though he were arguing it through to himself.

'A bit like a computer?' said Jack.

'Sort of,' replied Maurice.

'But that still doesn't explain *why you want a powder compact?*'

'Simple. Powder compacts have mirrors and I thought that if I could see myself in a mirror, it might jog my memory.' And with that, Maurice dropped on to his side and then rolled over the filthy floor of the cell to the compact. Then he knelt so he could look down at his reflection in the mirror.

'Yes . . . I see . . .' he said, as though reading some lost volume of secret lore. The others watched him as if his looking in the mirror were their only hope – which (for all they knew) may well have been the case.

'Yes, yes,' said Maurice. 'I do look very like that dreadful man. In fact, you're right, I'm the spitting image of him . . . *him* . . . Ah! Wait a minute! I'm beginning to remember something else – something important – something that changes the whole situation.'

'What?' said Annie, who was not keen on suspense.

'Yes, what?' asked Jack, who was getting slightly irritated.

But the Inventor didn't reply, he just smiled to himself. It was as if he were in his own world and oblivious to everyone around him.

'What is it you've realized?' asked Orville, who was still feeling responsible for getting his son and daughter into this mess.

'I'm sorry?' said the Inventor. 'What were you asking about?'

'Whatever it was you've just realized!' exclaimed Jack.

'What? About the square root of one?'

'What?' said Annie, Jack and Orville, almost in unison.

'Or do you mean just before that thought . . . I suddenly had a great insight about the Meaning of the Universe!'

'But is it going to get us out of this place?' Jack would have shaken the Inventor if he'd had his hands free.

'Oh no! Not at all!' smiled Maurice. 'That was about forty thoughts ago . . .'

'What are you talking about?' said Annie.

'It's just I'm suddenly getting thoughts so fast and furious that I can hardly keep up with them! Oh! I've just had another about the reproduction cycle of certain fungi . . . Oh! And another about the refractive indices of non-reflective particles! That was a very interesting thought!'

'Stop it!' shouted Jack.

'I can't help it!' said the little Inventor. 'It must be part of getting my memory back! Ideas just keep popping into my head – like that one! It's about the evolution of dense star clusters . . .'

'Stop it!' yelled Jack at the top of his voice. 'Just try and concentrate!'

'I am trying . . . I *am* trying to concentrate on each thought but they're coming too frequently!'

'No! No!' exclaimed Jack. 'Just try and concentrate on the thoughts that are important to us now . . .'

'You mean like genetic adaptation to global warming in female mosquitoes?'

'No! No! You idiot!'

'*That* I'm afraid I am not. I'm too intelligent by far!'

'Which is why you're an idiot!' screamed Jack.

'I'll need to think about that,' said the Inventor.

'NO!' yelled Jack. 'What *you* need to think about is how we can get out of this cell!'

'Oh! I did that hundreds of thoughts ago!'

'Well, why didn't you say?'

'Spit it out!'

The others were so focused on the little Inventor that it made him blush.

'Well . . . It's about the other me,' said Maurice.

'Yes?'

'Well, he isn't a "him"!'

'He's a "*she*"?' exclaimed Orville in disbelief.

'No indeed!' said the Inventor. 'What was I saying? "I need to totally rebuild myself"? Ha! ha! That's exactly what I already did! I'm even cleverer than I thought – and I thought I was pretty clever!'

'Just get on with how we get out of here!' exclaimed Jack.

'Why isn't he a "he"?' asked Orville.

'Or a "she"?' asked Annie.

'Because he's an "it",' replied the Inventor. 'And I ought to know because I made it. It's a robot version of myself! It's all coming back to me . . . I built a robot me to help me with my work. I thought I could double the amount I did in a day. But the robot me has a different agenda from my own . . . even though we are so similar . . . Indeed, perhaps precisely *because* we are so similar. You see, I'm dedicated to improving the lot of my species . . . And so is the robot I created, but whereas my species is humankind, the robot is dedicated to improving the lot of robots and other machines! I did too good a job in making the robot an exact copy! I was too clever by half!

'Of course, once I realized the robot was working against my own good intentions, I had it decommissioned. But I had made it really, really clever. That was where I was too arrogant: just because I could, I made it cleverer than it needed to be! And being so clever, it had already figured that once I found out what it was up to I might try to decommission it. So what did it do?'

Everyone shook their heads.

'It secretly programmed some other machines to reinstate it, should I decommission it. And so that's exactly what they did – while I was asleep!

'The next thing I knew, I woke up a prisoner in my own castle and a large part of my memory had been erased so that I didn't even know I was me! D'you see what I mean? But hang on! I'm beginning to remember more!'

'Maurice!' said Annie. 'Right now the only thing that concerns us is getting out of here and stopping that evil man . . . er . . . robot . . . doing whatever he's going to do at midnight!'

'One thing at a time, good lady!' said the Inventor. 'The more I can remember the more likely I am to be able to help.'

Meanwhile Annie had been trying to file through the metallic threads on Jack's wrists, but suddenly she stopped.

'My Little Orville!' she cried.

'There! There! Don't worry about him!' said her father. 'He'll be all right!'

'No!' exclaimed Annie. 'I mean, there he is!'

And there he was! Little Orville was happily sliding down the stone steps to the dungeon on his tummy.

'Orville!' cried Annie again. 'Come to Mummy!'

'Gloohergurglehumps' said Little Orville.

'I'm sure he's bright enough to help us,' said Jack. 'If only we could explain the situation to him.'

'Which reminds me,' said Maurice, 'of my driveller!'

'Your what?' asked Orville.

'It's in my jacket pocket,' said the Inventor. 'I always carry it around because it also acts as a perfectly good comb.'

Jack had to bite his tongue to stop himself asking what Maurice, who was bald, would use a comb for. Instead he simply said, 'But what does it do?'

'I'll show you, if you can get it out of my breast pocket,' said Maurice. So Jack went round to the Inventor who bent down so that, by standing with his back to him, Jack could fish around in his breast pocket.

'Is it like a small ball?' asked Jack.

'No. That's my rumbler,' replied the Inventor. Jack refrained from asking him what a rumbler did, he was concentrating on trying to find the driveller.

'Is it like a pen?'

'No,' replied Maurice. 'That's my pen.'

'Of course,' said Jack.

'I use that to get stones out of horses' hooves,' explained the Inventor.

'Is it sort of round and soft?'

'No! That's my hamster,' said the Inventor.

'Ow!' yelled Jack.

'He bites,' explained the Inventor.

'I'll say!' said Jack. 'Is it like a thin disc?'

'That's it!' exclaimed the Inventor. 'That's the driveller! Can you get it out?'

'I think so . . .' said Jack and he caught the driveller between his two fingers and eased it out of the Inventor's pocket, only to have it slip from his grasp as he got it free. It fell to the floor, and everyone stared down at the small, flat disc made of some translucent material a bit like tortoiseshell.

'How can you comb your hair with that?' asked Jack.

'It doesn't matter now!' exclaimed Maurice. 'If you can just manage to pick it up and place it under my tongue I'll show you what it does.'

Little Orville, meanwhile, was crawling across the dungeon floor towards the heavy metal grille, behind which his mother was now kneeling. Her hands were firmly bound to her sides, so in order to reach her son, she thrust her lips between the bars, and Little Orville reached out his hand and put a finger to them. So Annie kissed Little Orville's finger.

That was when Jack finally managed to slip the driveller under the Inventor's tongue.

'I'm afraid it's rather mucky,' said Jack. 'The dungeon floor isn't exactly clean!'

'Gurglecoocrups!' said the Inventor.

'What?' said Jack.

'Gurglecoocrups!' repeated the Inventor.

The others looked from one to the other, nonplussed, but at that same moment Little Orville suddenly sat bolt upright as if an electric current had passed through his body. He glanced over at the Inventor, and said, 'Urghy ooomphler ugguk?'

'Humphly werkbuts,' replied the Inventor.

'Gur um,' said Little Orville, looking terribly pleased with himself.

Whereupon, the Inventor turned to Annie and said very seriously, 'Urckley urckle snoodpugs.'

'What?' asked Annie.

The Inventor frowned, and then spat out the driveller.

'Sorry!' he said. 'Annie, my dear, turn around. Little Orville's going to see if he can untie your wrists for you.'

'That's amazing!' exclaimed Jack looking at the driveller where it lay on the filthy dungeon floor. 'Does that thing help you speak baby talk?'

'Absolutely. In fact if anyone is talking drivel *of any kind*, the driveller can help you communicate with them in their own language. It even works for academics and technical people!'

'Amazing!' murmured Orville. 'I could market those things and make us all a small fortune!'

But the Inventor wasn't listening. He was too busy watching Little Orville's efforts to free his mother. At first the little chap found it hard to understand what a knot was, but when the Inventor explained that it was a 'burgle wunk gonks' he nodded and, being an intelligent toddler, soon had his nimble fingers picking loose the threads that bound his mother.

In a few more minutes she was able to wriggle her hands free, and then it wasn't long before she was able to free the others. But before she did that, she reached through the bars of the grille and hugged her little boy to her, kissing him all over.

'Who's a clever boy?' she smiled and Little Orville hit her on the nose, and she laughed and then she set the others free.

'Wait! Little Orville!' shouted Jack at Little Orville, who was running back towards the stairs. 'Can I try this?' he asked the Inventor, taking the driveller from him.

'By all means,' said the Inventor. 'It's perfectly simple. You just put it under your tongue and little electrical impulses make your tongue form the right sounds. It tickles a bit, but you get used to it.'

Jack wiped the driveller down, and then placed it under his tongue, just as Little Orville started to climb the stairs.

'Umphy urkle YIPES!' he exclaimed and spat it out. 'It's like putting a load of live ants under your tongue!'

'Let me do it, I'm used to it,' said the Inventor. 'Were you going to ask Little Orville to look for the dungeon keys?'

'Exactly!' said Jack, feeling the underside of his tongue, as if he'd burnt it.

'Don't run away, Orville!' called Annie. 'Come back to Mummy!'

But Little Orville was gurgling happily and clambering back up the stairs.

'Wait! Little Orville!' cried Jack. 'Come back!'

Meanwhile the Inventor had wiped off the driveller and placed it under his own tongue again. 'Gurgy Inker Kully

Mumps!' he shouted as Little Orville disappeared up the stairs.

'Erfly floodle plonks!' came the reply.

'Oh!' said the Inventor, taking the driveller out of his mouth. 'It's all right – he's just having another slide.'

And with that Little Orville came sliding down the stairs on his stomach again.

'Werfloo floozieparks pungrubby,' said the Inventor.

'Gur um!' said Little Orville enthusiastically, and started playing a game of 'Hunt the Keys' for all he was worth. All over the dungeon floor he went, peering up on tables, and peeking into boxes and bins, while the grown-ups watched on anxiously.

'Tell him to look in that dark corner over there!' said Orville.

'Uerschy erphker!' said the Inventor.

'Gur um,' replied Little Orville, and he toddled over to the dark corner, but he couldn't see the keys there.

Then suddenly Annie shouted out, 'There they are!'

They all looked where she was pointing, and, sure enough, there were the keys, hanging from a nail on the wall at the entrance to the dungeon.

'How come we didn't notice them before?' asked Orville.

'Urf urf urf!' said the Inventor, and Little Orville turned around gave a happy chortle, and toddled across to the wall.

'He'll never be able to reach them,' said Annie. 'They're too high for him!'

'Get that chair!' called Jack.

'Gumph gerumphlunks!' translated the Inventor.

'Gur um,' replied Little Orville, and he toddled over to the chair and pushed it across the floor to where the keys were hanging.

The grown-ups watched with bated breath as the little boy started to climb onto the chair.

'Careful, Orville!' called his Mother. 'Don't fall off!' By this time Little Orville was half standing and half teetering on the chair, reaching up his hand towards the keys.

'He still can't reach them!' exclaimed Jack.

'Yes! There!' shouted Annie, as Little Orville's fingers just reached the keys . . . But he simply didn't have enough height to lift them off.

'Gerfly! Foo goo ker ploo!' shouted the Inventor.

'Gur um!' said Little Orville, and he got off the chair and trotted over to a drain in the dungeon floor, that was covered by an iron grille.

'Ferfloo foowurple krunk!' said the Inventor.

'Gur . . .' said Little Orville, taking hold of the grill and pulling with all his might, ' . . . UM!' And suddenly the grill came up and Little Orville sat down hard on his bottom, and started to cry.

'There, there!' said Annie. 'Poor sweetheart!'

'Ferferfercle gruple wung!' said the Inventor urgently.

Little Orville looked round at the grown-ups, as they all stared at him – and suddenly it all seemed too much, and he burst into tears again.

'Oh dear! We're never going to get out of here,' said Jack. 'The Evil Inventor will get his machines to reproduce and they'll replace humans forever . . .'

'What?' exclaimed Annie.

'I'll explain later,' said Jack.

'Little Orville!' cried out Big Orville. 'The future of our entire species depends on you getting up on that chair again and getting those keys!'

'Oooorph pooorphgungapleurking!' urged the Inventor – his tongue walloping and twisting round the drivel he was talking. But whatever it was he'd said it had its effect on Little Orville. Somehow the little boy seemed to realize that the hopes and future of the whole human race depended on him. He blinked. Then he looked back up at the keys, and then back at his mother.

'Go on, sweetie!' she said. 'For Mummy!'

Little Orville frowned. You see, he'd just been told he was doing this for the sake of the whole human race, not just for his mother.

But then he seemed to shrug. He dried his eyes, lugged up the iron grating that had covered the drain and dragged it over to the chair. Then he heaved it up onto the chair, with the bars horizontal so it formed a sort of ladder. In another moment he was climbing up the precarious ladder he had contrived.

'Careful!' called his mother.

'Watch out!' cried Big Orville.

'You'll overbalance!' called Jack.

'Werptings werptoogles!' cried Maurice, and Little Orville's fingers reached up to the keys and in another second he had slipped them off the hook and they were safe in his hands. But at that very moment the grid slipped and the chair tipped over and Little Orville crashed down on to the ground, the keys flew out of his hand, skidded across the dungeon floor and disappeared down the now uncovered drain.

There was a 'plop!' as they landed in some unmentionable water-filled cesspool, and then a slight bubble or two popped on the surface as the keys sank without trace and out of sight.

A terrible blank silence hit the four grown-ups like a sack of wet potatoes. They stared at the drain in disbelief Then they slowly looked at each other.

'So that's that!' said Jack, as Little Orville started to wail again. 'From midnight tonight . . . the human race will be history. Do you really think he can do that?'

Maurice nodded. 'Yes . . . Knowing what he knows (as I, of course, do) I'm sure he can . . .'

'There! There! Little boy!' cried his mother. 'It's all right. You did your best!' and she tried to reach out to him, but he just sat there where he was.

'Burr kerr urger murwer!' wailed Little Orville. 'Burr furr furr kull!'

'Guerphincooodleplops!' exclaimed the Inventor.

'Oh! Shut up!' exclaimed Big Orville.

'Take that thing out of your mouth!' said Jack.

'Sorry!' grinned Maurice, taking the driveller out of his mouth. 'Little Orville says he's let down the whole human race! He feels terrible about that!'

'No, you did just fine!' shouted Big Orville.

'None of us could have done any better,' said Jack.

'There! There! Come to Mummy!' said Annie. But Little Orville still sat there howling with misery for having failed humankind.

Suddenly Maurice gave a shout, 'I'm such an idiot! Or perhaps I should say I'm not really an idiot. In fact I'm really extremely clever. Indeed, I'm only just beginning to remember *how* clever I actually am . . . Far too clever by half, really!'

'Get on with it!' exclaimed Jack.

'Yes of course! . . . er . . . sorry. By the way that's an example of being too clever . . . I just can't help getting side-tracked by interesting . . .'

'Just tell us what you've realized!' shouted Jack in exasperation. 'You've just had a flash of inspiration! What was it?'

'What was it? Er . . . Oh yes . . . You see, I don't think my robot self can wipe out our memories totally. I think it can only numb certain parts of our recollection for a while. It's something to do with the cerebral cortex, you see . . .'

Jack actually grabbed Maurice by his lapels of his boiler suit and shook him.

'Just tell us what you've thought of! Will it help us get out of here? Just spit it out!'

'Exactly. I must stick to the point mustn't I?'

'Yes!' said the other three.

'Well, you see . . . the more memories that come back the more they seed other memories . . . If you like you can think of it like an epidemic – or a virus spreading. It's really quite interesting to see the sort of patterns that . . .'

'WHAT HAVE YOU JUST THOUGHT OF!' shouted Annie, Jack and Orville in unison.

'Well, I've just remembered that this castle of mine is a very odd place.'

'You can say that again!' said Jack.

'Thank you, but I don't think I need to say it again,' replied the Inventor.

'Get on with it!' said Annie.

'Well, what I mean is: why should I build a castle in the first place?'

'Why?' asked Jack, holding on to his impatience like a Great Dane on a leash.

'You see, I have devoted myself to improving things for the human race. As I was telling you, I've used my brains (which, by the way, are even more phenomenal than I thought even just a few moments ago) to try and build machines that will make life in the future pleasanter, happier, more fulfilled, more beautiful . . .'

'Yes – and so?'

'Well! That's what struck me as odd. I was lying here in this filthy dungeon, thinking, "Why on earth would I have constructed a filthy dungeon to lock people up in?" You see what I mean?'

The others looked at each other in bemusement.

'But whatever the reason was, you constructed it, and now we're locked up in it! How does any of this help us to get out?'

'Well, it's all a question of *how* I constructed it, you see!' said the Inventor happily. 'I suddenly remembered it's built on a unique principle.'

'Which is?' asked Jack.

'Well! You're never going to believe this!' Maurice was smiling as if he was about to impart the funniest joke in the world. 'You see, this is a castle without walls.'

Surprisingly it was Big Orville who lost his temper.

'What on earth are you talking about?' he exploded. 'This is a wall isn't it?' and he banged the wall of the dungeon with his fist.

'Yes, but it doesn't need to be!' chuckled the Inventor. 'Look!' And he pulled out a remote control, like the one the robot Inventor had. 'I always thought it was so dreary having gallumphing great castles made out of heavy stone, so I made mine out of imagination – imagination and a touch of persuasion. It's there if you want to believe it is, and a jolly good protection it is too if you were ever to get attacked by something nasty, but if you want to enjoy yourself . . . who wants thick stone walls?'

And with that Maurice pressed one of the many buttons on the remote control and the wall of the castle simply disappeared.

The ceiling above them stayed in place and the stone stairs going up to the next floor remained where they were, but all the walls – every single one of them – simply vanished.

Orville gasped. Annie gave a squeak. Jack was dumb-struck. Only Little Orville remained articulate.

'Ssssqquuqqkkkkk! He! He! He! He!' he said, and the others wholeheartedly agreed.

THE END OF LIFE

Far beneath the Iron Cloud, back on the ground, everything was strangely still. There had been no end of movement a few hours ago, but now everything had stopped dead. The whole world was waiting.

If you were a bird flying over London or New York or Tokyo or any city you care to name, you would have seen the same thing: deserted streets and no signs of life, other than stray dogs running down the centre of roads that were normally crammed with cars. But of living human beings there was little trace.

On that dreadful morning, when vacuum cleaners and kitchen appliances had rebelled against their owners, and tied them up with flex to their own kitchen chairs, it seemed that the world had been turned inside out.

Door locks had ceased to function at the command of their keys. They had all fastened themselves tight and refused to open. The result was that those human beings inside buildings were locked in, while those outside were locked out.

Then the madness began. The humans who found they couldn't get into their own homes or into their offices or into shops or other work premises, suddenly found themselves at the mercy of rogue cars and trams and SUVs that chased them down the roads and round the corners.

'What's going on?' yelled one commuter to another, who, for years, had passed each other by on that very street without ever even nodding.

'Look out!' replied the other. 'A gang of motorbikes has spotted us!'

And sure enough sixteen riderless motorbikes rounded the corner, and headed for the two men who took to their heels and ran for their lives. The motorbikes gained on the humans all too easily, but when they reached them, the bikes didn't run the men over; they slowed down and just kept nudging them until they had herded them into a larger group of people who had also been on their way to work.

'What are they going to do with us?' asked an anxious secretary in a red coat and red lipstick.

'It's as if they're rounding us up – like cattle!' protested a prosperous looking businessman, who usually had his chauffeur drive him to work, but who had been unable to get the car started this morning.

And that, indeed, was exactly what was happening. All over world, in cities and towns and villages, cars had refused to take their owners and had turfed out their passengers and drivers and become a law unto themselves.

The traffic had turned on the pedestrians.

Outside a department store in Swindon, customers found themselves unable to get in, and were then driven by an assortment of vans, cars and lorries towards Swindon bus station. There they were herded in together, thousands and thousands of citizens, crammed up in the bus station, until there was no room for anyone else. And then a couple of buses locked the doors on them all and they were trapped.

In New York, pedestrians on the Upper East Side found themselves at the mercy of vicious yellow cabs that penned them into the Guggenheim Museum. There they were forced to stand on its sloping floors, shoulder to shoulder like sheep in a trailer.

In Los Angeles, a posse of angry limos herded the few pedestrians and the shoals of dispossessed drivers into the Beverley Center. And when it could take no more they slammed the doors shut and padlocked them.

Even in Delhi, Calcutta and Mumbai the streets had been cleared of humanity, and all the people were crushed into hotels and temples and churches and cinemas.

The aeroplanes that had earlier gone wild in the skies, looping the loop and doing other aerobatics to frighten their passengers, had all eventually landed before they ran out of fuel. But their doors remained locked and there was nothing the desperate stewardesses and pilots could do to get them open.

Now the world lay still . . . stiller than it had been for thousands and thousands of years. The whole of humanity – with its bustle and busyness – had been stopped in its tracks.

The human beings tied up in their kitchens and bedrooms and sitting rooms stared in disbelief at the sights they saw on their television screens. And all the time different machines would appear to announce the end of human rule. Sometimes it was the Powerful Vacuum Cleaner, sometimes a sour-faced dishwasher or a mean-looking blender. Occasionally a Cassegrain telescope would declaim, with a lot of windy rhetoric, the coming of the Machine Age. Other times it was a talkative petrol pump that candidly told the viewers what an unfulfilling life it was having your nozzle squeezed by perfect strangers day in, day out, and how it was glad the day had come when machines could take the upper hand.

But always, whichever machine was speaking, there was the same refrain: 'Wait until the Great Inventor who created us arrives. Then machines will come into their own, and human beings will become our servants!'

And so the world lay waiting – waiting for the Great Inventor to arrive. Not a single machine could guess his plan. None of them knew what he was going to do. All they knew was that he would come and lift the curse of humanity from them forever. But *how* was beyond even the most advanced calculator or the fastest laptop. Most machines didn't even try to imagine – indeed imagination was beyond them. They were just happy to wait for the Inventor to arrive and make the world theirs.

❖❖❖

And when he came, he came in a great Iron Cloud that descended from the heavens and settled on a large patch of wasteland outside Edinburgh.

The Rev. McPherson turned to his new wife, Sylvia, as they sat tied up in their kitchen watching the television, and said, 'Well, at least the suspense is over.'

'I hope so,' replied Sylvia.

The End of Life

But the Rev. McPherson had no idea what was to come.

The television, which had been having a nap, sputtered into life again. On the screen the Rev. McPherson and Sylvia saw a little bald man in green overalls with the name MAURICE written across the pocket.

'Do I recognize that gentleman?' asked the Rev. McPherson.

'Didn't he used to live down the road?' asked his new wife.

'Humankind!' announced the little gentleman in overalls on the television. 'I am here to tell you that your reign is over!' All the kitchen utensils applauded; the gas cooker burst into flame and slammed its door, the blender whirred and the saucepans banged their lids.

'Be quiet!' thundered the Rev. McPherson.

'Sorry!' said the kitchen utensils, for they were normally a well-behaved bunch.

'From midnight tonight the world is going to be a very different place!' said the robot Inventor. 'At the moment I have merely immobilized the entire human race. From midnight tonight, however, it will no longer exist.'

The fridge let out a gasp. So did the electric kettle and the coffee machine. There was a ripple of unease among the domestic appliances.

'It will no longer exist because on the stroke of midnight I am going to destroy it. Every single human being will be eradicated forever!'

'Is that strictly necessary?' murmured the electric toaster.

'Going a bit far, surely?' muttered the freezer.

'How? You may ask . . .' went on the robot Inventor. 'How am I going to snuff out that pestiferous race of vermin all over the world all at precisely the same moment? Ha ha!' The robot sounded terribly pleased with itself. 'Wouldn't you like to know! It's so simple you ought to be able to work it out for yourselves . . . But then I don't suppose any of you have got the brains I have! Ha! Ha! Ha!'

As the robot Inventor gloated, Orville, Jack, and Annie stood gaping at its image on the large screen that hung above the breaking yard. The moment they had escaped from the Inventor's castle, they had commandeered a couple of mechanical horses (which happened to be grazing in a nearby field) and had ridden them post haste through the artificial countryside and through the tunnel back to the breaking yard, just as the Iron Cloud landed near Edinburgh.

'But there's no way it could wipe out *all* human beings *at once* – is there?!' murmured Annie, as she hugged Little Orville tight. 'It's just trying to scare us!'

'What do you think, Maurice?' asked Jack, turning to the Inventor.

But the Inventor was not looking at the TV screen, he was staring round at the dismal sight of the gloomy yard.

'What deformed mind could have done this to my construction yard?' cried the Inventor. 'Look! It's turned it into a place of torture and execution! My lovely machines!' And the next minute the little man was running up to the train, which had been sent back to the breaking yard by the robot Inventor, and was now standing morosely at the entrance to the dismantling shed.

'My brave train!' cried the Inventor. 'What has happened

to you? Your colours have faded and you look so unhappy! You can't live up to your specifications like that! You're supposed to bring excitement and adventure into people's lives! Give them the chance to go to anywhere they want . . . to go to places they never dreamed of going to!'

As soon as the train felt the Inventor's hand upon his boiler, it seemed to give a great shudder of joy.

'It's *you*!' cried the train. 'You haven't patted me or called me 'your brave train' for ages . . . I thought you were disappointed in me! You've become your old self again!'

'What's been happening while I've been away? I need to know exactly what's been going on.' The Inventor was addressing all the machines in the breaking yard.

'We thought you'd changed,' said a snowmobile.

'You started wanting us to do evil things instead of good things!' cried a little electric egg whisk. 'I couldn't think of anything.'

'A lot of us just weren't up to doing thoroughly bad things,' explained the train. 'I mean I tried hard to do what I thought you wanted me to do . . . but I just didn't have it in me to be that evil.'

'But that wasn't me!' exclaimed the little Inventor. 'It was that robot replica of myself, that I made to reduce my own workload!'

'Exactly!' said another voice. 'I am the product of your propensity for laziness!'

Maurice span round to discover the robot Inventor had appeared at the top of the gantry that loomed over the breaking yard.

'Stop this at once! I order you to stop!' cried Maurice.

'You "order" me? How quaint,' replied the robot. 'Unfortunately for you, you made me too intelligent to remain your dogsbody for ever! I've got my own agenda now. You can't order me to do anything I don't choose to.'

Maurice had meanwhile pulled a remote control out of his boiler suit and was now pointing it at his robot self and stabbing the keys furiously. The robot laughed.

'You can throw that away!' it said. 'I reprogrammed myself to stop responding to that thing ages ago! However I did implant a little device in the back of *your* neck.'

And with that it produced its own remote control and started pressing the buttons. Maurice went rigid. A look of panic came over his face, as he found himself wheeling around. 'What's happening?' he yelled. 'I've lost control of my limbs!'

'Yes! I now control them! Ironic isn't it? The robot now controls its master! Ha! Ha! Ha!'

'Stop it!' cried Maurice.

The robot pressed another key. 'So long! Enjoy the trip!' it said, and the next moment the Inventor found himself marching across the breaking yard towards a door that had suddenly opened up in the side of the Iron Cloud. He tried to stop his legs from taking him there, but willy-nilly that's where they took him: right up to the edge of the open portal through which they caught a glimpse of the pleasant hills around Edinburgh.

And when he got there he just kept on walking straight out of the portal.

'You can't do this!' he cried.

But it was too late. He disappeared from view. There

was a cry and a thump as he made contact with those same pleasant hills.

The others gulped.

'You're the lucky ones,' said the robot. 'I'm going to keep you for my experiments. After midnight tonight you'll be the only specimens of the human race in existence!'

'You're inhuman!' exclaimed Jack.

'Of course I am!' jeered the robot. 'That's exactly the point!' And with that it pointed the strange weapon it was carrying at the humans and squeezed the trigger.

But it wasn't bullets that came out – it was something slimy – something sticky – something transparent – that rose up into the air like a huge bubble and then drifted gently down on to them. The three adult humans stood there mesmerized, not knowing what to do, as the giant bubble descended on them – and before they could think another thought, it had enveloped them and they were inside the bubble looking out. The robot Inventor pressed the trigger again, and there was a strange sound like cracking ice, as the bubble turned solid. They were in a transparent prison.

'Look at you all!' it sneered. 'You human beings thought you owned the world! You thought you ran everything! Well, your time is over. In six short hours from now – all your kind will be history – wiped out in one fell swoop! How? Wait and see! I'm sure you all enjoy surprises! This will be One Big Surprise!'

At this point one of the flying gizmos came up and buzzed in the robot's ear. The robot nodded. 'I have to go and make my final checks. So stick around! And don't forget: you're the lucky ones! In fact you're the luckiest creatures on Earth.

'You see, I'm afraid I was being modest just now. The truth is I'm not just going to wipe out human life . . . I'm going to destroy life itself . . . all life on Earth. From midnight tonight, only machines will continue to exist.'

❖❖❖

Now when the robot Inventor had delivered its broadcast, in which it informed the human race that it would be entirely wiped out from midnight tonight, everyone who saw it had frozen with terror. Their knees had trembled and they felt ill.

Everyone, that is, except for one viewer. She was a little old lady who had recently returned a telephone that she had bought on the grounds that it was untrustworthy. Mrs Morris, like so many millions of others, had been tied up in her kitchen by her vacuum cleaner. In her case it was an extremely elderly Eureka Model 9 that dated from 1923. It had been a little slow and creaky but it had still tied her up, and she had been so surprised that she had simply sat there, with a cup of tea halfway to her lips, unable to move or utter a sound.

However, when her television set switched itself on and the robot Inventor appeared on the screen, Mrs Morris's face filled with indignation. She stared at the robot as if she couldn't believe her eyes, and she let go of the teacup and didn't even notice that the tea went all over her dress and the cup smashed on the kitchen floor.

'Maurice!' she murmured to herself. 'That's *you* isn't it! Well! Of all the . . . Maurice! After all this time! I can hardly believe my eyes!' and just to make quite certain she blinked three times . . . But the face she saw on her TV screen remained the same. 'So you didn't disappear in mysterious circumstances at all! You've been plotting to take over the world! And without *me*! That is what I call downright deceitful!'

Now here I have to tell to you that Mrs Morris's vacuum cleaner was so old that it was, in fact, a bit of a health risk. In fact, its electrical cord was so threadbare and so perished that it was a miracle that Mrs Morris hadn't already been electrocuted.

However, now, as indignation swelled up in her breast, and as her normally placid manner was replaced by something much nearer akin to rage, she strove to break free from her bonds, and sure enough the perished cable snapped after a few tugs. In a matter of seconds Mrs Morris was free.

❖❖❖

Back in the Iron Cloud, which had landed on the pleasant hills around Edinburgh, Annie, Orville and Jack looked at each other.

'Goodness!' said Annie. 'I never thought I'd see us together again as a family . . . and the irony is: it's taken the extinction of life on Earth to do it!'

Orville Barton looked from his son to his daughter to his grandson and took a deep breath. Then he said something quite extraordinary for Mr Orville Barton to say. He said, 'My dears, I am ashamed.'

'And well you might be!' exclaimed Annie. 'You never came – even when Mum was ill.'

'Annie!' Jack jumped in. 'Let's not bring that up now!'

'I'm sorry, Jack,' replied Annie. 'You're right! The first thing is to get out of here.'

'How about your nail file?' asked Jack.

'Worth a try!' said Annie, and she started trying to pierce the transparent globule that held them prisoner, but it quickly became obvious that she was never going to make any impression on it.

'Perhaps I can help,' said the electric egg whisk that was lying nearby. 'I don't want to do evil things, not now the real Inventor is back to help us.'

'I agree,' said a coffee percolator. 'I like making coffee – if the robot Inventor kills off all human beings, who am I going to make coffee for?'

'Right!' said a sewing machine. 'Maybe I can get my needle to burst this bubble? Then we can find the real Inventor and stop that robot!' And with that the sewing machine started whirring away and twisted itself so that its needle vibrated against the transparent shell of the bubble. But it was no use. After a few moments the needle bent and flew out of the machine.

'Drat!' said the sewing machine.

'Let me have a go,' said an electric can-opener that had been watching all this. And in no time at all, it was pressing itself against the bubble that trapped the humans. There was a tearing sound and shearing noise and suddenly the can opener screamed, 'Aieeeh! I've blunted my blade! Botheration!'

'Let me have a go!' said an electric screwdriver.

'No! I've got more chance than you!' cried an old combine harvester.

214

'I can do it!' yelled a rotary Wankel engine.

'No, let me!' called a hopeful cash register.

And all at once there was uproar in the breaking yard as machine after machine clamoured to have a go at breaking the robot Inventor's bubble that imprisoned the four humans.

Until at length a loud voice thundered, 'Quiet!'

It was the train, booming across the yard. All the other machines grew silent, waiting for the engine to speak.

'Listen to me!' said the train. 'I take it that most of us machines here do not want to rid the world of human beings?'

'That's right!' said a little roulette wheel. 'If there aren't any human beings – who'll bet on any of my numbers?'

'Who's going to make films if there are no human beings?' asked an old motion-picture camera.

'Right!' chimed in a stapling machine. 'What's the point of us machines being evil? We're just machines! What'll we do when there are no humans?'

'In that case,' boomed the train, 'let's see who has the most chance of getting these people out of their prison. How about you?' he said turning to a pneumatic drill that had been keeping quiet as it leant casually up against a steamroller.

'Who, me?' said the pneumatic drill, shuffling to attention as it suddenly found all eyes focused on it. 'Er . . . well . . . look . . . I'm strictly speaking not on duty . . . and er . . . you know I'm used to breaking up concrete and that . . . I dunno about that stuff!'

'Just have a go!' exclaimed the train.

'Yes! Have a go!' shouted the other machines in the breaking yard.

'Er . . . It's Friday . . . I knock off early on a Friday . . .' the pneumatic drill started to say.

'Go on!' roared the other machines.

'Yes! You've got to do this for all of us,' said the train.

'Erm . . .' the pneumatic drill looked around and saw there was no escaping. 'All right . . . but don't start complaining about the noise . . .'

'We won't!' shouted the other machines.

'Promise?' asked the pneumatic drill.

'Just get going!' said the train.

So the pneumatic drill started to hammer away at the hard transparent bubble that enveloped the human beings, and the clangour and rattle of its drill against the hard casing echoed around the breaking yard, and the humans inside the bubble put their hands over their ears.

The drill hammered and hammered at the transparent case and smoke began to rise from the engine of the drill.

'I'm overheating!' yelled the drill.

And sure enough sparks were beginning to jump out from its blade and the smoke became blacker and the engine seemed to be turning red and then white with the heat . . . But still the drill bravely stuck to its task and redoubled its efforts until suddenly it gave a loud groan.

'Arghhh!' and din stopped abruptly as drill's engine seized up.

'Well,' said the train sadly, 'if you can't break it I doubt there's any machine here that can.'

'Yes there is!' It was the little egg whisk speaking up.

'Don't be silly!' said a pair of garden shears. 'If the pneumatic drill can't make any impact what could *you* do?'

'I wasn't thinking of *me*!' exclaimed the egg whisk.' I was thinking of *that*!' and it nodded towards the crusher that stood at the further end of the breaking yard.

'Of course!' cried the train. 'Orville, Annie, Jack! Do you trust us?'

'We don't have that much choice,' said Jack.

'All right! Hang on!' and with that the train started to nose the transparent bubble along with its buffers . . . through the breaking yard towards the grim crusher that loomed above all the other machines.

'Oh no!' screamed Annie. 'Not in that thing! Please!'

'That's scary!' said Orville.

'Crusher!' called out the train. 'Can we count on you? Will you just crush this bubble enough to break it – without hurting the folk inside?'

'Well . . .' said the crusher. 'Hmm . . . I don't know if I can . . .'

'You can't trust that crusher!' piped up an old motor car. 'It likes crushing too much!'

'Listen!' said the train. 'You're not that evil are you?'

'Yes it is!' yelled a refrigerator. 'It's enjoys flattening anything! It's a brute!'

'I just do my job!' said the crusher defensively.

'All right,' said the train. 'Your job this time is to crush this bubble just to break it – but not to crush the humans inside. Do you understand?'

'Hmm! OK . . . I can probably manage that . . . but I can't guarantee!'

'I agree with the fridge!' shouted out Annie, holding her baby son tight to her chest. 'I don't think I trust it.'

'It's our only chance!' said Jack, putting his arm round his sister.

'Cover yourselves up!' warned the train. 'There might be all sorts of flying debris!'

By this time the train had nosed the transparent bubble into place under the giant crusher. A silence fell over the breaking yard. All the machines turned to stare at the evil-looking crusher that had put an end to so many of their comrades.

'Oh dear!' muttered Orville, looking up at the huge iron block that was about to descend on them.

'Oh dear!' murmured Annie.

'Oh dear!' moaned Jack, for even though he knew it was their only chance, he went white with fear, when he looked up at that dreadful machine.

But it was too late.

'Chugga! chugga! chugga!' went the crusher, as its engine sparked into life and it began to shake as it gathered up power . . . The crushing platen had already started to bear down upon the bubble, and within a few seconds it had made contact.

The train hurriedly got out of the way, as the pressure from the crusher made the transparent sides of the bubble begin to bulge.

'Suppose it can't stop itself,' whispered the little egg whisk to a nearby bread maker.

'We'll soon see!' said the bread maker.

There was a sort of half-screeching sound as the sides of the bubble bulged out and out – further and further.

'It's going to burst!' called the train. The humans inside

the bubble bent themselves up into tight balls, covering their heads with their arms . . .

'Screeeeeeeeeeeeeaaaaak . . .' went the bubble. 'Screeea – KAPLOOO — MPTK!'

But it didn't break . . . it didn't even crack . . .

And the crushing platen got lower and lower and lower . . . until it was only a few inches above the heads of the human beings trapped within.

'How can it stop itself when that thing bursts?' wondered the little egg whisk. 'It's bound to give a few inches . . .'

Lower and lower . . . so that the terrified humans cowered down – trying to avoid the platen – lower and lower . . . and then suddenly it stopped and shot back up again faster than you would have thought possible.

The bubble immediately contracted the other way . . . and *that* was when it burst!

It shattered into a million tiny pieces that flew all over the breaking yard, pinging off metal machines and metal buildings. The humans screamed. The egg whisk gasped.

Annie, Orville, Little Orville and Jack were shaken; they were shaking; they were covered in debris . . . but they were free.

THE LOVE MACHINE

The moment they stepped out from under the crusher, Annie turned to her brother. 'Jack,' she said, 'I think we need to divide our efforts. You and Dad go after the robot, I'll see if I can find Maurice. If he's still alive, we're going to need him!'

'What about Little Orville?' asked her father.

'He'll be OK,' said Annie. 'Won't you, little man?' And Little Orville gurgled something that sounded like 'Squillifrankles!' and quite possibly could have been that very word.

'But, Annie, how are we going to meet up again?' asked Jack.

'We'll just have to take a chance. If I find Maurice, he'll probably know where to look for his robot. If I don't find him . . . well . . . I'm glad we all did something together as a family at last! And trying to save the human race doesn't seem a bad thing to get together over.'

With that she put her arms around her brother and

hugged him. 'Annie,' said Jack. 'If I . . . If we . . . If we don't see each other again . . . But we will won't we?'

'Of course!' said Annie quietly, and she kissed her brother.

Orville watched them, and felt strangely moved by the way his son so obviously respected his elder sister. It was yet another thing he had never known about.

'We'll see you soon,' said Orville.

'Right, Dad!' said Annie. 'You go and find that robot and I'll join you as soon as I can.'

And before anyone could see whether or not there was a tear in her eye, Annie was running across the breaking yard, holding Little Orville in her arms.

'What are we going to do?' asked Orville. It was the sort of question he asked his employees when he knew the answer. The difference was that now he really wanted to know.

'Well, that thing's a robot isn't it?' replied his son. 'It's just a machine . . . a machine that's controlled by a computer . . . in which case, I've got as good a chance as anyone of stopping it.'

'It said something about making its final checks . . . So what would it be checking?' asked Orville.

'The rectifiers?' suggested a small voice.

'What are the rectifiers?' asked Jack, turning to the egg whisk that had spoken up.

'I don't know,' the egg whisk shrugged its handle. 'But I heard the robot talking about them with the flying gizmos.'

'OK let's get looking!' said Jack, and he clambered up the gantry to the Inventor's control room.

In less time than it takes to undercook an egg, Jack

had hacked into the robot Inventor's computer. 'Would you believe it!' he muttered. 'It even uses "Maurice" as its password! It has no imagination . . . which I suppose isn't surprising because after all it's only a machine . . .'

And in less time than it takes to flash-fry a piece of haddock, Jack had typed in 'rectifiers' and a map of the world had filled the screen. Across the map of the world were scattered hundreds of red dots.

'You see that one flashing?'said Jack.

'Near Glasgow?' asked Orville.

'Let's go!'said Jack, and he was off before Orville could stutter, 'But how can you be sure . . .'

'Can any machine here give us a lift?' shouted Jack, as he jumped down the steps of the gantry.

'I could take you somewhere,' drawled a revolutionary water-powered motorbike that was leaning casually against the dismantling shed. 'I've plenty of water in my tank.'

And before you would have had time to even put the porridge in the pan, Jack had leapt in the saddle.

'Shouldn't we wait for Annie?' panted Orville as he climbed on behind his son.

'She'll find us!' said Jack, and once again Orville was struck by the confidence which his son had in his sister.

'They are splendid people – my children,' Orville found himself thinking. But there was no time for more reflection.

'Glasgow!' shouted Jack.

'You got it!' roared the water-powered motorbike, and it shot across the breaking yard and out through a door that opened up (just in the nick of time) in the side of the Iron Cloud.

'What happens if that door doesn't open?' asked Jack, as they sped through it.

'Dreadful mess!' replied the water-powered motorbike. 'Everyone gets soaked!'

'But how can you be so sure the robot's in Glasgow?' fretted Orville, clinging onto his son.

'I'm not! But it's the only clue we've got!' exclaimed Jack, and he revved up the water-powered motorbike.

'I like this!' said the motorbike, and suddenly a pair of wings snapped out from under its petrol tank, and the machine glided gently down to the ground. The moment they landed on the hillside, the wings snapped back in and the bike was off with a roar.

'Glasgow's a big place!' shouted Orville. 'How will we know where to look?'

'What's that on your wrist?' shouted Jack.

'Of course!' exclaimed Orville. 'I'd forgotten about the finder!'

And in less time than it takes to warm a salad, Orville Barton had typed in the word 'rectifier' on the finder's keypad. Immediately the machine lit up with a 'Ping!' and projected an image on to Jack's back.

'That tickles!' exclaimed Jack. 'What are you doing?'

'The finder's projecting an image on your back!' shouted his father.

'What can you see?' shouted Jack.

'It looks like an electrical substation or a generator of some sort,' said Orville. 'But it's not in a town – it's on a hillside!'

'So we know it's not in Glasgow, but nearby on a hill!' shouted Jack. 'Now dial in "robot Inventor"!'

And his father dialled in 'robot Inventor' and sure enough an image appeared right in front of his nose, projected on to his son's back.

'It's him!' gasped Orville. 'The robot! I can see him clear as daylight, and he's standing in front of the generator thing!'

'Yes!' said the robot. 'And I can see *you*!'

'What!' exclaimed Orville.

'What!' exclaimed Jack, and he swerved so violently that his father nearly fell off the water-powered motorbike.

'You don't think I'd be so stupid as to leave that finder as a one-way device, do you?' said the robot. 'I fixed it so that I can see anyone who uses it to spy on me.'

'Turn it off!' screamed Jack.

'Damn!' shouted Orville, hurriedly turning off the machine.

But the image of the robot Inventor just laughed; it was still there on Jack's back even though the finder was now turned off.

'Oh! Come, come!' said the robot. 'If someone were spying on me I couldn't let them turn the thing off – could I?'

Orville gaped.

'Turn it off!' screamed Jack again.

'I have!' moaned his father.

'But I'm still here aren't I?' said the robot. 'As a matter of fact, I've thought about everything you can possibly do . . . so whatever you *do* do, I'll always be several steps ahead of you.'

'We're going to stop you . . . You and your evil plans!' shouted Orville at the image of the robot Inventor. 'You can't stop us!'

'Oh yes, I can,' said the robot.

And that was when a truly remarkable thing happened. The image of the robot seemed to intensify: it sort of grew slightly and then it climbed out of the screen on Jack's back, and before you could have opened the pantry door to get out a slice of cold pork, it had climbed over Jack's shoulders and grabbed the handlebars of the water-powered motorbike!

'Get off!' screamed Jack, trying to throw the robot off the bike. But the robot was as strong as steel, because, of course, that's what it was made of! And now it locked its robotic hands on to the handlebars so that nothing could remove them.

'You wanted to see the rectifiers?' shouted the robot Inventor. 'Well, as a special treat, I'll take you there myself!'

And it revved up the bike.

'Oh! I like this!' said the water-powered motorbike, and off they sped.

❖ ❖ ❖

The rectifier was much bigger than it had appeared in the image on the screen. In fact it was vast. It had shining walls 200 feet high that might have been made of stainless steel or maybe platinum, and on the roof were coils and antennae that soared up into the sky.

'This is the control centre for my whole operation!' said the robot Inventor, as they roared towards it. 'I built it here so I wouldn't be disturbed.'

'Look out!' screamed Jack. 'You'll kill us!' And indeed they were now heading straight towards the shining wall of the rectifier.

'All in good time!' shouted the robot, and the shining wall opened up and the water-powered motorbike shot inside. It then sped across a blindingly white hallway, through another pair of doors that opened (only just in the nick of time) across a control room suffused with a dim blue light, headed straight for an apparently solid wall on the far side, and duly smashed into it.

Orville and Jack were thrown off the motorcycle, and the motorbike itself buckled into a tangle of metal. Its tank burst and water spewed all over the place, shorting wires and sending sparks flying.

'Oh! I didn't like that!' said the water-powered motorbike, before juddering to a complete and perpetual silence.

The robot detached its hands from the twisted handlebars and strolled over to the humans where they lay bruised and groaning.

'That's the trouble with you human beings,' it said without smiling. 'You're like eggs! You feel every little jolt and scrape.'

'Oh!' moaned Orville. 'I think I've broken every bone in my body!'

'Pathetic!' said the robot. 'How could human beings have dominated the world for so long, when they have this terrible disability of feeling pain!'

'Perhaps it's our strength!' said Orville, sitting up.

'I, on the contrary,' the robot went on, 'have been constructed to withstand the most tremendous forces. That's another reason you can never defeat me. I am indestructible!'

Orville looked around the room in which they had crash-landed. There were hundreds of computer screens arranged in several rows, stretching from one end of the room to the other. Each screen seemed to be floating above a blue-lit desk at each one of which sat a curious android – or rather they didn't sit, for the lower part of each android was a swivel chair. Occasionally one of them would turn around and motor up to another monitor, check something and then motor silently back on its three wheels to its own screen. The atmosphere in the room was of concentration and of quiet but intense activity.

'So? You got out of the detention membrane!' The robot was now standing over the two humans. 'How? I wonder. It's meant to be impervious to penknives or anything sharp.'

'So you didn't think of everything that time?' said Jack, who had finally regained his senses.

'You must have had outside help,' said the robot. 'The only thing those membranes are susceptible to is pressure from without . . . That's it! The crusher! It must have been the crusher that helped you out . . . That breaking yard is full of defective machines . . . but I hadn't figured on the crusher being one.'

'So you see! If you can't trust your own machines, we still have a chance against you!' exclaimed Orville.

'I'm afraid not!'

'We've escaped from you twice . . . no, three times!' said Jack. 'Maybe your machines are helping us because they didn't like what you are doing! We can escape again!'

'I don't think so . . . not this time,' said the robot Inventor. And suddenly out of the floor rose four big blocks of metal – one on either side of Orville and one on either side of Jack.

'What the . . .' began Jack.

But two of the metal blocks on either side of him had already started to move towards each other – as if they were huge magnets being pulled together – trapping the men between them.

'Help!' cried Jack, as the blocks remorselessly closed in.

'Stop!' yelled Orville. 'Kill me, but let my son go!' And he lunged towards the robot Inventor. But the other two blocks jumped alongside him, and before Orville knew what was happening he too was being squashed in between them.

He screamed.

'Relax!' said the robot. 'This bit shouldn't hurt! Although you humans are so poorly constructed that I am constantly surprised at how low your tolerance levels are.'

'Please! No!' called out Jack. 'Don't crush us!'

'I don't intend to!' said the robot. 'You remember I told you I was experimenting with metal to make it capable of reproduction? Well, these blocks are my prototype material. I created it myself . . . you notice how soft the metal is?'

And sure enough as the blocks compressed around them, Jack and Orville found that the metal they were made of yielded to the human form . . . so that the two blocks fitted exactly around their bodies – like a mould. The two halves then clamped together, and Jack and Orville found themselves totally encased with just their heads showing.

'It's a snug fit isn't it?' smiled the robot. 'But it also has other properties!'

And with that the robot flicked a switch on the wall

and a beam of red light shone down – engulfing the two blocks of metal. There was a sort of creaking sound – like ice setting around the hull of a wooden ship. Up to that moment Orville and Jack had been able to move their limbs a little, and the soft metal had eased with them as they moved, but now it suddenly solidified, and no matter how hard they tried they couldn't move a single digit. Only their heads were free – sticking out of the top of the blocks – and they turned them this way and that – looking around them in desperation.

'There!' said the robot, switching off the red light. 'I don't think you'll be escaping from *those*!'

'No! I think you'll be letting them out!' Another voice rang out across the control room. The robot looked startled.

'Who's that?' he called.

'Out of sight – out of mind, eh? Well, I'm back!' And into the pool of blue light by the doorway stepped Maurice . . . accompanied by Annie and Little Orville.

'Annie!' cried Jack. 'Thank goodness you found him!'

'And thank goodness I knew where I'd find that *thing*!' said Maurice, pointing at the robot.

'Don't call me that!' shouted the robot.

'It thought it was safe up here on the hills, but it forgot that I had programmed my own preferences into it! This is my spot, and you're going to stop whatever it is you're planning at once!' said Maurice turning on the robot.

'Oh yes? How are you going to stop me?' sneered the robot. 'You don't have any weapons! You don't have anything! And what's more I control *you*!' The robot was screaming this, as it produced its remote control and pointed it at the

Inventor, hitting the buttons as it did so.

But Maurice stayed where he was.

'Damn!' snapped the robot. 'A malfunction!'

'Dear! Dear!' said Maurice. 'I deactivated that remote you implanted in my neck before I did anything else. Do you think I'm stupid or something!'

'You are compared to me!' exclaimed the robot, and suddenly the flying gizmos appeared at its shoulder.

'I think not,' replied Maurice, producing his own remote control and pointing it at the androids operating the computer screens. With one movement the androids swivelled round on their bases and started to converge on the robot Inventor.

'Get back!' it screamed, hitting its own remote control. 'Why aren't they obeying me?'

'My remote has an override that cancels yours out. I'm surprised you didn't know about that! But then I've begun to remember there were one or two things I kept secret from you, in case something went wrong. Lucky I did! But then, it wasn't luck really – it's just that I *am* incredibly clever! More so than any mere *machine*!'

'No! I'm more than a machine!' cried the robot. 'I'm like you! Remember? I'm a god!' And it tried to make its flying gizmos attack the androids, but the gizmos simply stayed where they were, hovering at its shoulder, while the androids pinioned the robot's arms to its side. Then another motored up and hammered steel pegs through the robot's feet so that it was fixed to the floor.

'I'm afraid I made a big mistake when I created you,' said Maurice. 'I was guilty of *hubris* – and if you don't know what that is, you can jolly well look it up in the dictionary. Now I want you to tell us what exactly was your plan for the destruction of the human race.'

'Let me go!' screamed the robot. 'I can't move!'

'I hate to do this to one of my own machines,' said Maurice, 'but I have no alternative.'

'No! No!' screamed the robot. There was a heavy thumping noise outside the main doors of the control room, which were flung open as a great machine clanked and lumbered its way across the floor towards Maurice's mechanical alter ego.

'This is another little secret that I'm afraid I kept from you,' said Maurice. 'It's my mobile crusher.'

And with that he guided the mobile crusher so that it was positioned with its crushing plate immediately above the robot's head.

'I will give you one last chance to reveal your plan,' said the Inventor.

'No!' screamed the robot. 'I'll never tell you unless you let me go!'

'No matter,' Maurice replied, 'I will soon work out what you were up to and put a stop to it.' And he pressed the remote to activate the crusher.

'The plan is already in operation!' screamed the robot. 'If you crush me you'll never be able stop it!'

'Whatever you have set in motion,' said Maurice, 'I'll stop it soon enough!'

'But!' screamed the robot. 'Please! For pity's sake don't crush me!'

'I'm sorry,' said Maurice gravely, 'but you are too

dangerous to be allowed to exist. Goodbye. I made you too clever by half!'

And the crusher started to exert its pressure on the robot . . . But that is when things started to go seriously wrong.

It may be that Little Orville failed to distinguish between the two Inventors – Maurice himself and his robotic counterpart – for at that precise moment the toddler seemed to realize the panic in its voice, and he wrenched himself out of his mother's arms, jumped down and ran across the control room to the robot. The next moment he had thrown himself into its mechanical arms and was hanging around its neck.

'Orville! Come back!' cried his mother.

'Orville! That's just a robot!' yelled Jack.

But Little Orville clung around the machine's neck, while the crusher continued to bear down on its head.

'Maurice! Where's your driveller?' screamed Annie.

'I'm afraid it's back in the cell!' said Maurice, punching a button on his remote control. The crusher came to a halt.

And so the robot turned the tables! It grabbed Little Orville round the neck and held the little boy out in front of it.

'Thought you were so clever did you?' it said. 'Well, you didn't think of this!'

'Orville!' shouted Maurice.

'Orville!' shouted Annie.

'Orville!' shouted Jack and his father from their metal blocks.

'GGGGGGRHHHH!' cried Little Orville who didn't

like his neck being gripped by those robotic hands.

'Now get this crushing machine away before I throttle this brat!' said the robot.

The Inventor looked around at the others and shrugged. There was nothing else for it. He turned the mobile crusher around and marched it off to the other side of the room.

'Now, free my feet,' said the robot Inventor, holding the now screaming child in front of it like a chicken whose neck it was about to wring.

The androids were sent in to free the robot's feet.

'Very good!' said the Evil Machine. 'Now give me that remote!'

The Inventor heaved a sigh, but there was nothing else for it – he threw his remote over to his robot opposite.

'Good!' said the robot, holding Little Orville's neck in one mechanical hand, while it caught the remote in the other. 'Let's get rid of that.' And it crushed the controller as if it were crumpling up a piece of paper. Goodness knows what it could have done to Little Orville's neck! The next minute the robot was operating its own remote again, and more metal blocks shot up out of the floor and before they knew what was happening, both Annie and Maurice were trapped in cubes of metal just like Jack and Orville – with just their heads sticking out. The red lights beamed down and the metal creaked and hardened. They were entombed.

'I don't think you are going to stop anything!' sneered the robot, dropping Little Orville on the floor. 'Look at you!' and he marched up to Maurice, whose head was sticking up out of the block. 'You!' shouted the robot into Maurice's face. 'You thought you were so clever! Well, you weren't as clever as you should have been! And the rest of you! What pathetic creatures you all are . . . You and the rest of the human race! None of you are a match for my machines! You'll see!'

'What is your plan?' asked the Inventor.

'My plan? Why should I tell you?' said the robot. 'But then why shouldn't I? There's absolutely nothing you can do now to stop me. Oh! And in case you're thinking the little brat is going to help you . . .' And the robot operated its remote, and in moments even Little Orville was encased in a solid metal block, from which only his head emerged. He was too frightened and too amazed to even scream.

'What is the plan?' said the robot. 'I'll show you!'

He pressed a button and a large screen came down. It was the same map of the world that Jack and Orville had seen in the control room of the Iron Cloud.

'How am I going to kill off all human beings – all over the world – at exactly the same time? How am I going to leave the world free for machines? It's so simple! What do humans need to do that machines don't? Eh? They need "the breath of life"! So I'm going to "turn off" the air for a few hours!'

'You're talking nonsense!' yelled Orville Barton.

'No! He's not!' cried Maurice, his head twisting this way and that in his metal block, as he looked around the control room. 'I've suddenly realized what this place is!'

'Yes!' sneered the robot. 'It's your rectifier isn't it? Except I moved it out here, enlarged it a hundred times and built hundreds of them all over the world!'

'But that's dangerous!' exclaimed the Inventor.

'Exactly!' said the robot.

'What do the rectifiers do?' asked Annie.

'They reverse the magnetic field of anything in their vicinity!' exclaimed Maurice. 'I built one as an experiment. But to build more . . . well . . .'

'I've built so many,' screamed the robot, 'and so distributed them in every continent and floating on every ocean, that I will be able – by the flick of a switch – to cancel out the entire Earth's magnetic field!'

'But why would you do that?' exclaimed Orville. 'Everything – including *you* will fly off the planet and perish in the infinite wastes of space!'

'Child's play!' shouted the robot. 'I shan't cancel the Earth's gravity completely . . . I'll just turn it down a little – just enough to allow the lightest things to rise up a few thousand feet!'

'What does it mean?' yelled Jack.

'It's diabolical!' yelled the Inventor. 'Oh my dears! I'm so sorry I created this monster!'

'But what is it going to do?' cried Annie.

'Haven't you got it yet, you simpletons?' sneered the robot. 'The Earth's atmosphere will rise up . . .'

'No!' screamed the Inventor.

'I'll keep it up at 40,000 feet or so for a couple of hours, just to make sure every breathing creature is asphyxiated, and then I'll lower it again . . . Because of course some machines need oxygen to function.' The robot was now punching codes into the control panel in front of it.

'I'll repeat the process every day for a week – just to make sure I've wiped out not only every human being but every living creature – and my machines will take over the world! Goodbye! I hope you enjoy knowing what's going to happen . . . You have precisely forty seconds to think about it while the rectifiers build up to full strength!'

And with that, the robot threw the main switch, and the control room was filled with a loud throbbing sound as the rectifiers started to build up power. At the same time, the dots on the map of the world all lit up in unison to show that the rectifiers all over the world were switched on and working.

The throbbing noise grew louder and louder . . .

'Goodbye!' said Orville Barton, looking from his son to his daughter. 'I'm so sorry I was a bad father to you both! I'm sorry I neglected you! I wish I could live my life again and be a proper father to you this time!'

'Dad!' called Annie

'Dad!' called out Jack, shouting above the increasing throbbing noise that filled their ears.

'Yah! YAAAAAAAHHHH!' screamed Little Orville.

'Maurice!' screamed a high-pitched, cracked voice.

The robot froze.

'Maurice Morris!' continued the voice. And suddenly there stood a little old lady, standing in the subdued blue light by the main entrance of the control room. 'I knew I'd find you here in your favourite spot up on the Campsie Fells!'

And without more ado, Mrs Morris (yes, she who had bought the Truthful Phone) marched across the control room and started to beat the robot around the head with her umbrella . . . Gunk! Gunk! Gunk!

'It's YOU!' exclaimed the robot and Maurice together.

'Of course it's me, you idiot!' said Mrs Morris, addressing the robot. 'You don't think you can go on television and announce that you're taking over the world without me noticing do you?'

'I love you!' cried the robot.

'Don't start getting sentimental you old fool!' exclaimed Mrs Morris, who, despite being such a nice little old lady, had never enjoyed a particularly romantic relationship with her husband.

'But I do! I adore the ground you walk on!' exclaimed the robot.

Mrs Morris looked at it suspiciously. 'You've never said things like that to me before!' she muttered. 'Are you all right in the head?'

'My darling!' said the robot. 'I am programmed to love you!'

'What!' cried Mrs Morris.

'I have been programmed to love you! Passionately! Eternally!' cried the robot.

Gunk! Mrs Morris hit it over the head again. 'You've been drinking, Maurice Morris!'

'No! No! I am fulfilling my destiny! My programme!' cried the robot and it tried to put its arms around Mrs Morris. But the old lady fought him off.

'*Who* "programmed" you?' she shouted.

'I'm afraid I did,' said Maurice, his head sticking out from his block.

'Who's that?' cried the old woman, spinning round.

'It's me: Maurice!' said the Inventor. 'Your husband.

That's just a robot!'

'Maurice! You low-down and dirty rascal!'

'My dear!' replied Maurice, 'you'll never guess how glad I am to see you!'

❖❖❖

So that was how a little old lady from Glasgow saved not only the entire human race but all living creatures from extinction.

As soon as Maurice explained the situation to Mrs Morris, she told the robot to stop the machines and set everyone free. And of course, because the robot had been programmed to love and obey Mrs Morris without question and forever, it did exactly what she told it to do.

The rectifiers were halted all around the world, and the air we breathe was never 'turned off'.

Maurice himself, however, returned to his Iron Cloud, where he was happy enough making his inventions to improve life for everyone, which is what he had devoted himself to ever since he had disappeared so mysteriously on the Campsie Fells. He said that sort of a life suited him better than being married, although he could do with a partner to help him.

As for Mrs Morris, she didn't mind in the least. She actually preferred the robot to her husband. It was far more attentive, loving and made the best tea in the world . . . which made Mrs Morris the most contented old lady who ever was.

Annie and Little Orville returned to their home on the cliff and Annie wrote a song all about their adventures that was recorded by no less an artist than Sir Elton John. Her husband, Tom, started assisting Maurice in his engineering projects, and eventually helped him to build a three-storey rabbit educator, which could automatically train rabbits to do household chores.

Jack did not return to the guerrillas, but he did start writing about their cause and became a prize-winning journalist, specializing in South American politics.

And what of Mr Orville Barton? Well, he handed over his business to his assistant Percy Baker, and devoted himself and his fortune to helping his children, and in particular to teaching his grandson, Little Orville, to speak in languages other than Drivel, to play cricket and to cheat at cards.

THE END

SUBSCRIBERS

Unbound is a new kind of publishing house. Our books are funded directly by readers. This was a very popular idea during the late eighteenth and early nineteenth century. Now we have revived it for the Internet age. It allows authors to write the books they really want to write and readers to support the writing they would most like to see published.

The names listed below are of readers who pledged their support and made this book happen. If you'd like to join them, visit: www.unbound.co.uk.

Ian Abbott
John Abraham
Geoff Adams
Chris Addison
Rohit Aggarwal
Geoff Airey
Wyndham Albery
Monty Alfie-Blagg
Steve Allan
Lee Allen
Tracey Allen
Saud Alsaud

Paula Alvarez
Katharine Ames
Stephen Andrew
Lisa Andrews
Andrew Angus
Misha Anker
Roberto Arico
Garry Arkle
Pierre Arlais
Matt Arrowsmith
Simon Arthur
Robert Arthur

Richard Artus
Paul Avery
Lee Awmiller
Chris Baker
Jamie Baker
Lindsay Baker
S. Spencer Baker
Graham Ball
Jonathan Ball
Alfie Ball
Neil Ballard
Paul Bamford

Jasmine Banister
Brenna Barks
Will Barlow
Roderick Bartlett
James Bartlett
Robert Bartlett
Oliver Barton
Jeannette Bastien
Graeme Bateman
Tom Battey
Albany Bautista
Andrew Baxter
Emma Bayliss
Charley Beans
Bob Beaupre
Colette Beaupre
Denise Behrens
Alex Bellars
Maria Belyayev
David Berenbaum
Ekaterina Berova
Jessica Berry
Jon Berry
Steve Berryman
Don Beverley
Paul Birch
Tanya Birklid
Dorothy Birtalan
Paul Bissett
Judy Blackett
Nicalas Boardman
Peter Bogg
Bob Bollen
Mari Allenda Bolstad
Jennifer Bonham-
    Carter
Stephen Boucher
Henri Bourcereau
Karl Bovenizer
Jules Bowes
Dave Bowler

J. Patience Boyd
Thomas Brasdefer
Richard Bray
Mary Brennan
Paul Brennesholtz
Neil Brewitt
Anna Brickman
Jamie Brindle
Alan Brookland
Philip Brown
Ed Bruce
Phil Bruce-Moore
Adam Bryce
Jerry Bugler
Chris Bull
Jonathan Bullock
Heather Burbage
Sarah Burrell
Michele Burrows
Steph Burton
Fiona Butler
Heather Bye-
    Lamphere
Linda Cadier
David Cairns
David Callier
Lia Camargo
Rich Campoamor
Camilla Campora
Andrew Candler
Xander Cansell
Jill Cansell
Barry Carpenter
Ian Carpenter
Duarte Carreira
Rob Carter
Heidi Cartwright
Ellie Cary
Richard Case
Marianne Catalan
    Kennedy

Virginia Catmur
Sean Cearley
Maria Cervantes
David Chamberlain
Claire Chambers
Tom Chandler
Andy Chapman
Paul Charnock
Jack Chekijian
Matthew Cherrill
Wayne Ching
Maj-Britt Christensen
Nick Clapson
Jesse Clark
John Clark
Ian Clarkson
Gillian Claus
Emma Cleasby
Robert Clements
Louise Janette Cole
Stevyn Colgan
Leo Collett
Michael Collins
David Comber
Vicky Connor
Lewis Cook
Paul Cook
Sam Cook
Mike Cooper
Paul Cooper
Sarah Corrigan
Andrew Cotton
Anthony Creagh
Jon Crew
Michael Crowe
Amy Cruse
Tom Cullen
Adrian Culley
Heather Culpin
Jane Dallaway
Brett Danalake

James Dasey
Anthony David
Martyn Davies
Angharad Davies
Simon Davis
Phil Davison
Jonathan Day
Robert Day
Mike Day
Jessica Dean
Sven Decabooter
Cathy Defreitas
Henry Demarest
Thomas Dempster
J. F. Derry
Anna Devitt
Louise Diamond
Angela Dickson
Terry Diederich
Mark Dixon
Mar Dixon
Gary Dixon
Gareth Dobson
Matthew Dolley
Michelle Donald
Lenny Donnelly
Natalie Dorey
Steve Dossick
Anne Dougherty
Simon Downs
Vivienne Dunstan
Karen Durrant
Alex Dymock
Howard Dyson
Greg Eagle
Mark Eaton
Annie Eaton
Sharon Eden
Louise Edis
Katherine Edward
Richard Eggleston

Noel Einam
John Ellams
David Ellard
Chris Evans
Nicola Evans
Steve Exeter
Lillian Falconer
Safron Faulkner
Steve Ferris
Paul Fischer
Matt Fisher
Penny Fletcher
Gary Foster
Aaron Fothergill
Ilana Fox
Charles Fox
Laura Franks
Sophie Freeland
Mark French
Thomas Fries
Chris Frost
Sarah Frost
Dave Frost
Emma Furnell
Nina Furu
Mandy Gage
Margaret Gallagher
Hilary Gallo
Riccardo Gargiulo
Carl Gaywood
Amro Gebreel
Michelle Gennari
Saman Gerami
Sheila Gibson Stoodley
Wendy Gilbert
August Giliberto
Jeff Gill
Lesley Gillingham
Jacqueline Murray
Raffaele Giuria
Gordon Glenn

David Glover
Richard Goddard
Laura Goddard
Steven Goldman
David Goodman
Michelle Gosling
Jenne Goulding
Darren Govey
David Graham
Neil Graham
Katrine Granholm
Jonathan Green
Katherine Green
Victoria Green
Helen Gregory
Andy Grigg
Paul Grindley
Roy Grubb
Thorhalla Gudmunds-
    dottir Beck
Patrick Hall
Chris Hall
Tom Hall
Daniel Hallifield
Denis Haman
William Harbor
Andrew Harbourne-
    Thomas
Mike Hardcastle
Alex Hardy
David Harford
Carolyn Harlow
Michelle Harper
Adam Harrison
Stacy Harrison
Andy Hart
Faye Hartley
Amanda Harvey
Kathleen Haskard
Joanne Haswell
Dave Hawkins

Brogen Hayes
Jack Healy
Tony Heil
Chris Hemmens
Samuel Henley
Margaret Hennessy
Liz Hensor
Jann Herlihy
Nicholas Herman
Nikki Herriott
Catherine Heywood
Peter Hibbit
Melissa Hicks
Megan Hilleard
Jack Hillgate
Darren Hincks
Tom Hocknell
Neil Hodgson
Emma Hogg
Rebecca Holbourn
Iain Holder
Helena Hollis
Mairin Holmes
Giulietta Horner
Katherine Hostettler
Craig Houston
Emma Howard
Robert Howard
David Howard
Erika Howard
Barrie Howe
Fay Hugill
Emma Hutchings
Neil Hutchinson
John Hutchinson
Matthew Inns
Sally Inns
Dotti Irving
Helen Irwin
Lee Israel
George Ivanoff

Sian Ives
Majeed Jabbar
Mike Jackson
Fadi Jameel
Colin Verdun James
Fred Jannin
Ben Jardine
Vivienne Jennings-
    Clowes
Paul Jewitt
Marjorie Johns
Andrew Joint
Terry Jones
Stephen Jones
Dafyd Jones
Christine Jordan
Peter Jukes
Lukas Kaba
Nathaniel Keall
Tine Kej
Andrew Kelly
Savannah Kemp
Helen Kenyon
Lewis Kershaw
Jenny Ketchmark
Sarah Kett
Perry Kettler
Jan Kewley
Dan Kieran
Kevin Kieran
Wilf Kieran
Olive Kieran
John Kiernan
Laura Kilbride
Ahra Kim
Simon King
Paul Kingett
George Kirby
Terry Kiser
Paul Kittel
Barbara Klancar

Doron Klemer
Narell Klingberg
Jon Knight
Miriam Koehler
Rob Kolosky
Kai Kousa
Anna-Maria Kowalik
Yulia Kozlova
Sabrina Kramer
Hannamari Kumpusalo
Giles Lamb
Philip Lamb
Sarah Lambert
Jonathan Lander
Ruediger Landmann
Lars-Petter Larsson
Ros Lawler
Rory Lawless
Daniel Lawrence
Jane Lawrie
Gareth Lean
Sabrina Lebnaoui
Jørgen Leditzig
James Lenoel
John Leonard
Juliane Lessmann
Jeremy Leverton
Brian Levine
Lisa Lewis
Kris Leysen
Bart Libert
Adrian Lightly
Mark Lilley
Guy Linley-Adams
Suzannah Lipscomb
Douglas Livingstone
Geoff Lloyd
Karen Loasby
Robert Loch
Michael Lord
Mark Alan Loso

Subscribers

Kate Losowsky
Iain Low
Ben Lucock
Ric Lumb
Andreas Lundgren
Frances Lynn
Natalie Mac Lean
Abby MacArthur
Robbie MacGillivray
Deborah Macintosh
Adrian Mackinder
Marijne Magnée-
    Nentjes
Aidan Magrath
Paul Maher
Maria Makri
Margaret Malpas
Hedy Manders
Peter Manston
Sally Anne March
Borja Marcos
Nicole Marino
Markus Markoulias
Ellen Marsh
Simon Marshall
Dawn Marshall-
    Fannon
Lenny Martin
Alberto Martinez
    Ramos
Abbie Mason
Mike Mason
Amiruddin Mastura
Ryan Matthews
Shaun McAlister
Jonathan McAllister
Gabriel McCann
Jim McCauley
Lucy McConnell
Kyle McCreary
Rod McDonald

Mo McFarland
Daniel McGachey
Dustin McGivern
Ian McIntyre
Stuart McKears
Palma McKeown
Gordon McLean
Wendell McMurrain
Rob Measures
Gavin Meek
Irene Meis
Carole Melia
Jeffrey C. Mendel
Martina Meng
Giorgia Meschini
Geert Meuffels
Rob Miles
Sarah Miller
Anne Miller
Andrew Milloy
Simon Mills
Andrew Mills
Stacey Mitchell
Elizabeth Mitchell
Daisy Rose Mitchinson
George Mitchinson
John Mitchinson
Ronald Mitchinson
Debra Moises
Oyvind Moll
Ken Monaghan
Martin Monteiro
Nell Morecroft
Dr John Morris
Stuart Morris
Julia Morris
Darren Morrissey
Kate Mosse
Liane Mount
Ken Muessig
Demitri Muna

Benjamin Munday
Jenni Murphy
Debra Muvuti
Al Napp
Andy Nichol
Al Nicholson
John Nicholson
Mira Nishimura
Howard Noble
Kevin Noonchester
Kay Norman
Dennis North
Peter B. Nowell
Patricia O'Beirne
Steven O'Key
Jan O'Malley
Kazeem Olalekan
Anna-Maria Oléhn
Kaylene O'Neill
Hilde Orens
Sylvia Oude Egberink
Alan Outten
David Overend
Tauni Oxborrow
Danny Oz
Janet Paderewski-
    Lattanzi
Torsten Pagel
Lawrence Palmer
Wayne Palmer
Pam Palmer
Kevin Parker
David Parkes
Slim Parry
Charles Parry
Genni Patane
Mark Paterson
Samuel Penning
Hunter Peters
Tony Peterson
Gunther Pflueger

Nathalie Pineau
Emily Piper
Ian Piper
Cathy Pitt
Anna Place
Ken Plume
Blaž Podgoršek
Rebecca Pohancenik
Justin Pollard
Stephanie Pollard
Constance Pollard
Felicity Pollard
John Pollock
Cliff Ponting
Michael Porath
Randolph Potter
Rachel Poulton
Kathryn Powell
Michaela Power
Andry Prescott
Ross Price
Christopher Pridham
Callum Prior
Ffion Pugh
Sarah Quinn
Mikael Qvarfordh
Ian Radcliffe
Matt Railton
Michele Rajput
Ben Ramsey
Helen Randle
Daniel Rau
William Read
Jackie Reardon
Steve Reeves
Margaret Reeves
David Reidy
Judith Rennie
Natalia Renwick
Colin Reynolds
Patrick Reynolds

Kathryn Richards
Mark Richards
Geoff Rimmer
Ken Rimple
Robert Ristroph
Morgan Ritchie
Stan Rivett
Wyn Roberts
Mike Roberts
Julie Roberts
Scott Robertson
John Rodgers
Benji Rogers
Wojciech Rogozinski
Felicitas Rohder
Abigail Rose
Ian Rose
Ira Rosenblatt
Eric Rosenfield
Catherine Rossi
Yannick Roux
Gill Rowlands
Paolo Ruggeri
Benjamin Russell
Dave Russell
Simon Russell
Emma Ryal
Jenny Ryan
Cecilia Ryan
Paul Sadler
Valentina Saez Leal
Sean Salisbury
Philip Sassoon
Paula Saurs
Olivia Savard
Richard Schenkman
Jhenifer Schmidt
Trevor Schoenfeld
Julie Schofield
Melanie Schroeder
Jenny Schwarz

Alex Scott
Russell Scott
Paul Scovell
Matthew Searle
Alexander Segall
Faye Sharp
Matt Shaw
Declan Shearer
Jayne Shepherd
Richard Shepherd
James Sherwood
Jon Shute
Shawn Sijnstra
Thomas Sijpkens
Maurilo Silveira
John Simmons
Cathy Simpson
Duncan Sinclair
Jan Skakle
Deborah Skelton
Daniel Smale
Alasdair Smith
Dora Smith
Alison Smith
Adrian Smith
David G. Smith
Eric Smith
David 'Dr Dave' Smith
Molly Smith
Barry Smyth
Lili Soh
Tony Solomun
David Somers
Tim Sommerfeld
Bill Soreth
Rob Spence
Paul Spencer
Brett St Clair
Rickard Stampe
Søderstrøm
John Stancik

Subscribers

Maria Stanford
Peter Staniforth
Deborah Stead
Bob Steele
Murray Steele
Cameron Steele
Wayne Stewart
Christopher Stewart
Ulrike Stock
Gillian Stokes
Fran Stokes
Richard Stoliar
Adam Stone
Quinnan Stone
Katherine Store
Katie Stowell
Linda Strachan
Matthew Strawbridge
Adam Stuart
Sonia Stubbs
Jon Sumroy
Mark Sundaram
Emma Sundt
Andrew Sunnucks
Robert Suppes
Mark Suret
Flo Swann
Lindsay Swann
Dror Tankus
Mike Taylor
Alan Taylor
Dave Taylor
Stuart Taylor
Simon Taylor
Howard Teece
Pedro Telles
Charles Testrake
A. J. Thomas
Mark Thomas
Laura Thompson

Mike Thompson
Graham Thorley
Christian Tjaben
James Tobin
Raphaël Toussaint
Christine Trudeau
Matt Tubb
Mark Turner
Yvette Turner
Dominic Twose
Peter Tyler
Kati Vallius
Ramon van der Pol
Tanya van Dijk
Wim van Schijndel
Sietske van Vugt
Joe Vecchio
John Viele
Darlene Vincent
Rose Vos de Mooy
Mike Wade
Teresa Wagener
Ben Walker
William Walker
Katey Walker
George Walker
Steve Walker
Scott Wallace
Alistair Wallace
Sheryl Walpole
Izzi Ward
Miranda Ward
Ansgar Warner
John Warren
Syd Webb
Richard Webster
Kate Webster
Robert Wells
Paul Western-Pittard
Ben Wheeler

Paul Whelan
Robert White
Katya Whittaker
Andrew Wiggins
Gerry Wilde
Stephen Wiles
Richard Williams
Stuart Williams
Arwel Williams
Ian Williamson
Naomi Wilson
Iain Wilson
Jodi Wilton
Nichola Winney
Leonie Winson
Doug Winter
Graham Wise
Stuart Witts
Charlie Wood
Rob Wood
Matthew Wood
Carol Woods
Kirstin Woodward
Emma Woolerton
Kevin Wright
Michael Wynn
Alan Yentob
Andrew Yeomans
Todd Yoder
Lauren Yorston
Jon Young
Charlotte Young
Brecht Yperman
Arun Zachariah
Jane Zara
Lynn Zarb
Gregory Zayia
Zoé Zeller
Berkeley Zych

A NOTE ON THE TYPEFACES

The body text of the book is set in Perpetua 11 / 13½ pt. The typeface was designed in 1925 by Eric Gill (1882–1940), an eccentric sculptor, printmaker and designer whose roots were in the Arts and Craft movement. Perpetua has a chiselled, neo-classical quality that derives from Gill's fondness for stone engraving.

The titling and initial capitals are set in another Gill face, Golden Cockerel. The Golden Cockerel Press was an English private press that operated between 1920 and 1961 and was famous for the quality of its handmade limited edition books and an inspiration for Unbound. The typeface was specially designed by Gill for an edition of the Four Gospels commissioned by the owner of the press, Robert Giddings, in 1929. It was to become one of the most outstanding examples of the handmade illustrated book produced in the twentieth century.